VALERIE NORRIS

The April Letters

Published by
Llyfrau Cambria Books, Wales, United Kingdom.
*Cambria Books is a division of
Cambria Publishing.*
Discover our other books at: www.cambriabooks.co.uk

For my husband, Chris Norris

PART 1

Chapter 1

2007

It was not such a small room after all. I had imagined it would be tiny, austere and airless, but in fact it was none of those. There was a shower room, chair, table, TV and even a DVD player, and – oh thank goodness – a small window. I had not dreaded the solitary confinement itself, only the thought of having no view of the outside world, nothing to remind me that, no matter what went on here, the sun still rose and set. Not that it was much of a view; just the corner of a car park with a few branches of a sycamore tree just visible over the high wall. But I could see sky.

My phone beeped. It was a text from Joy. We had said goodbye earlier that day, our words sounding forced and unnatural, like when you are waiting on a railway station platform. Her smile was as warm as ever but her eyes were pebble bright.

'You mustn't worry,' I had said. 'I'll be fine. This is much easier than before.'

I had to put on my glasses to read her message on the small screen:

How is it? The Ritz not the pits I hope?

Well, not quite the Ritz but better than I thought. A window and a TV. What more do I need, I replied.

Joy's reply came back instantly. *Good. Love you xxx*

1965

The beach was busy today. Donkeys trotted obediently up and down past rows of deckchairs, interspersed with children digging sandcastles, while the little waves gasped on the shore. Susan was watching a boy and girl nearby making a huge sandcastle, the boy exhorting his sister to help him dig out the moat. She watched with disdainful interest. A couple of years ago she would have been just as enthusiastic– she and Dad had built some wonderful castles. But now she had outgrown buckets and spades. Instead, she spent her time dipping into the sea with Dad, shrieking in mock terror when he splashed her, or sunbathing next to Mum and either reading her comic or book, sketching, or writing in her journal.

The warm August afternoon was winding down. Families were starting to shake out sand-laden towels, gather up thermos flasks and cardigans brought just in case it turned chilly. Mum and Dad were lazing in their deckchairs. At least Dad was lazing, his hands clasped behind his head as he tilted his face to the sun. Mum rarely lazed. She was knitting a white sleeve of a matinee coat for someone's new grandchild. Susan had forgotten who. Mum held it up and it hung delicately curved and spiders' web soft.

'Shall we go soon?' Mum said, stowing the tiny garment in her bag. 'We could start on the packing this evening, rather than leaving it all for the morning.'

Dad stretched and yawned noisily. 'I suppose so.'

Susan was lying on her stomach on a towel reading that week's edition of School Friend. 'Can we have ice cream, please?' she said. 'It *is* the last day.'

Mum groped in her bag for her watch. 'Well, I was thinking of calling in at that wool shop on the way back and getting some wool to start on your new winter cardigan, Susan. The shop closes at five, so there wouldn't be time for ice cream as well.'

'I could go on my own, down to the café,' said Susan. 'Could I? Please?'

Mum frowned. 'What do you think, John?'

Dad's eyes were still closed. 'Susie's a big girl now, I don't see why not.'

'Don't you want to choose what colour wool you want?'

'I know what I want. Red this time. Bright red.'

'Oh… I was thinking more of dusky pink? It would go with your blue skirt. And your grey trousers.'

Susan sat up and wiggled her toes in the sand. 'Red will go just as well. And it's more grown up than pink. Pink's for little girls.'

Mum sighed. 'Alright. Red it is. And just be careful going to the café. You can be about half an hour, and then come straight back to the boarding house.'

Dad opened his eyes. 'Oh, take your time,' he said. He leaned over and whispered something in Mum's ear, pushing the strap of her swimming costume down off her shoulder and kissing the indented place where her strap mark was. She giggled and blushed. 'John,' she murmured. But she didn't pull away.

Susan thought how pretty Mum was when she smiled like that. But then, she was pretty when she was serious, too. She jumped up and bundled her books into her bag. 'So I can go, can I?'

'Yes, off you go then.' Mum started to gather their paraphernalia. 'Don't be late for tea though, you know Mrs Chalmers is always on the dot with the meals and doesn't like it if we're late.' Earlier in the holiday they had tumbled breathlessly into the dining room for tea, unwashed and dishevelled after a walk along the cliffs that had taken longer than they had expected. Mrs C had served them their slightly dried up steak-and-kidney pie with a stony expression. They had giggled about it in the bedroom afterwards. Dad had said she had a face like a smacked bottom.

'Oh, and Susan…' Mum said.

'Yes?' said Susan, picking up her sandals.

'Make sure you take care crossing the road on the way back. It's ever so busy. Use the crossing.'

'OK,' said Susan over her shoulder.

The soft sand felt delicious under her bare feet, and she watched it squeeze through her toes as she walked along. The café was at the far end of the beach, with a few benches and a row of flags outside. Inside it was just as jolly and welcoming, with half a dozen Formica tables and black and white pictures on the wall of the seafront thirty years ago, and tomato sauce in large red tomato-shaped plastic bottles on the tables. Susan went to the counter, where the coffee machine was making whooshing noises like a steam engine while a man in an apron produced foamy coffee, with the foam so peaked it almost looked like the egg whites after Mum had whisked them to make meringue.

'Can I help you, love?' said the man, as he handed change to the couple in front.

'I'll have a 99, please,' said Susan promptly. This was her favourite; a cone of vanilla ice cream with a chocolate flake stuck in the top at a jaunty angle. It wasn't often that she had one though, because it was an extra threepence for the flake.

'That's eight pence, please,' said the man.

Susan burrowed into her little leather purse that had a cat's head on the front. She hesitated. 'Could I have a glass of lemonade as well, please?'

'That's a shilling altogether,' said the man, gushing the fizzy drink from a large bottle into a glass.

Susan sat down at one of the tables, and carefully licked her ice cream all around the edge, savouring the cold creaminess on her tongue. She would leave the flake until last. The café was quite busy, with even more people sitting outside on the benches. Susan felt it was somehow more grown up to be sitting inside. From behind the counter a transistor radio was playing the latest Beatles song. She hummed along, twisting her pony tail with her free hand. There was a mirror on the other side of the room and she caught sight of herself. She looked away quickly then dragged her eyes back to look again. She was neither fat nor thin, her hair was mousy brown as were her eyes. Ordinary. Not like mum, with her rich dark hair and serene expression. At school there was a statue of the Virgin Mary with the baby Jesus. The statue always made her think of Mum. She had never told anyone that, because it didn't seem quite proper.

As she frowned at herself in the mirror, she realised that a little boy with a runny nose at the next table was watching her, so she got out her notebook and a pencil and opened it up to the latest entry. She was writing a story. Like all her stories, it was an adventure. The heroine was called Anya, and she was feisty, brave and beautiful like a good heroine should be. The adventures happened in a school in an imaginary country. Susan jotted a few sentences down but she kept getting distracted by the boy who had started whining because he wanted an ice cream and his mother said that it would spoil his tea. So Susan gave up and packed Anya and her friends back into her bag and concentrated on her ice cream instead.

Tomorrow they would go home and then it was only one more week until school started again. She quite liked school, and when she went back she wouldn't be one of the new girls anymore, she would be in the Lower Fourth, the second year. And she would see her friends Melissa and Jane again. She had had Jane round for tea once in the holidays, but Melissa had gone away to stay with her grandparents. During last year the three girls had made their own special place behind some bushes in a corner of the school grounds, where they went during break time. Jane had said at the end of term that they would probably be too grown up to go there when they went back after the summer. Susan had agreed, but secretly she hoped that they would. It was fun to having their own secret place.

Then she remembered that Mum had said she would take her shopping next week for new school shoes and a proper bra. So far she had only had a training bra and she had grown out of that during the summer. Automatically Susan folded her arms over her chest and she could feel her breasts pressing against her arms. It was like they didn't belong to her. Although she was partly proud of her new shape, she was a bit scared too. It was as if someone else had taken over her body. Mum said they might even go to Burlingham as a special treat. That was something to look forward to. She loved the trip on the train, pressing her face against the window and watching the houses shoot by outside. They would go to the shops and then have fish and chips at lunch time.

Susan nibbled rodent-like down her flake, making the crumbly chocolate last as long as possible. A man was buying a cup of tea at the counter. 'Alright if I sit here, love?' he said. Susan nodded, and as he sat down on the opposite side of the table the dark brown tea sloshed into the saucer. Susan took a gulp of her lemonade. It tasted much too sweet after the ice cream. The man nodded at her and lit a cigarette. To be fair, all the other tables were taken. Susan glanced at him. He was a bit younger than Dad and had hair down onto his collar and a long fringe. He didn't look at her; he drew deeply on his cigarette and the acrid smell enveloped her. She shifted on her seat and took another swig of the lemonade. She wished now that she hadn't wasted her pocket money on it. She decided to leave the rest of it and go.

Outside the sun was still shining and Susan took a deep draught of the tangy sea air. Now she felt rather silly for leaving; after all, the man hadn't been nasty in any way. But her mood had been broken. She hurried up towards the boarding house, aware that she had been quite a while and not wanting Mum and Dad to worry. Dutifully she crossed the road at the crossing, like Mum had said. Then up ahead she saw a crowd gathered on the pavement. There were policemen and an ambulance. The back doors of the ambulance slammed shut and she watched it drive off. The slamming of the doors echoed in her head, and a worm of apprehension moved inside her. Without knowing exactly why, she began to run towards the crowd. There was something on the edge of the pavement. Susan saw it and stopped. A paper bag had split open, and balls of red wool were oozing out into the gutter.

***

It was a dream, it had to be. One of those ragged dreams where nothing makes sense and you are so glad to wake up. Except that she didn't wake up. She had burst into the boarding house, heart pounding. The worm inside her had turned into a snake and it was eating her. Dad was there except that he wasn't Dad; his face was different and there was nothing behind his eyes. Even his voice wasn't Dad's when he told her what had happened. She didn't say anything; it was all part of the dream. A policeman and a policewoman were there, and Dad had to go with the policeman. The policewoman smiled at Susan and said in a gentle voice that if she had nowhere else to go then she would be looked after at the police station. But Mrs C said that Susan had better stay with her, that she would give her tea in her own rooms. Susan obediently went with her. It didn't much matter either way. You didn't have much choice in a dream.

Susan sat on the sofa in Mrs C's living room. Mrs C had put the television on for her while she bustled out to the kitchen to make the dinner for all the guests. Susan watched meaningless shapes spin across the screen, while sounds gabbled at her. In the room a miasma of years of fried food and cabbage seeped in from the kitchen. The room was cluttered with all sorts of things: piles of magazines, miscellaneous boxes, untidy paperwork. There was a clothes horse where a pair of elastic stockings drooped like sad flags, and saggy curtains with big sunflowers on them. The two young girls who helped Mrs C poked their heads furtively round the door and looked round-eyed at Susan, whispering behind their hands and nudging each other. Eventually Mrs C brought Susan her meal on a tray. Battered fish, chips and mushy peas; the usual Friday evening fare. Susan tried to eat some, but it was hard to make the food go down. A clatter of dishwashing was going on in the kitchen, the girls chattering loudly. One of them brought Susan a glass of squash, and gave it to her without looking at her. Later on Mrs C brought her a cup of cocoa and said she had better go to bed. Susan asked when Dad would be coming back but Mrs C said she didn't know. She asked if she was alright and Susan nodded. She didn't know what else to do.

The bedroom was silent. Could it possibly be to the same room that Susan had seen earlier in the day? Then, they had been collecting their swimming costumes and towels, peering out of the window and wondering if the bright weather was going to last for the last day of their holiday. Now, Susan took her nightdress out from under the pillow. Her bed was a little camp bed on the floor, the other side of the room from the big double bed. This morning they had talked about how next year Susan would have to have a room of her own. She turned out the light and got into her bed. She tried to close her eyes but they wouldn't stay closed. Whether they were open or closed, what she saw were those red balls of wool bleeding into the gutter. The ambulance came, and Mrs C's stockings were turning into snakes and slithering towards her...

She started as the door opened and she realised that she had been asleep after all and had been dreaming. Under the slits of her eyelids she could see Dad's feet as he crept in the darkness. She heard him get into bed. It must have been hours later when she woke to hear a sound that she couldn't first identify. Then she realised it must be Dad crying, a muffled combination of moaning and whimpering. She wondered if she should go to him, but she didn't move. She couldn't bear to hear what he might say, scared of the dream becoming worse. She tried to cry too but she could only squeeze a few tears out from the hard knot in her chest.

Next morning Dad held her hand while they sat on the bed and he told her that she was going to have to be brave. Very brave. His voice was dull and squashed. When they went downstairs for breakfast Mrs C said she had laid a table for them in her living room, where they wouldn't be disturbed. Mrs C's eyes slid over them and she ushered them quickly into the room as she heard the footsteps of other guests on the stairs, the laughing cheery voices. Dad said to her that he would have to go out again, and he thought it would be better for Susan if she stayed there, if that was alright. Mrs C hunched her shoulders and pursed her mouth. She said she supposed she could allow Susan to sit in her living room, but they would need to empty their bedroom first, because it needed to be cleaned for the next lot of boarders. So Susan sat again in the stuffy room with the sunflower curtains and the piles of papers. The stockings had gone. She had her book with her, and she turned the pages while words trickled in front of her eyes. After a while she heard Mrs C in the kitchen and she asked her where Dad had gone and if she knew when he would be coming back. Mrs C said he had gone to see about the body being taken home. It took Susan a minute to realise that she meant Mum. The body meant Mum. Mum isn't a body, she wanted to say.

When Dad came back he asked if he could make a trunk call. He would pay for it, of course. Then they took the two suitcases round to the car. They had just thrown everything in the suitcases anyhow, not folded neatly like Mum would have done. Susan opened the back door of the car and slid into her usual place.

'You might as well sit in the front,' said Dad.

It wasn't a treat like it normally would have been. There was no normal now. As they drove out of the town onto the main road, she glanced at Dad's face. It was blank, like a mask. They drove on in silence, the miles eating up the hedgerows and villages as they headed inland towards the Midlands. Susan stared at the swirly pattern in the woodgrain of the dashboard. It always reminded her of the waves of the sea.

'I phoned your Aunty Pat,' said Dad. 'At least I phoned the woman down the road and she said she would run up straight away and tell her. I'll have to tell everyone else later.' For a while he didn't say anything else. Then he said, 'All these years. All these years and it's all over. I can't believe it. I can't see how I'll be able to open the garage this week. It's never been closed except the fortnight when we go on holiday. And Christmas. When I took it over, all I wanted to do was to make it a success. Something to be proud of. Smith's Garage - good service, good value. I built it up on reputation and fine workmanship. Now what's it all worth?'

He didn't seem to know she was there and the bitterness in his voice was something she had never heard before. 'You've still got me Dad,' she whispered.

***

When they pulled up at the house Aunty Pat was already there, having let herself in with the key that was hidden in a gap in the wall. She ran down the passage towards them crying noisily, folding both Dad and Susan in her arms, one arm round each. The slight smell of stale sweat, cheap perfume and cigarettes was comforting in its familiarity. The warmth of her body seeped through to Susan as they all clung together rocking and crying. When at last she let go Susan felt herself trembling and she wiped her eyes on the back of her hands. Aunty Pat's mascara had wept black tears onto her cheeks.

'Thanks for coming, Pat,' said Dad.

'What sort of a big sister would I be if I hadn't come straight away? When Doris came to tell me I just grabbed my bag and got the next train. She'll cook for the boys tonight.' She put her hands on Dad's shoulders and looked up into his face. 'What happened, John? What happened to Jean?'

9

Dad sighed and crumpled down onto a kitchen chair. After a minute he began. 'We were walking down the street, going back to the boarding house. Then this car just comes out of nowhere. It veered straight off the road and came straight at her and just... and just mowed her down. I managed to jump out of the way, but she didn't have a chance. It ran her down then crashed into a shop front.' Dad was staring at his hands as if he was wondering what they were. 'The police think he had a massive heart attack at the wheel. He's dead, anyway.'

'I can't believe it,' gasped Aunty Pat. She put her arm round Susan again and drew her in. Susan could feel her shaking. It was frightening and comforting all at once. Susan nestled in and closed her eyes while the adults talked. Aunty Pat let go to light a cigarette.

'Why don't you take your things upstairs while Pat and I talk,' said Dad. Susan got her bag from the hall and did as she was told.

The steep stairs with carpet going threadbare on the eleventh step. Granny and Grandad's clock which stood guard at the top of the stairs and Susan could never remember having worked. Mum's odd job and sewing room, the metal hulk of the sewing machine standing silent amidst the reels of thread, colourful as wildflowers, scissors, odd bits of fabric, and the cornucopia of her overflowing workbasket.

Susan stared at the room as if it were a picture. She moved on to her own room next door. Still Edward Bear on the bed, his chubby teddy body long since devoid of much fur. Books along the top of the chest of drawers, Monopoly and other games beneath it. A corner of her peach coloured nightie poking out from under the pillow. She registered all these things in quiet amazement. How was it possible for everything to be exactly the same and yet totally different?

***

Jean Smith had been well liked and her untimely death unleased a river of shock and sympathy for the family. 'I can't believe it,' people said over and over again. 'And her only in her mid-thirties.' John too was universally liked and had earned respect as an honest dealer, someone who kept his word, worked hard and was usually smiling and whistling. Always time for a quick word, no matter how busy he was. You knew where you were with Smith's Garage – Repairs and Service. And as for that poor girl, left motherless. People called with gifts and offers of help. A box of eggs left on the front step, a bunch of flowers, a scrawled note.

The funeral was two days after the new school term started, so it was decided that Susan would stay off school until it was over. Dad had rung them up to explain. They said that it would be better for Susan to get into as normal a routine as possible, once the funeral was over. Her new form teacher, Miss Mitchell, was very kind. She saw Susan on her own and said she was so very sorry and Susan could come and talk to her whenever she needed to. 'Yes, Miss, thank you Miss,' muttered Susan, her eyes following a crack in the wooden floor. She went to find Melissa and Jane at break time. The first minutes, while they didn't know what to say, were excruciating. Nobody acted normally, and Susan retreated behind a wall in her mind.

One Saturday she had walked into town to buy something for tea when she bumped into Melissa and Jane. They had been to a matinee at the pictures to see a Walt Disney film and they were obviously dismayed to see Susan. Susan asked them if it had been good. Jane blurted out that they hadn't asked her to go with them because they thought she wouldn't have time, now that she had to help her Dad in the house. Susan said it didn't matter. Which it didn't. From the far off place inside her she actually felt rather sorry for their discomfort. They went their separate ways, Susan with her bag of groceries and ham for tea that night. Then Melissa, her round plain face puckered, called back over her shoulder and said that next week they were going to the pictures again and would Susan like to come. Susan said she would see.

Susan's life solidified into a pattern. A new pattern, the new, bewildering, normal. She went to school, she did her homework, she helped Dad with housework and shopping. Aunty Pat came alternate Saturdays, which was all she could manage because she worked in the week and the train journey took the best part of an hour. She talked to Susan, took her out shopping and made sure she had all she needed for school. The other weekend John and Susan drove to Pat's house for Sunday lunch. Sometimes Susan cried for her mother, little secretions

11

of misery wrung out of her, but more often she simply felt lost and confused. She was dimly aware that Dad was suffering too. She would have liked to talk to him about how much she missed Mum and how these feelings sometimes threatened to rear up and consume her, but she didn't want to cause him any more sadness than he already had.

For Sunday lunch Pat had cooked shoulder of lamb with swede, potatoes and tinned peas, and there was apple pie and custard for pudding. Dad and Pat sat at opposite ends of the kitchen table, while Pat's three boys and Susan sat at the sides. Susan watched her two elder cousins eating. They ate with concentration, elbows projecting as if to stabilise themselves, hardly seeming to draw breath as each mouthful disappeared in a gulp. They picked up their bowls to get a better angle to scrape the last of the custard out. Her other cousin, Frank, was sitting next to her, and he ate more steadily. Lionel and Norman were several years older than him, and they were only fourteen months apart, so their constant edgy antagonism had passed Frank by.

Frank nudged Susan under the table with his foot. 'Lionel's got gravy down his front,' he whispered to her. 'Serves him right for being such a pig.'

Pat scraped her chair back from the table and stood up. 'You two can clear up,' she said, nodding towards her two elder sons and clattering the dishes together. 'The twins can go and play in the front room.'

'We're supposed to be going to Mario's this afternoon,' complained Norman.

'It can wait,' said Pat, smoothing her miniskirt over her thighs. 'You spend too much time in that coffee bar as it is, playing the juke box and whatever. I've been hard at work all week and spent all morning cooking your dinner so now I'm going to sit down with your Uncle John and relax for a change.'

'I've been hard at work all week too,' said Lionel.

'You've been working for five minutes, my lad, whereas I've been slaving away at that factory for years now. Too many years.'

'We can all help,' said John, getting up from the table and starting to collect together the pudding bowls.

'Don't you dare, John. They can do it.'

12

Frank nudged Susan again and jerked with his head in the direction of the front room. Susan gladly followed him. There was always a variation of the same argument every time they visited. It part fascinated, part repelled her.

They threw themselves down on the sofa in the front room and the noises of the kitchen receded.

'Do you fancy a game of cards?'

'Not really,' said Susan.

'Cluedo?'

She shook her head.

'Well, what do you want to do?'

Susan shrugged and fingered the corner of the sofa arm where it had become threadbare. 'I don't know.'

There was a time they would have run giggling upstairs and played dressing up in Aunty Pat's bedroom, holding their breath and hiding under the bed with all the dust when someone came to look for them. They had played doctors and nurses sometimes too, although in that game all Frank had wanted to do was to show her his thing.

By bizarre coincidence, Susan and Frank had been born on the same day in the same hospital. Frank was the elder because he had entered the world a few hours earlier than Susan, a fact he was always ready to bring into play when needed. The arrival of the two babies, 'the twins' as they became known in the family, had cemented a strong bond between their mothers. Jean and Pat, who at that time lived only a few streets away from each other, spent hours talking and drinking tea while the twins played together. When they were small Pat and Jean used to look after each other's children, although it was far more usual for Jean to be looking after them both, Frank often turning up with dirty knees and missing buttons, both of which would get seen to by Aunty Jean. She read them stories, Rupert Bear being their favourite, while they sat one on each side of her. More recently, after Pat and Ray moved away to Burlingham, the two women still saw each other quite often, because it wasn't too far on the train. Up until a couple of years ago there had always been a joint birthday party for the cousin twins, with jelly, pass the parcel, and an iced birthday cake, all courtesy of Jean.

Frank had little squinty eyes behind his National Health glasses and was slightly plump and rather shy. He and Susan used to play together well, mainly because Susan usually let Frank have his own way. But they had grown apart in the last year or so. It started when they both moved up out of junior school, Susan to her local Grammar School and Frank to the city Secondary Modern. That, and puberty on the horizon, had set them on different tracks. The death of Susan's Mum had only accelerated what was probably inevitable.

'Are you sad today?' said Frank

Susan didn't answer. Sad. What a strange little word to describe so much.

'I know you're always a bit sad now. It's just that today you seem more sad.'

Susan sighed. 'Not really. Not *more* sad.'

Frank got up and fished around in his pocket. 'Here,' he held something out to her. 'You can have this.'

'What is it?' Susan had been on the receiving end of the contents of Frank's pockets before and so she was cautious.

'It's a conker. It's a really big one, my best one, but you can have it. It might cheer you up.'

Susan took the shiny brown nut and rolled it around in her fingers. 'Thanks.' She realised he was being kind, in his own way.

'What's it like?' said Frank.

'What's what like?'

'Having your Mum die. Is she in heaven, like a guardian angel? Do you think she's sort of looking down on you?'

Susan rolled the conker round in her palm. It was so smooth. Was Mum looking down on her? If only she knew. If only she could talk to her. 'I don't really know. I just know I miss her. I just…'

Susan bit down on the rest of the words. It was like a river. A big raging river, and it would grab her and drag her down if she let it. She mustn't let it.

'Is she, sort of, a ghost now?'

'Not in a scary way. Sometimes at night I think I can hear her, but Dad says that's just my imagination.'

'I liked Aunty Jean. I liked the stories she used to read, and the cake she used to make and the way she always smelled of soap.'

In the silence that followed they heard Aunty Pat yelling something followed by the bang of the front door. They looked out of the window to see Norman and Lionel swaggering down the road in their denim jeans and Lionel pulling on a black leather jacket.

The clock on the mantelpiece ticked. It was almost falling off the shelf because of the clutter of bills and letters stuffed behind it.

'I know your Mum's dead, but at least she loved you,' said Frank after a bit. 'Not like my Dad.'

The bitterness of his words cut through the grey fog in Susan's mind.

'Of course your Dad loved you. Why wouldn't he?'

Frank shook his head. 'Then why didn't he stay with us?'

Susan could only vaguely remember what Uncle Ray was like, and it must be three years now since he had left. He had shouted at the boys a lot and she had been a bit frightened of him, although he had never shouted at her.

Frank took his glasses off and rubbed his eyes with his fists. Susan didn't know what to say. Frank had never before wanted to talk about his Dad.

'Do you ever see him? Does your Mum know where he is?'

'Mum thinks he's in London somewhere. Living with his new woman.' Frank polished his glasses on the corner of his shirt, then put them back on and inspected Susan through the newly cleaned lenses, as if seeing her in focus for the first time. His eyes fixed on her chest.

'You're growing a lot,' he said. 'This time last year you didn't have any bosoms and now look.' He licked his lips. 'Can I see them?'

Susan sighed and crossed her arms over her chest. At least Frank was back to normal 'No, Frank. Not now, not ever.'

Chapter 2

I find the quietness in here odd. In my room - my little cell - it's almost silent, yet you can always detect a background murmur, a hum of distant clatter, voices, trolleys, telephones; life being lived on the other side of the door, without me.

Matthew says that the first week will be the worst. After that, it's just a matter of passing the time, he says. I like Matthew. He has a rakish glint in his eye and spiky red hair that stands up like a cockatoo's comb. And his uniform almost looks like it's been ironed, with creases down the trousers. Actual creases! What's that all about?

Life went on; days, weeks passed. Susan and Dad muddled through the churn of their daily lives as best they could, helping each other, talking but not talking. Dad had shrivelled. She wanted to tell him how much she longed for Mum, but how could she when she knew how much he was suffering himself. He was kind to her, in his sleepwalking way. Neighbours and friends helped with chores, shopping, washing, but as the weeks went by their support became less and less. Everyone had their own busy lives. So apart from when they had fish and chips from the fish shop on a Friday, they fell back on simple meals – meat pie in a tin, eggs, sausages.

Aunty Pat took Susan shopping sometimes, to get a new bra, or new shoes for school, or just to look at the fashions. It should have been Mum doing these things; the two of them sitting together in the Oxford Street Tea Shop, with their packages under their chairs, Susan watching her mother's slim hands pouring the tea, the tea cups clinking on the saucers, sharing a tea cake between them and sometimes fondant fancies. Mum dabbing her mouth with a napkin, Mum fingering the silver heart locket round her neck, which had been a present from Dad on their first wedding anniversary. Susan had loved those shopping trips, just her and Mum together. Now with Aunty Pat, they sat in the steamy fug of Bill's café by the station, where the coffee machine screeched and whined and the cups were white Pyrex. Susan never let on to her Aunt the lacerating pain she felt of those first shopping trips.

Mum's clothes hung dejectedly in her wardrobe, limp as washing on a still day. Susan would go into her and Dad's bedroom and secretly press her face into skirts and dresses, many of which Mum had made herself. She unscrewed the tops from perfume bottles and the lids from jars of face cream that stood on the dressing table, and closed her eyes so that she could inhale the scent and conjure up the past. Then in the New Year Aunty Pat said wasn't it time that poor Jean's clothes were got rid of and, if it would help, she would see to it and take them to the Salvation Army. So she had arrived early one Saturday morning and instructed Susan and Dad to go out for the day. Susan waited until after school on Monday, when Dad was at work, and crept into the bedroom. All the jars and pots had vanished. She looked at the impassive wardrobe door, brown and solid, and knew that she had to open it. Inside the coat hangers stood silent and bare like winter branches. She closed the door and never looked inside it again.

***

It was on a cold day during February half term that Susan came across her mother's recipe books in a kitchen drawer, behind the string, elastic bands, pens and other household clutter. She saw the books and drew back her hand, uncertain whether to touch them or not, whether to invite the anguish. Yet comfort too; seeing, touching, experiencing things that had been precious to Mum kept a part of her alive. The books were falling to pieces from years of thumbing and perusing, covered here and there with floury fingerprints. Odd and ends of recipes cut from magazines or scribbled on torn scraps of paper were wedged in between the pages. Susan could almost see Mum weighing ingredients, chopping onions or stirring bubbling saucepans, all the time a half smile, half frown of concentration on her face. Cooking was an art to her, and she infused her love into each meal she produced. The image of her mother presiding over the cooker was so vivid that Susan could have reached out to touch her, and the familiar, bewildered pain ambushed her. All these months and sometimes it still sliced her through.

She took the cookery books over to the kitchen table and sat down with them. There were torn out pages from magazines clipped in the back and scribbled notes in margins in Mum's curly writing, amending some of the recipes. Shepherd's pie (*'can add carrots for a change'*), beef stew, toad-in-the-hole (*'drain off the fat before adding the batter'*), bread and butter pudding. The sight of her handwriting, unique and familiar, had brought her mother even closer; it was as if she were reading over her shoulder, pointing out details. Susan could almost hear her breathing, could almost catch the faintest linger of her Camay soap. Then, before she could capture the moment it had evaporated and she was left staring at a list of instructions on a page, the book dry and lifeless as autumn leaves under her hands.

She turned over a few pages and after a while she started to read some of the recipes. Although she had loved to watch her mother

18

making meals, she had never actually made one herself. In the last few months before she had died Mum had encouraged her to help by chopping vegetables *'be careful, that knife's really sharp'* or stirring pots on the stove *'cock the lid just a little bit, to let the steam out. That's perfect!'* Susan sat back, remembering the satisfying clunk-clunk-clunk on the chopping board as the knife rendered a carrot into a pile of orange coins or the tangy prickle of tears under her eyelids as she cut up an onion. Mum had intended to pass on all her cooking skills. They had been making cakes together since before Susan went to school, usually fairy cakes in little corrugated paper cups. Susan was always fascinated by how they went into the oven as gooey as mud and magically came out as golden spongy delights, ready to be crowned with a pert blob of icing. By the time she was eleven she could knock up a batch of fairy cakes, scones or a Victoria sponge all on her own. Funny, she hadn't thought about doing that since Mum had died. Anyway, baking wasn't *real* cooking, not like being able to prepare a proper meal from scratch. *That* was real cooking.

She was still poring over the cookery books when Dad came in for his lunch.

'Hello Princess, make me a cheese and onion sandwich, will you,' said Dad from the doorway, kicking off his work boots and stripping off his greasy overall, which he discarded to the floor like a shed snake skin. 'I haven't got much time, I'm trying to squeeze another couple of jobs in this afternoon,' he added over his shoulder as he strode to the sink and rubbed green gloopy Swarfega into his dirty hands. 'And pop the kettle on.'

Although the house was just to the side of her father's garage, normally he took his lunch sandwiches with him to eat in his office, that is, the little cluttered alcove behind the workshop that he called his office. But because this was half term, he popped back to eat his lunch with Susan every day. Dad had always given himself heart and soul to his business, but just lately he worked even harder. Susan had realised that this was partly to fill the enormous gap in his life, but also that word of his reliable service had spread and people kept on coming back to him, and that he didn't want to turn down good money. 'I want to make sure you don't want for anything, Princess,' he would say.

19

Susan cut thick, wonky slices of bread on the wooden breadboard. The bread was a bit stale and she asked if she should make cheese on toast instead, but Dad said he didn't have time. She presented the sandwich and the tea, sweet and dark as he liked it, in front of him. 'You need to have something too,' said Dad between mouthfuls.

'I will, later,' she replied. His eyes strayed to the books on the table. She hesitated, not wanting to upset him. 'Look Dad, I found Mum's recipe books.' He put down his sandwich and picked up the book, reverently as if it were a precious relic. He turned the pages and traced his finger, the grime engrained under his nails, over her writing in the margins. She saw that he was overcome, just as she had been, and wished that she had put the books back in the drawer before he came in. 'I haven't seen her writing for a long time,' he whispered. 'I'd know it anywhere.'

'I'm sorry. I didn't mean to make you sad.' She couldn't bear it when Dad was unhappy like this, and more especially when she had caused it.

He brushed the back of his hand over his eyes. 'It's alright, love. It doesn't take much to make me sad. Even now.' They sat in silence, both feeling the presence and the non-presence of the woman they loved. Dad sighed and resumed eating.

The idea suddenly burst from nowhere. 'I could make some of these recipes,' said Susan. 'I used to watch Mum, and I was starting to help her quite a bit before... before... last year.' She turned the page and pointed to a picture. 'Look, beef stew with dumplings.' The illustration was tempting, with the soft fluffy dumplings nestling in the rich brown of the meat and gravy. 'I could do that. It would be a change from what we usually have. Can I? Please?' The idea gathered momentum in her mind. She could almost smell the food and see the shadowy figure of Mum in her apron at the cooker, humming and stirring.

Dad glance at the clock, drained the last of his tea and stood up. 'If you want to. But don't spend too much money and be careful with what you're doing.' He planted a kiss on her head. 'I know you're a sensible girl. Now I have to get going.'

Susan's first attempt at home cooking was a disaster. She had gone to town the next day, eager with her new project, and bought a pound of stewing beef, carrots and onions. But when they tried to eat it the meat was tough, almost inedible, and tasteless too because she had put no seasoning with it. They had to open a tin of baked beans instead. Dad was tolerant, especially when he saw how crestfallen Susan was, but he also made it clear that he needed a meal he could actually eat when he came in hungry after a hard day's work, and that maybe Susan was being a bit too ambitious.

The next day, being still half term, Susan went back to poring over the recipe books. She also borrowed some books from the library on basic cookery, so that she could read about the cookery terms themselves rather than just the recipes. She followed the text and instructions with fascination; it was as if secret rites were being revealed to her. She found out that 'simmer' meant to be just very gently boiling, and that this was important to tenderise the stringy stewing meat. She discovered that when the recipe said to 'simmer for three hours' boiling it fast for one hour to save time, as she had done, would not work. 'A stew boiled is a stew spoiled,' was the wise advice. The words unpacked themselves from the page into her mind, and she had her first inkling that cookery was a fusion of skill, art and the right amount of intuition. She pored over the books for hours, savouring the words, which became edged with mysterious arcane poetry for her: *'roll in flour and fry gently until brown…' 'season to taste with salt and pepper…', 'roast until the juices run clear…'.*

Fortified with new knowledge, this time she bought some minced beef, stock cubes and herbs. She carefully allowed the instructions to speak to her, confident now with the terms, and made a cottage pie. She didn't tell Dad in advance. If it had turned out badly, she would have thrown it out and heated some shop bought pies in the oven instead. Instead, it was perfect; rich dark gravy lapping around tender meat and juicy carrots, topped off by the contrast of creamy mashed potatoes crisped to peaks on the top by a blast under the grill. Just like Mum used to make.

***

Soon Susan was making most of the meals that Mum used to make,

21

and branching out to more exotic dishes such as spaghetti bolognaise and curry. She took over doing all the shopping. Then she also began to notice when the carpets had bits on them and when there was dust on the sideboard, and she duly got out the vacuum cleaner and the duster. It was so pleasing to see the house clean and fresh after she had finished. She widened her scope, eagerly looking for what else she could do. Soon she was busy every afternoon and evening after school and every weekend keeping house. It focussed and steadied her. She was walking in Mum's footsteps, being like her. It gave her a warm feeling to present a meal to Dad and have him sigh, replete with pleasure, afterwards. The gaunt look was beginning to disappear from his face, and the stress furrows were softening. It was so good that she could help him. It felt like keeping Mum alive. It was odd; she was stepping into Mum's shoes, running the house in the way that Mum used to and yet, although she knew Dad did look after her, there were times when it felt like it was she who was the grown up.

***

There was just over a week left until the end of the summer term, and a stir of excitement, of restlessness, was whispering through the girls' school. The July weather had turned hot and school windows were thrown open in the classrooms while the girls sweltered in their identical stripy summer dresses. At break time that morning Susan had been on the edge of a group of girls who were sitting on the grass talking about the forthcoming school holidays. Several of the girls were making daisy chains and putting them round each other's necks, or on each other's heads. Jane, lying down with her head on Melissa's lap, said she was going with her family to a caravan for a fortnight. No-one asked Susan what she was doing. In fact, she didn't know. They had always been on holiday as a family, usually to the same resort, but that just wasn't possible now. Not that she and Dad had talked about it, but they both knew they couldn't revisit the place where it had happened. Dad had vaguely mentioned that they might go away for a week somewhere. But nothing had been arranged, and neither of them felt much inclination.

Susan finished off her daisy chain by joining the first daisy to the last, and hung it round her own neck. 'That looks nice,' said Jane, glancing up and threading the fifth daisy onto her chain. They heard the bell ring for the end of break time. 'Oh… I haven't got time to make mine into a necklace now,' said Jane, and threw it down onto the grass. The girls got up and brushed grass off each other as they made their way back indoors, lingering as long as they dared. Susan picked up Jane's discarded daisies and followed at the back.

The next class was Geography. Susan quite liked Geography. She liked learning about the way the earth was formed; estuaries and rift valleys, mountains and glaciers. It probably came third on her list of favourite subjects, after English and History. In the last few weeks though, she had struggled more to keep up, because the housework and cooking didn't leave her much time for homework. At the end of the class Susan gathered up her books, carefully wiping her mapping pen on a piece of blotting paper before stowing it in her satchel. As she left the classroom her form teacher was waiting at the door. 'Good morning, Miss Mitchell,' girls chorused cheerfully as they passed her. They were all going to miss her next term when they moved up into the Upper Fourth. She was one of the most popular teachers, young and smiling. She wore flowery dresses that ended just above her knees and she had a soft cloud of untidy hair. More than one girl had a crush on her.

'Ah, Susan,' she said in her chirpy high voice. 'Can I have a quick word with you?' She guided Susan to the side of the corridor. One or two girls glanced half-curiously in her direction before they hurried on to the next class. Susan flicked an enquiring glance at her, her satchel clutched to her chest, before she dropped her eyes to the floor.

'How are you, Susan?'

'I'm alright, Miss.'

There was a pause. She felt Miss Mitchell's bright sparrow eyes on her.

'Susan, I'd like to have a little chat with you and your father. In the next few days if that's possible.'

Susan licked her lips. 'He has to work in the garage every day, Miss.'

'I know, I know.' She pushed back her hair from her eyes where it immediately flopped down again. 'What I was thinking is that I could call in at your home. What time does your father finish in the afternoon?'

'About five o'clock. But sometimes later.'

She nodded. 'Do you think you could ask him if I could pop round tomorrow about five-thirty for a chat? Just for a few minutes. You can let me know in class tomorrow morning. Is that alright?'

'Yes, Miss. Can I go now please? Only I'm late for French.'

'Of course. If your teacher asks you where you've been, just say I wanted a word with you. She'll understand.'

***

'You're sure you don't know what she wants?' Dad had rushed in at five o'clock and hurriedly washed and changed into trousers and a shirt, and was now running a comb through his hair.

Susan was opening a pack of Garibaldi biscuits and putting them on a plate. 'I've told you. She just said she was popping round for a chat.'

'Teachers don't just pop round to your house for nothing.' He frowned, his voice edged with concern. 'There isn't anything you haven't told me, is there? You haven't got into any trouble at school?'

'Dad, I told you, I haven't got a clue what she wants. Maybe she just wants to see if I'm OK. She's really nice.' Susan tried to say all this with conviction, but she was well aware that she hadn't been doing her homework properly for weeks. But surely Miss would talk to her in school about that?

The knock on the door was prompt at 5.30pm. From the kitchen Susan could hear the voices in the hall: *Hello, I'm John Smith, I don't think we've met before, it was always Susan's Mum Jean who used to go to the parents' evening and things, I used to leave all that to her...* Susan could tell from his forced jollity that he was nervous. She clasped her hands tightly behind her back and waited while Dad showed their visitor into the front room. Susan had run the duster over the furniture in there straight after she had come in from school. She took a deep breath and joined them.

'Hello Susan,' said Miss Mitchell, smiling warmly in that way she had which made her cheeks crinkle. 'I was just saying to your father what a nice room this is.' She looked around her, taking everything in. 'Oh is that your mother?' She had homed in on a picture of Mum on the sideboard and bent down to study it. The picture had been taken five years ago on Mum's thirtieth birthday. She was wearing a pink summer dress with a matching cardigan in a slightly darker shade and her silver locket. Susan felt vaguely exposed by the scrutiny. Miss Mitchell was out of place here.

Miss Mitchell straightened up and turned her gaze to study Susan. 'I can see your resemblance to your mother, Susan,' she said.

'My Jean certainly was a looker,' said Dad. Susan frowned slightly; she didn't think she looked anything like Mum. Mum was tall and slender, and she had had wonderful, glossy dark hair with a natural wave to it whereas her own hair was straight and mousy. 'Susan, put the kettle on, will you,' said Dad. 'I expect you'd like a cup of tea? And do sit down.'

When Susan brought the tea tray and put it down on the coffee table, Dad and Miss Mitchell were chatting and laughing like old friends. The room was cosily filled by a comfy three-piece suite, well-worn now, a coffee table in front of the fireplace, a sideboard, a glass-fronted cabinet containing the best glasses and tea service, and a couple of small extra chairs. Miss Mitchell was sitting in the chair that used to be Mum's, with the standard lamp behind her. Susan felt hot all over and her hands trembled as she poured the tea. Silence fell as they all sipped.

'I expect you're wondering why I'm here,' said Miss Mitchell, putting her teacup down and clearing her throat. It occurred to Susan that her teacher was nervous. Miss Mitchell looked from one to the other of them, and then fixed her eyes earnestly on Dad. 'My colleagues and I have been keeping a very careful eye on Susan this year. After the awful tragedy.' She took a breath. 'And it did seem, in the first few weeks, that you were coping very well, Susan. A bit quiet and withdrawn, but that was understandable.' She turned back to Dad. 'Her work was of the same high standard that it had been during the first year. But in the last few months there has been a change.' Susan felt her cheeks going red. She stared at the carpet, where there were a few small burn marks in front of the fireplace, evidence of the odd spark jumping out when they had had a log fire at Christmas. You had to look carefully to see the burn marks, though. 'But now I'm sorry to say that all of my colleagues who have been teaching Susan this year, and myself, have noticed a marked deterioration in her work. She either doesn't do her homework or it is inadequate, and consequently she is falling behind in class. We chatted about this just after Easter, didn't we Susan?' she finished.

'Yes, Miss,' muttered Susan. It was all going to come out now, and Dad was going to be angry with her.

'But... but,' Dad looked from one to the other. 'You never said anything to me, Susan!'

Susan twisted her hands but didn't reply.

'Could you talk to us about this?' said Miss Mitchell gently. She reached out and laid her hand briefly on Susan's. 'We are all worried about you and we'd like to help.'

Eventually, with Miss Mitchell's encouragement, Susan told her. She told her how she had started cooking, how much she enjoyed it and found she was good at it. Then she found she could apply the same sort of skills to all the housework – shopping, washing, cleaning. She really liked doing it; it made her feel good, but it took up a lot of time. Every now and then Miss Mitchell interrupted to ask a question. Dad said nothing; he just slumped in his chair.

'Let just make sure I have this right,' said Miss Mitchell. 'Susan, now you do all the housekeeping yourself?' When Susan nodded, she continued, 'Well, I can see that you make a wonderful job of it, but things can't go on like this. You're only thirteen, and your school work must come first.'

Dad seemed to wake up. 'You must think I'm such a bad parent, letting Susan take all this load. I didn't realise she wasn't doing her homework. And... and... well, she just sort of took over the house, bit by bit, like.' He shook his head and sat forward, clasping his big hands together. 'I can see now I should have realised. Things will change though, you'll see.'

Miss Mitchell went on to tell them there had been talk of Susan having to repeat the year. But if they could guarantee that Susan would in future attend to her school work as a priority, then at the staff meeting next week Miss Mitchell would state her view, after this visit – this unofficial visit – that Susan should be allowed to progress as normal to the next year. They talked a bit more, and Susan agreed that she would spend time in the summer holidays catching up on her school work.

Susan sat motionless on the sofa, hearing Dad still apologising as he showed Miss Mitchell out. He came back into the front room and threw himself down in the chair, wiping his hand over his face. Susan dragged her eyes up to look at him. As she opened her mouth to say how sorry she was, Dad got up and came to sit next to her on the sofa. He took her hand.

'I'm so sorry, love. You seemed so confident, so grown up, I just let you get on with it.' He sighed. 'You should have kept up with your school work, though. And I should have checked, I should have checked.' He shook his head 'Whatever would Mum think.'

That was too much for Susan and, although she tried to gulp the tears back, she started to cry. 'There, there, love.' He wrapped his arms round her while she cried against his chest. He smelt vaguely of grease and oil. Comforting Dad smells.

'So, what are we going to do,' he said when she was quieter and had wiped her face on the back of her hand. 'I suppose we'll have to get someone in to help three or four days a week, a part-time housekeeper. It'll cost, but it has to be done. I know I could do more, but, well, you know that I'm not very good at this housework lark.' He stroked her hair. 'Not like you.'

The Garibaldi biscuits that Susan had arranged on the plate were untouched, next to the empty teacups. Susan wondered now why she had bought those instead of shortcake or Bourbon creams. Dad nudged her gently. 'We'll get something sorted before you go back to school in September. Yes?'

So Susan agreed. What choice was there?

'I'll tell you another thing,' said Dad. 'That teacher, what's her name… Miss Mitchell, she came here to look us over. To see what sort of a home I'm bringing you up in.' He scratched his chin. 'She was kind enough with it though, and not too obvious. And, even with all that untidy hair, a nice looking woman too. Yes, there hasn't been a woman as pretty as that in this house since your mother.'

Chapter 3

It was true what Matthew had said and what I had expected anyway. For the first days I just lay on my bed and the world went on without me. Or it might not have done, I didn't know or care. Then I started to sit in the chair more, putting it by the tiny window so that I could see the corner of the staff car park and the sycamore tree over the wall. The edges of the leaves were starting to turn brown like rust on an abandoned car. I spent minutes, hours, watching those leaves.

There was a rubbish bin and three car parking spaces in my field of view. Sometimes I would see a person leaving their car or going back to it as they started or finished their shift. The person I saw most often was a plump woman, late thirties perhaps, light brown fleece bundled over her cleaner's uniform, gaping bag slung over her shoulder. She would always be dragging heavily on a cigarette as she walked, as if she needed it after a hard day, and she was usually texting on her mobile phone with her other hand. What was she saying? *Just leaving, put pizza in oven in 10 mins?* or *Just leaving, will pick up Indian?* I started to script her life in my head. Her name was Donna, she was married to Dave who was on the dole and they had two kids. Donna, Dave, dole? Perhaps not.

I tapped my fingers on the table. Yes, today I felt ready. I was starting to settle down and the wheels in my brain were turning. I got out my laptop and turned on the word processor. The empty page offered itself to me, naked and enticing.

Dad found someone to come in and help with the house. Mrs Dobbs was a large woman in her sixties and she suffered with a chest complaint. She would gasp and wheeze about the house like a defective steam engine. Susan relinquished her role as housekeeper reluctantly. Still, she had to admit that Mrs Dobbs was a reasonable cook and in time a tolerable routine settled down on the household. Susan was still able to practice her cookery, which had now become her main hobby, on a weekend. She worked hard at her school work and, being a bright girl, was able to catch up where she had fallen behind. By the end of the Upper Fourth, she was back on schedule and she pleased Dad by having very good end of year exam marks.

***

A new school year. The girls, like noisy exotic birds, chattered to each other excitedly and exclaimed over what they had done in the summer. The Lower Fifth! They would be embarking on two years of work towards their O-level exams, having made their subject choices at the end of the summer. Basically, the choice was sciences or arts, and Susan had chosen arts. She had tentatively renewed some of her friendships, but she tended not to see friends very much out of school because she liked to cook and clean at the weekends. On Sundays they still usually saw Aunty Pat and Susan's cousins. Occasionally she went to the pictures or to a birthday party.

Susan settled straightaway into the new school year. She had looked forward to going back to school; the summer holidays sometimes still held a sad hollowness and a reminder of that summer two years ago when everything had changed. Now that she was back at school the daily routine held her safely, and in general she enjoyed her lessons and life was bearable.

Madeleine, the most popular girl in the class, had a new haircut. Her long ponytail had gone and she was perched cross-legged on her desk, showing off her new cropped bob to the admiring circle of girls who were invariably clustered around her. Madeleine's aunt was a teacher in the school, so she was a source of news and gossip – not all of it reliable. Susan joined the edge of the circle just in time to hear, 'Yes it's true. Cross my heart and hope to die! The new teachers this year are *men!* She paused for effect while everyone exclaimed their disbelief. They were a *girls'* school! Men teachers? But how exciting if it were true!

'Are they young?'

'What are they going to teach?'

'Will they be teaching us?'

'What do they look like?'

Madeleine drew herself up and told her audience that there was a young one – *only just out of teacher training college* - was going to teach Physics and one who was older (but she didn't know how old) was going to teach English and some Religious Education. There were groans and complaints from those in the class – the majority - who weren't taking Physics as one of their options. Susan smiled and listened but didn't join in. She didn't really see what the fuss was about. It didn't make any difference if the teachers were men, as long as they were fair and not too strict. Just then any more speculation in the class was stopped as their new form mistress came in and told them to go to their desks quickly and silently. This year for the first time their desks were allocated alphabetically, so Susan found herself again next to Jane, whose surname was Sims. They smiled at one another and gave a thumbs-up sign.

It happened that their new timetable showed that they had an English class later that morning, so they didn't have long to wait to find out if what Madeleine said was true. They waited before the class in a simmer of suppressed giggles and speculation. He was late! After a few minutes the door was pushed open and thirty pairs of eyes swivelled to get the first view of who came in.

It was indeed a man. He was carrying a battered briefcase plus four books under his arm, and he was breathing slightly heavily. Chairs scraped the floor as the girls duly rose to their feet. Their new teacher was medium height, not slim but not plump, with dark hair cut quite short at the back and wavy on top, and heavy framed glasses. He wore a nondescript suit and a tie which was slightly askew. His clothes were comfortably rumpled; not exactly untidy but not smart either. You couldn't say he was old, but certainly not young either. The atmosphere in the room sagged. He was not the handsome prince they had pinned

31

their hopes on.

He surveyed them solemnly. 'I'm Mr Morgan. Good morning, class.'

'Good morning, Mr Morgan,' they intoned.

'I'm sorry I was a little late. As you know, it's my first day and I had some difficulty finding my way around. Anyway, I'm here now. Sit down, please.' He had a pleasingly melodic voice, with a slight accent that Susan couldn't place.

Madeleine put her hand up. 'Please Sir,' she said. 'My desk is right at the back but I can't see the board properly without my glasses. Please can I come and sit at the front, near you?'

'I'm not going to be writing on the board very much this lesson. And next time it would be as well to remember your glasses.' A slight pause. 'Now then, I'd like to go through this term's syllabus with you.'

Jane caught Susan's eye and they both bent their heads to hide their smirks. Susan couldn't recall ever seeing Madeleine wearing glasses.

***

Mrs Dobbs had been, by mutual agreement, not working for them during the summer, and was due to start again when Susan went back to school. But then in the middle of the school holidays she called to see them and told them, in her husky apologetic voice, that she wouldn't be able to carry on because her husband wasn't a well man and he needed her at home. Susan felt a froth of panic rising in her. She had become comfortable with Mrs Dobbs. The arrangement had settled into a groove that suited them all. She hadn't realised until now, when it was about to change, that she had been quite content with this rhythm, and Dad felt the same. His life too was shaping into a new pattern. With Susan fifteen next birthday, he had started in the summer to go out to the pub on a Friday night, and sometimes Saturday too, or to go out somewhere with his mates on a Saturday afternoon after the garage had closed. Susan didn't mind.

Dad had put an advert for a new housekeeper in the local newspaper, and also a card in the newsagent's window. One day near the end of the summer holidays Susan arrived home after swimming at the local town baths with Melissa and Jane, her wet towel and swimming costume rolled up and tucked under her arm. Dad was in the garage office as Susan was walking past to the house, and he banged on the window to get her attention.

Susan diverted and went in. A car, a Hillman Minx, was up on the ramps with its bonnet open and another two cars were waiting alongside. The radio, which was always blaring out in the garage, was playing the song that was top of the charts that week, about San Francisco and wearing flowers in your hair. Susan loved the song, and had a secret yearning be a hippy and wear flowers in her hair. Joe, the middle aged mechanic who had been with Dad ever since he started the business, was working on the elevated car, socket in hand, and black with grease.

'Hello love, we haven't seen you in here for ages. Are you alright?' he called to Susan. Susan liked Joe. When she was little he used to bring her a chocolate bar sometimes.

Dad poked his head round the door and beckoned her into the office. The office was an untidy mess of overflowing filing cabinets and a desk tottering under various bills, invoices, letters, MOT certificates and other thumbed paperwork. Susan always wondered how Dad managed to find anything.

'Good news, love.' He swivelled round in his old office chair, which had stuffing poking out of one side. 'Someone has answered the advert for our Mrs Mop. She rang up. It was a bad line and I couldn't hear her very well, but she's calling round later. Six o'clock.'

When Susan answered the door at precisely six o'clock the person who stood on the doorstep couldn't have been less like Mrs Dobbs, or less like a Mrs Mop at all. She and Susan stared at each other across the threshold for a moment without speaking. Who is this, thought Susan.

'I have come about the job,' she said in a rich, low voice. 'My name is Wanda.'

Susan blinked back her confusion. 'Ah... You'd better come in.' She stepped back and showed her into the front room while she fetched Dad.

'She's here,' she whispered to Dad. 'I don't think she's going to be any good, though.'

Dad also had to hide his surprise when he saw the girl sitting on the sofa, looking not much older than Susan. Her hair was cut very short, almost like a boy's, she had a pale solemn face, and she was small and scrawny. In her jeans and blue shirt, she might have been playing the part of a waif in a film. She sat very still with her hands linked in front of her. Dad cleared his throat and asked her what experience she had. She quietly told them, in her accented voice, that she had kept house and looked after several brothers and sisters in Poland, while her mother worked. Her father was dead. She and her mother now lived in England and she was looking for part-time work. She was twenty-two years old. She asked if she might see the kitchen, and enquired what sort of meals they would want. Dad jumped up and showed her through, explaining that they weren't fancy eaters. In the kitchen she gazed round inscrutably, nodding her head, and smoothed her hand over the table. Susan wanted to say, what are you looking for? Dirt? You won't find any here. When Dad asked her when she could start, Susan couldn't believe her ears.

After Dad had shook hands with Wanda and she had left, Susan and Dad had an argument – a rare thing for them and so all the more upsetting. Susan wanted to wait to see if more people responded to their advert, or to put some more 'help wanted' cards in newsagents. She's too young, insisted Susan. And she's… she's… well, she seems a bit odd. What does that matter, countered Dad, as long as she can do the job? We might as well give her a try. It ended up with Dad shouting that he was the one who was going to be paying the girl's wages, and that Susan could like it or lump it. Susan flounced up to her bedroom and curled up in a ball of spiky misery on her bed. Edward Bear was there on her pillow and she buried her face in his diminished fur. Whatever would Mum have thought about this foreign girl coming into their home?

***

Over the weeks and months, Susan had to admit that Wanda turned out to be the answer to their prayers. Three days a week she became used to coming in from school and finding Wanda cleaning or preparing the evening meal. She was like a shadow, gliding round and doing her work efficiently and unobtrusively; humbly, almost. At first she talked very little to Susan, apart from queries about household things (*where is floor cleaner, do you want that I change the sheets next time I come, do you and your father like swede...*). This was unlike Mrs Dobbs, who had always been ready to put down her duster and chat. Then gradually Wanda started to ask Susan what she had done in school in school that day, and listen carefully to her answer, nodding and even smiling sometimes. When she smiled it was as if a little pixie who hid behind her eyes popped out for a minute. What really made Susan cautiously warm towards her was that Wanda didn't seem to think it was strange that Susan enjoyed cooking and had been keeping house until a year ago, and they would consult together about meals and recipes. Susan asked her where she had learned to cook – because she produced some delicious casseroles – and Wanda told her how she had learned from her grandmother as a child in Poland. Then, Susan would sense her withdrawing, as if she had shared more of herself than she intended.

If Susan found herself able to tolerate Wanda, Dad positively liked her. But then, there were not many people that Dad didn't like and get on with. As the months went by Dad seemed to know a lot about Wanda, and Susan was surprised to discover that on the three days that she worked Wanda made lunch for Dad and sometimes they ate together in the middle of the day, in the kitchen. 'Well, she makes me a good hot lunch, soup or something, and the least I can do is give her a bit of company,' Dad told her. 'And, her being such a thin little thing and all, I insist that she sits down and shares it with me. She didn't want to at first, but I insisted.' Susan said nothing. Was she imagining it or was Dad being a bit defensive? The she told herself not to be so mean. It was nice for Dad to have some different company.

From Dad she found out that Wanda lived with her mother. Her father had been killed in the war and eventually she had come with her mother to England four years ago. She was reluctant to say any more about her history, Dad didn't like to ask about other brothers and sisters, who had not come with them.

One day when Susan came home from school Wanda was dusting the shelves in the front room. She had moved all the ornaments and photographs off to have a thorough clean. Mum had dozens of little ornaments and trinkets, mementoes of places they had visited. Susan stiffened as Wanda picked up the picture of Mum and Dad on their wedding day, their heads inclined together and the cloud of Mum's white veil trailing over her shoulder.

'It is your Mother, yes?'

Susan nodded.

'She is very beautiful.'

'Yes,' whispered Susan, caught unawares by the stinging that came to her eyes, that could still happen unexpectedly sometimes.

To her surprise Wanda put down her duster and put her arm around Susan. 'It is hard,' she said simply.

The kind gesture was too much for Susan. She leant against Wanda and let herself surrender to a brief hug. It was strange being hugged by someone smaller than herself.

'I'm sorry,' she said, pulling herself away. 'I should be better than that now. It's been two and a half years now since she died.'

'It's alright, Susan. You know, I think you are very brave.'

'You do?'

'Oh yes.' She smiled and her nose crinkled up.

But there was a niggling shadow. Susan couldn't have said what it was that didn't seem quite right about Wanda. She was hiding something. Was it her foreignness, or was it the way she could be behind you when you didn't know she was even there? Or something secret?

***

The novelty of having a male teacher wore off as the weeks went by. In general the girls respected Mr Morgan. As teachers went, he was quite strict when needed, but they would grudgingly admit that he was fair. He kept order in class without ever raising his voice and he tried to make his lessons interesting. He didn't smile much though, and the girls weren't able to find out if he had a wife or girlfriend. On the whole they thought he didn't look the type; he was much too studious. After a time, they lost interest.

For Susan, by the time it was nearly Easter Mr Morgan's English classes had become her favourite lessons, and his passion for the subject had melted into her. They were reading and analysing the *The Mayor of Casterbridge*, and Susan was totally enamoured of the story. Lucetta - what a beautiful name! And they were studying poems by Robert Frost. Susan knew them by heart and plump words about apple-picking and dark, deep woods bloomed in her head.

They also created their own beauty with the English language, writing poetry and essays for homework. Susan put her whole essence into this, and usually got a B+ or an A- with a *good work* or *well done* scribbled alongside in red pen. Often Mr Morgan would write long comments on her work, which showed he had really read it properly. Some of the other girls would say the same thing. They all wondered how he possibly had time to do anything else but teach. Maybe he *didn't* do anything else. But Madeleine said she had seen him shopping for groceries in the Co-op, one Saturday morning. She reported that she saw eggs and bread and tinned peas in his basket. So presumably he ate.

Chapter 4

I drew in a deep breath and rotated my shoulders to ease the ache from where I had been hunched over the laptop. The light was beginning to fade; I hadn't noticed. I stood up to stretch my legs. Four paces across the room and four paces back. Outside at the rubbish bin was a cluster of three smokers. Their arms wrapped around their bodies in lieu of coats told me that it was a cold evening.

I felt tired, stale. Was I pushing too much? I went to the sink in the bathroom and splashed cold water over myself. I watched in the mirror as the rivulets of water streamed over my bald head and coursed down my face like tears. I gently touched my wet scalp. Sometimes you can look in the mirror and hardly recognise the person in there.

One day at the start of the summer term Susan came home from school, laden with books as usual. She was hot and thirsty, because they had been playing tennis in the afternoon and the weather had turned sultry. She dropped her satchel on the kitchen floor and her blazer on the chair, ran herself a glass of water at the sink and gulped at it. She noticed out of the corner of her eye that Wanda had put a vase of wild flowers on the table. There were various bumps coming from above; that would be Wanda, she thought, as she headed to the living room with her glass. At the bottom of the stairs she stopped. Wanda was talking to someone, but not in her usual voice. This was sing-song speech. Then she started actually singing. Perhaps she's talking to herself, thought Susan. But then she heard a chortle of laughter. It sounded just like a small child.

Puzzled, Susan drained her glass and went upstairs. Wanda was in the bathroom, with her back to her, scouring the wash-hand basin. To Susan's utter amazement in the empty bathtub was a small child, scarcely more than a baby. The child was dressed in brightly spotted red and green dungarees and was playing with a pink plastic rabbit. He or she turned the most enormous dark eyes onto Susan with frank curiosity when she came in. Wanda spun round.

'Ah, Susan. I didn't hear you.' It was the first time Susan had seen Wanda anything approaching flustered. She peeled off her yellow rubber gloves and snatched up the child.

'So I see.' Susan extended a cautious smile towards the child, who was still gazing at her solemnly. The course of her life had hardly ever brought her into contact with small children. 'Hello,' she said, feeling foolish.

'Susan, I would like you to meet Katya.' Wanda kissed Katya's cheek. 'My daughter. I am very sorry I bring her with me today. My mother usually is looking after her, but yesterday she had some bad thing to eat and was very sick this morning. So I had to bring Katya. But my mother will be better soon, I am sure.'

'Oh... oh, I didn't know you were married.'

'I am not married, Susan.'

Susan didn't know how to reply. Wanda had regained her composure and waited with quiet dignity. To hide her discomfort,

Susan smiled again at Katya and reached out a tentative finger to tickle her cheek. The skin was pillow soft. The child dimpled and beamed back at Susan, exposing tiny white teeth.

'Oh…' Susan was captivated by the pleasure that this simple human response brought her. 'She's beautiful!'

'Would you like to hold her?'

'I don't think so… I've never held a baby before.' Susan stepped back uncertainly, but Wanda was already slipping Katya off her hip and passing her over.

Susan clutched the child to her, uncertain of how to grasp her. She felt robust and solid in her arms, heavier than Susan might have expected. She held her hand and the small fat fingers curled around hers. Susan laughed in delight and Katya copied her with a gurgle.

'How old is she?'

'She's fifteen months. I think she want to get down now.'

Susan lowered the now wriggling child to the floor and she tottered off on her little drunken legs, soon plopping down onto her bottom. 'She is only just starting to walk. Aren't you, *skarbie*?' said Wanda, her voice gentle.

'Does Dad know…, I mean, does he know about Katya?'

'He met her for the first time today, same as you. And, also same as you, he thinks she is a darling. Susan…' she paused. 'This does not change anything, you know. I will still be coming to cook and clean for you both.'

'Alright,' said Susan, trying to digest this complete surprise. Just when she thought she was starting to get to know her, Wanda was still an enigma. What else was there that she still didn't know?

***

They didn't see Aunty Pat so often nowadays. The pattern of having Sunday lunch alternate weeks in each other's houses had petered out as Susan and Dad had learned how to be a family on their own. And also, Aunty Pat seemed to go out a lot nowadays. She still kept in touch though; she and Dad would talk on the phone about once a week, and always Susan would hear Dad say 'Yes, she's alright,' so she would know that Aunty Pat had asked about her. Sometimes she herself chatted with Aunty Pat on the phone. 'I have to keep an eye on you, Susie, now that your Mum can't do it. Well, I'm sure she *is* keeping an eye on you, from up there. You know. In heaven…'

But today Aunty Pat was coming over to see them. They hadn't seen her for weeks through the summer and Susan was looking forward to it. She was fond of her aunt, who fascinated and shocked her all at the same time. Even though she would never say it out loud, in her heart Susan knew the difference between Mum and Aunty Pat: Mum was a lady and Aunty Pat wasn't. Still, she had a good heart and Mum had treated her like a sister. Today Frank was coming too. Susan's two older cousins were full grown men now in their early twenties and presumably had better things to do with their Saturdays.

Aunty Pat and Frank had caught the train from Burlingham to the town and then the bus to get to their house. From the window Susan saw the red bus drawing up at the stop just outside the garage, and then creak its way off down the road, having set down two passengers. Susan drew in her breath. Aunty Pat was wearing an orange miniskirt that was at least six inches above her knee, showing bare mottled legs underneath. She had had her hair cut into a jaw-length pageboy, with a long fringe. She was older than Dad so she must be what… she must be forty or more now, Susan calculated. Frank lumbered along beside her, fiddling with his glasses. He had shot up recently, and was now half a head above his mother. And if he was not slouching so much he would have been taller still.

They all exchanged hugs and kisses in the hallway. Susan tried not to stare at the black curtain of Aunty Pat's false eyelashes (this was the first time she had seen any, close to) and tried to avoid her pale pink lipstick when they kissed. Even so, she felt a surge of affection for her; she was nothing if not spirited. She and Frank hugged awkwardly and avoided each other's eyes. It was hard to believe now that they had giggled and played together so naturally a few years ago.

'You're looking well, John.' Aunty Pat looked her brother over when they were all settled in the front room with tea and cake.

Dad nodded through a mouthful of Susan's chocolate cake. 'Can't complain. Business is still good, and the darts team that I play with of a

Friday night is top of the league now.'

'I'm glad you're getting out and about. I go out a bit too. It makes a change from the telly.'

Frank grunted. 'A bit! It was nearly three o'clock in the morning when you came back last Saturday.'

'It wasn't that late, was it? I'd been to Top Rank, dancing. Then there's no buses back at that time of night, so I have to walk, unless I get a lift of course…' She paused. 'Anyway Frank, you're old enough to be in the house on your own now. When I was your age, I was out working in the factory, not still cosseted in school like you are.'

'How school going, Frank?' asked Dad.

Frank shrugged. ''S OK, I suppose.'

'It would be a lot better than OK if you pulled your socks up and did a bit more work,' said Aunty Pat, rummaging in her bag for her cigarettes. 'Like Susie here. I'll bet you're doing well, aren't you love?'

'She's always among the top girls in the class. I'm dead proud of her,' said Dad. 'Do you know, she's talking eight – no, nine, isn't it – O-level exams next summer!'

Susan felt herself blushing.

'Well, fancy that,' said Pat. 'What's your favourite subject, love? I bet it's cookery. It's got to be cookery, you're so clever in the kitchen!'

'I don't actually do cookery at school,' Susan replied. 'In the top stream we have to do Latin instead of Domestic Science.'

Frank pulled a face. 'Latin… whatever for? Where do they speak Latin?'

'Well, nowhere now,' Susan said. 'But it teaches you about the structure of languages. Anyway, English is my favourite subject. I like writing stories and poems, and reading literature. We have a really good English teacher.' She turned to Frank. 'Is Metalwork still your favourite thing at school? You used to be good at that.' She still felt a soft spot for Frank, remembering their childhood days together. He always seemed so disgruntled nowadays.

'Yeah, I like making things,' he said, brightening a bit. 'This term we're making a drilling jig.' He shot her a grateful look, and it was almost back to the unspoken communication they used to have between them a few years ago.

42

'That reminds me,' said Dad, jumping up suddenly. 'Frank, you'll never guess what car I've got in the garage at the moment, having its clutch replaced? It's an MG! Come and have a look.' Frank got up, almost eagerly, and Dad slung his arm round the boy's shoulders and clapped him on the back.

Aunty Pat sighed as she sat back and watched Susan gather up the tea things and load them onto the tray. 'I'm glad he takes an interest in our Frank. Your Dad is the nearest thing he's got to a father now.' Her face hardened. 'His Dad doesn't so much as send him a birthday card, the mean bastard. Excuse my French.' She followed Susan into the kitchen and leaned against the draining board while Susan ran hot water into the sink to wash up.

'By the way, is that girl still coming in to do for you? The foreign one?'

'Wanda? Yes, she comes three times a week. She's been coming for over a year now, apart from the holidays.'

'And your Dad only told me the other day on the phone that she's got a baby, and she's not married.'

Susan squirted washing-up liquid into the sink. 'Yes, a little girl. Katya. She's brought her here two or three times. But only when her mother – Wanda's mother, that is - can't look after her.'

'And where's the father in all this?'

'We haven't asked. Dad says she does her work here, and does it well, and that's all that matters.' It's nothing to do with you either, Susan wanted to add, but she didn't.

'Well, I think it's a bad example to you and I told your Dad that. But you know how easy going he is, he said he liked the girl.' She paused and fingered the long string of beads that were hanging round her neck. 'Susan, you never want to be getting yourself into trouble like that. You know that don't you?'

Susan dropped her head over the steamy froth and concentrated on scrubbing the inside of a teacup.

'Seriously now,' Aunty Pat persisted, 'Take it from me, there's plenty of boys out there who'd take advantage. And it's easy to get carried away. You know what I mean, don't you, Susie?'

Susan snatched up a tea-towel and nodded briefly.

43

'Have you got yourself a boyfriend yet? You can tell me, you know.' She put her hand on Susan's arm and said earnestly, 'You haven't got to let him go too far, but if you do, you must be careful.'

Susan dried the cups and said nothing. She was beginning to wonder if all this had been planned and Dad had deliberately whisked Frank away into the garage.

'But you do go out don't you, with your friends? To youth club, or maybe some dances?'

Susan shook her head. 'Sometimes I go to the pictures, or to someone's house for tea.'

'But no boys yet?'

Susan shook her head again, hoping this would soon be over.

'Well,' said Aunty Pat. 'That's a relief. But when you do start going out with boys — and you're fifteen, so it won't be long — you just come to me and I can tell you everything you need to know.' She leaned in confidentially. 'In fact, I've been out with a few men myself these last few months. Don't tell Frank though, he'd go bananas.' She winked at Susan. 'We'll have a chat again.'

***

'I have last week's homework to give back to you all,' said Mr Morgan from his desk at the front of the class. The red-covered exercise books were stacked neatly on the desk. He motioned to two girls at the front to hand round the books. 'There were some good efforts.' Susan took her book, and leafed through to her essay. C+. A change from her usually high marks, but this time she wasn't surprised; neither was she surprised to see a curt *see me* written next to the grade.

'Now,' continued Mr Morgan, taking his glasses off and polishing them on the small cloth he kept for the purpose, 'For that homework I asked you to describe a *place*; a place outdoors such as woods, fields, beaches or an urban settings that you knew well. Perhaps somewhere from your childhood that evoked emotions in you. I wanted you to make me see the place in my mind's eye; to see it how *you* saw it. We talked about this at length. Now,' he said again, 'For the next homework…'

44

The bell rang to signify the end of the class and, because it was the last class of the day, time to go home. He stopped speaking and waited patiently during the clamour of the bell. Some girls started fidgeting and furtively sliding books into their satchels. Susan waited, poised with her pencil and exercise book. 'For the next homework,' he began again, 'I would like you to do the same, but this time for an *indoor* space. So it could be a room, or a passageway, or a church, or a shop, for example. We will talk about this more next lesson, but for now I would like you to jot down some ideas.' Then he closed a textbook that was open in front of him and laid his hand on the top. Susan noticed that he always did this when he closed a book, as if in reverence for its preciousness. 'Any questions so far?' He looked around. 'Right, class dismissed.' The girls sprang up like greyhounds released at the start of a race, and started laughing and chattering. It was Friday; the weekend was here!

Two girls were waiting at Mr Morgan's desk. Presumably they also had *see me* written in red at the end of their essays, in Mr Morgan's flowing handwriting. Susan slowly gathered her things together – pencil case, exercise book, notebook, textbooks – and eyed the queue. Another girl joined it and then Susan tagged herself onto the end. For Susan, the 'see me' command at the end of her homework usually meant that he wanted to explain something that was simply too long to write at the end of the piece, or to ask her searching questions about what she had written. It would stimulate her and make her want to try even harder with her writing next time. Of course when they had another class to go to, the conversation would have to be very brief, so normally he saw girls at the end of Friday's class. He takes a lot of trouble with his teaching, she thought, as she watched him earnestly explaining a point to the girl in front of her. And he really seems to read everything properly, not just skim over it. The girl nodded dully and said, 'Yes, Sir.'

At last it was Susan's turn. She felt her heart beat faster as she silently laid her exercise book down in front of him. The C+ glared at her off the page.

'Ah yes, Susan.' He scrutinised at her short piece again and sat back in his chair. Chalk dust had settled on his tie like dandruff. Then he looked once more at her work.

'You start off really well. I liked the description of the beach. I felt that I could hear the waves and that I could really feel the sand between my toes, just like you did. Is this where you used to go on holiday as a child?'

'Yes Sir,' she said, her eyes fixed on the wastepaper bin by the side of his desk.

He frowned. 'But then, just as I was getting engrossed, your essay seemed to collapse. It becomes wooden and stilted, and you finish it very abruptly. I got the feeling there was a lot more to say, but for some reason you changed your mind. If it were someone else, I might have construed this as simply laziness, but because it's you, Susan, I was rather disturbed to have to give you a low mark.'

He stated all this simply and directly, as was his way. Although he had not asked her a question, she knew she was expected to say something.

'I just got fed up with it,' she said, feeling her cheeks grow hot. 'That's all.'

'Ah. I see. I wonder why.'

The classroom door was open and as girls passed by some glanced in, but no-one was curious. Their minds were on collecting their coats and hats from the cloakroom and going home.

Mr Morgan was perfectly still as he waited.

Susan drew in a breath. 'We used to go there every summer, every year for as long as I can remember. Then, three years ago, we stopped going.' Abruptly she bit her lip. Memories were pushing their way to the surface, things she didn't want to think about. 'That's where my Mum had an accident and died.'

'Ah…yes, I read in your file that your mother had died just before you started the Lower Fourth. I'm very sorry, Susan.' His voice was gentle.

She glanced at him in surprise.

'I read all my pupil's files,' he said. 'I like to know your backgrounds. Do you want to tell me what happened? You don't have to if you don't want to, but you see, terrible as that time was for you, you did make a free choice to write about it in your essay. That suggests to me that there's something inside you trying to get out.'

46

She shrugged, her eyes still on the floor. There were pencil shavings under the desk in front of her.

'One moment,' he got up and closed the classroom door. 'Let's sit down.' They both sat side by side at the desks in the front row. He looked out of place sitting at the small desk. 'Now, take your time.'

So she told him. She told him everything. It was like describing a film, scene by scene. At first, the words came out awkwardly, but then they seemed to be gushing out of her throat and she couldn't get them out quick enough. How she had gone on her own for an ice cream, how Mum had gone to the wool shop on the way back to the guest house, the ambulance driving off, the police, Dad telling her she had to be very brave, waiting for Dad at the guest house, the nightmare journey home, hearing that Mum had been mowed down by a car, that Mum was dead, she was dead...

Susan clutched the desk in front of her, unaware that she was doing it, hardly even aware any more of Mr Morgan's still presence.

The fountain of words kept on tumbling out, gathering momentum, welling up from some dark place inside her. She thought she might split in two from the sheer anguish of it. 'She was gone, Mum was gone, and it was all my fault...' she clapped her hands over her mouth, partly to catch the words and partly to muffle the frightening animal sounds that she was making.

'Susan, it's alright.' His voice was calm. He passed her a clean white handkerchief and she buried her face in it.

The corridor outside the classroom was growing quieter now, as girls hurried away to go home. Her breathing gradually slowed down and she was weak and trembling, but at least the fearful beast that had threatened to overwhelm her had backed away.

Mr Morgan leaned forward in his seat, his face intently looking at hers. She hung her head, embarrassed, ashamed, exhausted. 'What did you mean when you said it was all your fault?' She didn't reply. 'What did you mean, Susan? Tell me,' he said with teachers' authority in his voice.

'She went to the wool shop to get wool for *me*, to knit me a jumper. She wasn't going to go then, but I said I wanted her to. If she hadn't gone to the wool shop, for me, she wouldn't have been there, in that place, just where the car ran off the road. It was all my fault.'

She heard him make an impatient noise and the chair screeched back on the floor. He stood with his back to her. She waited. Whatever happened now, it didn't matter. Nothing could really matter.

He sat back down and faced her, his hands on his knees. 'Now Susan, I want you to listen to me.' This was the voice she knew, the voice he used in class to keep control, the voice they instinctively obeyed. 'What happened to your mother was an accident. A terrible, awful tragedy, but an *accident.* No-one was to blame. Not you, not anyone. I need you to believe me, Susan. It was *not your fault.*'

Not my fault... The sounds rolled round in her head like glass marbles, in the space just emptied by her outburst. She struggled to grasp the sounds, to give them meaning. 'Do you really think so?' she whispered.

'I *know* so.' His voice was still firm, but now she could hear the compassion in it.

'But... but Sir...' She hesitated, but then decided to plunge on, 'How could God have let it happen? My Mum was a good person, she never hurt anyone.'

'Ah, God.' He sighed. 'I don't know how to answer you, I only know that we have to trust. To trust that it's all part of a plan that we're not supposed to understand.'

They sat quietly side by side. The words ran through Susan's head: *not my fault... not my fault...* Was it true?

'I'm going to make a suggestion.'

Susan's eyes flickered. She felt so drained all she wanted to do was to drag herself home and curl up on her bed.

'You like writing, don't you, and you're good at it. I think you should write to your mother.'

'Write to Mum? But Sir...'

'Yes, yes, I know she's dead. But you could still unlock your thoughts and feelings and put them down on paper. Tell her how much you love her. Tell you how much you miss her. Tell her about your life now.'

Susan didn't want to seem rude. 'It seems a bit strange, writing to a dead person.'

'Well, I do it. My mother died last year, and I sometimes write to her.'

Susan gasped in frank amazement. He was smiling now and she thought how much kindness there was in his face. 'Yes, even teachers have mothers. I had mine for thirty-two years and I miss her very much, and I write to her to tell her so. And furthermore, I believe that somehow she sees my letters.'

That night Susan took a long look at the picture of Mum which was on her dressing table. She cried a bit when she got into bed and curled up with Edward Bear. Yet they were good tears. Something inside her had shifted.

Chapter 5

Matthew had let himself in with a knock on the door. I liked it that he accorded me that courtesy.

'All this writing!' He came to the side of the table to look over my shoulder at the computer screen. I instinctively pulled the lid down and he tactfully moved away.

'Is it a story, a proper story?'

'Yes, it's a story.'

'Ooh.' His eyes danced. 'What's it about? Is it full of romance, or is it a thriller or... I know,' he clapped his hands. 'A murder mystery! I just *adore* a whodunnit.'

'It's just a story.' I realised I was being overly protective, so I added, 'About a woman's life.'

'Aha. A saga then.'

'Hardly.'

He sat down on the bed. 'You're really not going to tell me, are you? Oh well, you seem to be enjoying it.'

'More than I thought. And more than anything, it passes the time.'

Dear Mum,

Susan put her pen down and gazed out of her bedroom window. There wasn't much of a view; she could see the small back yard with the washing line, the mute brick wall that marked the back of the garage premises and, beyond that, roofs of houses that corrugated away across the streets. Mum's sewing room, next to her room, shared the same view. Mum and Dad's room, or rather Dad's room now, looked out onto the garage workshops and the main road.

'I would love a little house on a housing estate,' Mum used to say, her eyes all soft and dreamy, 'a proper garden at the front and the back, with a lawn and flower beds. I'd have roses, and daffodils in the spring... oh and a lilac tree in one corner, and a little fence painted white, and a gate to match.' Then she would sigh and smile at Susan. 'But we can't always have everything we want, and we have to be thankful for what we have got. We're lucky that your Dad has got the garage, and that he provides for us so well. Always remember how lucky we are, Susan.'

Susan returned her attention to the white sheet of paper in front of her. For the last week she had been pondering the conversation with Mr Morgan. He had not treated her any differently in school afterwards, not asked how she was, yet she knew he was keeping an eye on her, and that made her feel safe. Protected. She looked at him now with new eyes. He was not just a teacher, he was a real person, a person who was compassionate and who had loved his mother and who was sad when she died. She even knew how old he was now. She knew she could have found some short-lived attention from the other girls in her class by revealing this pearl of information, but Susan was not interested in scratching for popularity. Anyway, she would have had to tell them how she came by the information, and that was completely private.

Sounds of a new hit record, *'Those were the days, my friend'*, were coming from the transistor radio beside her on her desk. The song was sweet and sentimental, with an ache behind the words. She picked up her pen again. The pain of not writing the letter, but knowing she must,

51

was beginning to be more than the pain she knew she would feel during the writing of it.

I miss you so much, Mum. Even though it's better than it used to be, I still miss you more than words can say. Sometimes I think I can't remember what you looked like, so I have to look at your picture. I have a picture of you right here next to my bed.

I've grown up since you last saw me. I'm fifteen and a half now. I like school and I'm doing well. I also like cooking and sewing, just like you did, although I'm not as good at it as you. But I do try to be like you. I have some friends at school, but I don't see them a lot. I prefer just to be at home. Dad is OK. You mustn't worry, I'm looking after him. He goes out with his friends some evenings and weekends, and he seems jolly most of the time. But I know he misses you.

Mum, why did you have to die? I know now it was just an accident, just something that happened. But why? I know it says in the Bible that you've gone to a better place. Are you happy there? Do you look down on me and Dad? Sometimes I imagine you there with the angels. Well, you are an angel yourself now.

Writing to you like this seems strange. I wish I knew if you can read this. Mr Morgan, that's my teacher, says that in a way you can, and anyway it doesn't matter. Just me writing to you and telling you how I feel is what counts. It's like my life is in two halves, when you were alive and after you died. Everything changed then.

My favourite subject at school is English. That's what Mr Morgan teaches. I still write short stories now and again (do you remember how I used to do that?), but more often poetry or essays of my own. Mr Morgan will look at things that you've written for yourself, if you ask him, and give you some feedback. He really is a good teacher, and a kind person too.

Susan paused and looked down in surprise at the page she had covered. Once she had started, her pen had found its own way.

Well, that's all for now,
All my love, Susan xxxx

***

52

Today was the day. Susan's stomach was churning with nerves, even though she knew she should be confident. At least, it was part nerves, part excitement. She stood behind the counter in the café, wiping the surface that she had just wiped five minutes before, and checking shelves that were perfectly well stocked. It was a hot summer day, and today she would have preferred to be out in the sunshine rather than working indoors. An elderly couple shuffled in. They were both wearing coats, despite the soaring temperatures.

'Two teas please, love.'

Susan served them with an automatic smile. 'Sugar's on the table.' Her eyes swivelled again yet again to the clock on the wall. Five minutes to go. She left the counter and went into the kitchen, where her employer was loading potatoes into the peeling machine, ready to make chips.

'Peggy, is it alright if I go now?'

Peggy paused, frowning, one hand on the handle of the machine.

'Do you remember, you said I could go early today because I have to go and get my O-level exam results from school?'

'Oh. I suppose so. I'll have to leave these spuds and serve then, won't I.' She wiped her hands on a grubby cloth. 'You will be in as normal tomorrow, though?'

Susan said that she would. She took off her overall and left, glad to be out from the clinging atmosphere of fried food and into the sunny August day. The bus was just coming. Peggy was not the most friendly of people and she hardly ever had a cheerful word to say. Still, Susan was glad to have a full-time job for the summer. And Peggy must think she was a good worker, because she had started the job there last summer and Peggy had asked if she would stay on and work Saturdays and holidays. Susan now had some money to call her own, and apart from things like buying records or the odd trip out, she didn't spend much and so she had quite a bit saved up. During the school holidays she worked all day except for Wednesdays and Sundays, but Wanda filled in at home over the summer so she didn't mind that her days were full.

Through the bus window she watched parades of undistinguishable terraced houses veiled with net curtains while the bus laboured up the hill. Then, they were approaching the school gates and all thoughts of Peggy and her café left her mind.

***

Susan was just about to fit her key into the front door when it sprang open.

'Dad!' she said in surprise. He must have knocked off early.

He pulled her in through the door 'Well?' he said, his eyes searching her face. 'Have you passed all nine?'

Susan took a deep breath. 'I got three Bs…' she paused.

'And what about the rest? Tell me!'

Susan couldn't hold back any longer. A beam erupted all over her face. 'And six As!'

Then it was all pandemonium as Dad hugged her and told her what a clever girl she was, and they danced around the hall together, whooping with laughter. Susan heard a little shriek and looked down to see Katya hanging onto her leg, wanting to join in with the dancing.

'Hello Katya, I didn't expect to see you here.' She picked the little girl up.

Katya grinned at her impishly, showing a row of perfect teeth. 'Cake,' she said. 'Mummy make cake.'

Wanda appeared in the doorway from the kitchen. Instead of the trousers and shirts that she normally wore, she was dressed in a pretty red frock with beige sandals. Susan had never seen her in a dress before.

'Hello Wanda! It's not your normal day is it?'

'No, is not. But your father asked us to come for tea, to celebrate with you. We knew you would do well. Congratulations, Susan. You are a clever girl and your father is right to be proud of you.' Wanda embraced her lightly and kissed her on the cheek, almost solemnly. 'I have gift for you.'

They went into the kitchen where the table was laid with cake and sandwiches that Wanda had prepared. She gave Susan a small parcel. Inside Susan found a silk scarf, hand stitched around the edges and having a turquoise-based paisley design. Susan was deeply touched to

54

receive such a beautiful present and thanked her. 'Now, you will sit while I do everything,' said Wanda.

'Sit by me, sit by me!' pleaded Katya. She clambered up onto a chair and experimentally poked her finger into the buttercream in the Victoria sandwich cake.

'You mustn't do that,' whispered Susan, as Katya licked the buttercream off her finger. Out of the corner of her eye Susan could see Wanda and Dad making tea. Wanda was spooning the tea leaves from the caddy into the pot. Dad leaned towards her and whispered something in her ear, lightly touching her on the arm. She looked up at him for a second, just one second, and her face suddenly glowed like the flare of a match. Susan blinked. But then before she could process what she had seen, Katya was tugging her arm for her attention, Wanda was bringing the teapot to the table, Dad had slipped into the chair alongside her and everything had swung back into focus.

***

The Sixth Form suited Susan. The work intensified, and she rose to the challenge. Classes were smaller and more intimate, and she found her niche among the most studious girls. She was studying for A-levels in English, History and Geography. A weighty combination, the headmistress had said to her at the beginning the year, but I know that it is well within your grasp to achieve good results. You are a capable girl. I am a capable girl, repeated Susan in her head.

Her favourite subject was still English, and the small A-level group was still taught by Mr Morgan. They were studying the role of women in Victorian literature, and Susan was glorying in *Jane Eyre*, which was one of her favourite books. But the best parts of all were the two after school clubs that Mr Morgan ran for the Sixth Form. These were a Book Club, where they would discuss 'the book of the month' that they had all read, and a Creative Writing Group, where they delved into the techniques of writing and shared their own efforts. The Book Club was very popular, whereas the creative writing group, being rather more challenging, had only attracted Susan and four other girls. Mr Morgan became quite relaxed and unteacher-like during both these sessions,

55

which he obviously enjoyed as much as they did. They found out much more about him: he enjoyed playing the piano, he liked walking and birdwatching, he liked some modern music, but mainly classical, he liked to watch films and some TV shows, and he was from Wales. That accounts for his wonderful accent, thought Susan, and she realised that he had reminded her of Richard Burton. Now she knew why. He also revealed that he was unmarried and lived alone, although this caused less interest than it would have done in the class a year ago. By now, Richard Morgan was not regarded as a potential heart throb; just an inspiring teacher.

***

It was nearly Christmas! Susan was looking forward to it, and she was going to cook her first turkey dinner. Dad had asked her what she thought of Wanda, Katya and Wanda's Mum coming on Boxing Day for tea. At first Susan was a bit surprised but then she thought, why not. The arrangement with Wanda had become more informal as the months had gone by, and Susan had become used to it. And she liked Wanda. After she came in from school Wanda would talk to her in her grave way, her big toffee eyes mournful until something made her smile and then her whole face lit up. Sometimes they would talk about things like clothes or music, or Susan's studies, or cookery, and she would seem almost like a friend or a sister. Then other times she seemed much older than her twenty-four years. She rarely talked about her past, and Susan didn't like to pry, although she couldn't help being curious about Katya's father.

Four days before the end of term Susan decided to come home at lunchtime, to wrap presents in the afternoon when Dad was not around, and to start some preparation for the big day. They were supposed to stay in school all day but, provided they didn't miss any lessons, Sixth Formers were allowed some leeway, and especially now in the last week of term. Susan was humming 'Oh Little Town of Bethlehem', which they had sung in assembly that morning, as she came in through the back door. It wasn't locked; they didn't lock it when Dad was working in the garage. Two empty soup dishes and the remains of a loaf of bread stood on the kitchen table, and the house was drowsy. Susan dropped her bag on the floor and went to the hall to hang her coat up. A slight rustling sound from the front room attracted her attention.

The back of the sofa faced the door, so what Susan could see was Dad and Wanda's heads close together, and his arm around her. Then he was kissing her, kissing her passionately. Susan gave a cry, and they both jumped up from the sofa, their faces stricken. Susan ran, she ran upstairs into her room and locked the door. She heard Dad thundering up the stairs behind her.

'Susan! I'm so sorry, we were going to tell you... just let me in and I'll explain. Susan!' He banged on the door. Susan lay curled up on her bed, feeling the thumping of her heart. Dad kept shouting, shouting through the door that he was sorry, until she heard Wanda's voice muttering low alongside his. She couldn't make out the words, but then everything went quiet and she heard their footsteps going back downstairs.

Susan lay, her gaze fixed on the raindrops that were trickling down the window like winter's tears. Gradually her thumping heartbeat slowed and she felt disconnected, floating almost. How can I have been so stupid? she thought. How did I not see? She remembered Dad mentioning that he had 'happened to see' Wanda in the pub a couple of times. And he had bumped into her when she had been out with Katya and they had taken her to the swings. When she thought back he had seemed slightly not normal when he told her, sort of too hearty and too jolly. How can I have missed this? she thought again. I'm just a stupid little girl. Still a child even though I'm nearly seventeen. She felt angry with herself, and angry with Dad for betraying her and betraying Mum with someone who was so much younger than he was. Curiously, she didn't feel angry with Wanda, only hurt.

After a while she got off the bed and wandered round her room, straightening pillows, touching books. She picked up the picture of Mum and Dad on their wedding day and traced her fingers over it. Oh Mum... She put the picture back with a sigh. Well, I can't stay in here forever she thought. I may as well face them now.

Dad was sitting hunched at the kitchen table and Wanda was

57

washing up the lunch dishes. Susan watched from the doorway. Everything was different now, everything was contaminated. It would never be the same again. Dad jumped up to hug her, but Susan wouldn't allow it. So he stood back and spread his hands miserably. Wanda turned and stood leaning against the sink. They never meant to hurt her, blurted Dad. It had all just happened, just out of the blue, they were so, so sorry, they were going to tell her, they were going to tell her soon...

Wanda stepped forward and put her hand briefly on his arm. 'John, let us be completely honest. Susan deserves that now.' She turned to Susan, her voice quiet and dignified. 'We thought that you might disapprove. We thought that you might stop us from seeing each other.' She glanced at Dad. 'At least, I did. And, Susan, I like your father's company and he likes mine. Over the weeks and months it has grown to be a bit more than that. But nothing changes how your father feels for you, you understand? He loves you. And I do not seek to take place of your mother. Ever.'

Susan looked from one to the other of them, Dad flushed and untidy, Wanda composed and quiet. No. It was just too much to believe, too much to take in. 'You lied to me,' she said, her voice trembling, 'You lied to me and treated me like a little kid!'

Dad shook his head beseechingly. 'No, no we never *lied* to you... we just put off telling you.'

'It's the same thing,' shouted Susan. 'How *could* you! What would Mum think, you taking up with someone nearly young enough to be your daughter?' The hurt rose up and threatened to choke her. She ran from the room and threw herself on her bed, sobbing. This time she didn't even bother to lock the door.

***

The Creative Writing Group had dwindled to just three girls, Susan, her old friend Melissa and another girl called Sally. It was the highlight of Susan's week. She had gained more confidence in reading her work out aloud to the group, and Mr Morgan's feedback on her contributions stretched and stimulated her. Always he was tactful and constructive, never seeking to humiliate any member of the group.

The group was held in the Sixth Form common room, in a corner space just off the main room that was reserved for meetings and small groups. Several low chairs were arranged around a central low coffee table. Susan sat down in one of the chairs with her notebook and pen, pulling her grey skirt down to cover her knees. She hadn't slept well last night, and her head was aching. After the awful scene of the previous afternoon, Wanda had gone home and Dad had tried to talk to her, but she couldn't bear to listen to him, and after a couple of attempts he left her alone.

In the main part of the room several girls were standing around by the notice board chatting. Since it was almost the end of term most of the notices, about various clubs and outings, had been taken down. Only a few Christmas cards and the poster and sign-up list for the Christmas dance, jointly arranged with the Sixth Form from the boys' school, remained. The dance was tomorrow. Susan had signed her name up. She was rather shy about dancing, but she liked the music. She had even bought a new dress for it. Now she didn't really feel like going.

As Mr Morgan arrived, he paused to chat with the girls by the notice board. They were teasing him good naturedly about coming to the dance, but he just smiled and shook his head, escaping to come over to where Susan was sitting. 'Well,' he said, settling himself down in a chair. 'I have had a message from both Sally and Melissa that they are not coming. They said they have too much work to finish before the end of term, but I suspect Christmas shopping.' He smiled faintly and rummaged for in his pocket for a handkerchief. 'So… we can still have our session as planned, or you can go Christmas shopping too.'

'I'd like to have our session,' said Susan, without hesitation. She could escape into the world of words, a world where she belonged and where life did not deal unexpected blows.

'Good,' he said. 'I read the poem you gave me last week.' He got out the single sheet of paper and Susan got out her copy. He read the words aloud slowly, in his mellifluous voice:

59

Sometimes
The lines between our eyes
Died.
'What's the matter?' you've asked.
'Nothing,' I've replied.
We sit there, heads bent, hands clasped.
Nursing our lives —
Love's wilderness.

He paused, as if allowing the full measure of the words to soak in. Susan looked at the sheet dully, the words now jarring in her head. Did Wanda and Dad have lines between their eyes? 'This is mature work,' he said eventually. 'And the way you have just a single word in the third line serves to add emphasis.' The group by the notice board had drifted out and it was just the two of them in the room, heads bent over Susan's poem. Susan put her sheet down and looked at him.

'Mr Morgan, do you think I could talk to you about something?' As soon as she had spoken she regretted her boldness.

'Of course.' He waited.

Susan took a deep breath. She might as well carry on now. She told him exactly what had happened yesterday, and how upset she was about it. He listened carefully, sometimes interrupting her to ask for details that Susan hadn't made clear, such as who Wanda was, and how long she had worked for them.

Eventually Susan's long speech died away. She waited, feeling foolish to have unburdened herself like that. But already it felt a bit better, just from having got the anger and shock off her chest.

For a time he didn't say anything, and Susan could almost feel him thinking, turning over what she had said, putting the pieces together. 'Coming upon your father and Wanda like that in an embrace must have been a big shock,' he said, his voice neutral. 'Let's see, it's been nearly five years since your mother died, hasn't it?' She nodded. 'And, did I get this right, you don't actually dislike Wanda?' Susan said nothing. 'So, now that you have had a chance to get over the surprise — and, let me say I think the way you found out was most unfortunate — what is it that troubles you so much?'

60

Two girls had come in and were making coffee in the main part of the room. After an incurious glance at Susan and Mr Morgan, they were opening a packet of biscuits and gossiping together as the kettle boiled. Susan examined her fingernails. 'It's just that... it's just... Dad and Mum were so happy together. They were like a pair of lovebirds. I don't understand how Dad can look at someone else when he loved Mum so much.'

'Well let's be clear. Has your father said that he loves Wanda? No? So, this relationship might not last. But also, it's natural that after this length of time that your father would want to have another relationship. How old is he?' Susan told him he was thirty-nine.

'He's a still a young man, only seven years older than myself. This is a *good* thing for him. He must have been lonely in the past few years. I know the woman in question is young, but sometimes age is irrelevant.'

Susan was silent, hearing what he said but still struggling with it.

'And, it would have been more difficult for you if it was someone you didn't like. Think about it,' he added.

Susan nodded reluctantly.

'Good. Do you still write to your mother, either in a letter or in your journal? Susan told him that she did occasionally. 'Well, why don't you put down on paper to her how you feel? I think she would be glad that your father is finding happiness.'

Susan allowed herself to start to relax, to let go of the knot of indignation inside her. 'You're very kind, Sir. Thank you.' She had called him 'Sir' automatically, even though since being in the Sixth Form he had said that Mr Morgan was more appropriate.

'It's part of what I'm here for.' He really did have a very kind smile. The kindness seemed to glow out of his eyes. 'And,' he continued, 'do keep up your writing. I feel it's an important part of your true self, as it is for me.'

'Next term, could we see more of *your* writing please?'

He sat back and stroked his chin. 'Maybe. The idea is more to encourage all of *you* to write. But we'll see... Anyway, Christmas is not far away. What are your plans?'

'My Dad's sister and my cousins are coming on Christmas day. Then Wanda, her daughter and her mother are supposed to be coming for Boxing Day. I suppose that will still happen...' Susan thought about it for a minute. 'Yes. I'd still like to invite them. And little Katya's very sweet.'

'That would be a nice gesture. Well, it sounds like your Christmas is going to be more lively than mine. I'm going to stay with my older brother and his wife in Somerset. It's not that I don't get on with him, but things can be a little... dull.'

'Oh.' She didn't know what else to say. She was curious – was his brother like him? What were they going to do? – but it seemed impolite to ask.

'And then two days after Christmas I will escape for a week's walking in Portugal. That will certainly refresh me for the rigours of the new term.'

Susan digested this unprecedented disclosure about his private life while he collected his papers and stood up.

'Oh, and I hope you're going to the dance tomorrow?' He asked her.

'Well I'm not exactly sure that I feel like it now...'

He stood up and fastened his briefcase. 'You should definitely go. Have fun, dance, get a bit silly. Merry Christmas, Susan.' He put his hand briefly on her shoulder as he left.

Chapter 6

Today and for the next three days Chris was on duty while Matthew was going away for a long weekend. Chris did the job, but without any of Matthew's chumminess, and I missed him.

I carried my bowl of porridge to eat by the window, to see what was going on outside. But it was lashing with rain and there was no-one about. I felt lonely so I texted Joy.

Gosh what a rotten morning. With weather like this I might as well be in here as anywhere else, haha! xx

She didn't reply. Then I realised she would be on her way to work and not looking at her phone until lunchtime. In here you lose track of the rhythm of the outside world.

Dear Mum

I didn't realise it had been so long since I had written to you – four whole months. Time goes by so fast, and I seem to be really busy all the time, what with my school work, helping in the house, working in the café on Saturdays and holidays, writing and listening to music (that's to relax). Everything is fine, though. You don't have to worry about me. After all, I'm seventeen and that's practically grown up! And, when I think about it, you had already met Dad when you were seventeen. I sometimes look at the photographs of you and Dad in your early courting days, going for walks, sitting in parks, holding hands. You were so beautiful.

So, what can I tell you? Dad and Wanda are still going out together. She comes most days and does the housework, and then she and Dad go out about two evenings a week, or sometimes they just stay in and watch telly. On weekends she often brings Katya with her. Katya is such a darling and she says the funniest things. You'd love her, Mum. That seems an odd thing to say, because if you were still alive we would never have met them. I think you'd like Wanda too, which is an even odder thing to say. I sometimes wonder what she sees in Dad, with him being so much older, but then when you see them together they always seem to be smiling or laughing and they don't seem to notice their age difference.

I love being in the Sixth Form. It's great to be doing only your favourite subjects, and to really get your teeth into them. And they don't treat you like a child. I did well in my end of year exams, Mum. I know I can say that to you without being boastful. You would be proud of me, like I know Dad is. I don't go out much, like most of the other girls do, but I don't want to. Some of the girls have boyfriends, but I don't want a boyfriend, I haven't got time for a boyfriend. When I see Aunty Pat or talk to her on the phone she's always on at me about boys, and how I must be careful, and how they only want one thing. Then she goes and contradicts herself and says that I should go out more, go to more parties and have fun! She seems to go out loads herself, and nowadays she's always talking about this boyfriend or that boyfriend. I don't see my cousins much at all. Last time I saw Frank he was working in one of the car factories. We don't seem to have anything to say to each other. Actually, I find him a bit peculiar nowadays, because he's often so grumpy.

As I told you, I'm still writing, poems and short stories mostly. And I do lots of reading. The Creative Writing group at school folded up because there weren't enough *people coming, so Mr Morgan and I just do it on our own now. I admire his work a lot (he's writing a short novel, but he doesn't know if he'll ever get it published) and he gives me feedback and criticism on my work. I'm never afraid to show him what I've written, never afraid that he's going to laugh or pull it to pieces. I don't show it to anyone else. We were meeting at school in the Sixth Form Common Room, but during the summer holidays he's been coming here to the house in an evening. He'll only come when Dad is here, he's very particular about that. He normally stays about two hours and the time just flies by. He's so easy to talk to. We often find that talking about our writing leads onto lots of other topics, and he tells me a bit about his life. He's travelled to other countries, which must be amazing, and he knows a lot about them. He's really interesting. Also he goes to church every week, and we've talked about that a bit. Perhaps I should go sometime. I remember you used to send me to Sunday School and I liked singing the hymns. Mr Morgan has gone away on holiday for two weeks now, walking in Italy, and I'm missing our sessions together. Still, I'm working several days in the café so I have plenty to do. I asked him if we could carry on as we are, just the two of us, when the term starts again. He thought about it a bit but said that it was only fair to give girls in the new Lower Sixth a chance to join. I suppose so.*

Only two weeks until school starts again, and then I'll be in the Upper Sixth! I'm not likely to be a prefect or Head Girl or anything though. They are always girls who do lots of sport and school activities, not quiet girls like me. I wouldn't want to anyway.

I love you Mum.
Susan xxxx

5 April 1971

Dear Mum

Oh Mum, so much has happened in the last month! First I had my eighteenth birthday. Well, you know that. Dad bought me a solid gold necklace and some Premium Bonds. Since last year you become an adult at eighteen, not twenty-one like before. So I'm now officially grown up! I can vote and I can get married if I like. As if I'd want to do that. I don't feel grown up though, Mum. I don't feel grown up at all.

And, speaking of getting married, that's what Dad and Wanda are doing. I suppose I should have guessed it would happen sooner or later. They had been mentioning it and dropping hints for a while, and now they've finally come out and said it's going to be late August or September. They said they want to wait until I'd done my A-levels in the summer. Then, they said I'll probably be going to University just after that. My room will be kept just the same, for me when I come home in the holidays, and they will turn your little sewing room into a bedroom for Katya. I know getting married is what they want, I know that, and I know it's right for them and that you would approve because Dad is happy again. Wanda is nice, but I can't help feeling pushed out. It's like they can't wait for me to go to university to have the house to themselves and, Mum, I don't think I want to go.

Everybody says what a marvellous opportunity it will be for me, how capable I am, how it will set me up for a good job, how it will broaden my horizons. It's what everyone expects of me. But I'm scared, Mum. It will be so big and I won't know anyone. I ended up making applications to three different universities and they've all made me offers. If I accept the offer of going to the University of Burlingham. Aunty Pat says I can lodge with her, so I won't have to stay in Halls of Residence. She's really enthusiastic about it and says we'll have lovely times together in the evenings. I think she imagines we'll do each other's nails and hair. It would save a lot of money though, because she says she wouldn't charge me much rent, and instead I could help out with the chores. Al least it would be somewhere that I know. As I'm writing this I'm thinking how proud you would be of me going to university. It's what Dad says too. So I suppose I shall go. It's just such a big step. Several other girls from the Sixth Form are going to various universities, but they are more confident than me.

The only person I talk to about how I feel about this is Mr Morgan (or should I say Richard? He says I can call him that when we are having our writing sessions on our own, but not in school. He made a joke of it and said it was his birthday present to me for my coming of age). Richard says he understands how I feel, because he was very shy when he was my age, and he dreaded going away to University. He went to somewhere near London to read Theology and English Literature. He says he was very homesick the first couple of terms but then he settled in and it was worth all the effort. He's really encouraging. After we've had our writing session (well, sometimes we don't do a lot on the writing, sometimes we just discuss all sorts of things) I always feel sort of... I don't know... refreshed and more settled.

But Mum, here's the worst. Richard's got another job, at a school in Wales, and he's starting it in September. It has much better promotion prospects than here, he said. Why didn't you tell me before? I said. He said he couldn't tell me until he'd sent his letter of resignation to the Headmistress and it was all official. He'll tell the rest of the girls next week when the summer term starts. I was SO upset. He kept saying it won't make any difference to me because I will be away at university, and he was sorry to see me so distressed. I said what about our writing sessions. I could have come home some weekends to continue them. He said I'll find that after a few weeks at uni I will have new interests, and I'll join all sorts of clubs and things, and not want to continue with our writing sessions anyway. He said that he hoped we would write to each other, though. I suppose I'll have to be content with that.

Mum, everything is changing. It's all changing so fast and I can't keep up. I don't want to keep up. I liked my life as it was. I think I'd be OK with everything if only Richard wasn't moving away.

I love you Mum. Please look down on me and help me,

Susan xxx

***

Susan lay on her bed listening to her favourite Bob Dylan album playing on her record player. The window was open, letting in the lazy summer day. In truth she was a bit bored. Her A-level exams were over and there was not really anything to do at school, and although technically she was supposed to be there, the girls from the Upper Sixth drifted in and out as they pleased. They spent most of their time rehearsing for an end of term show that they were putting on. In the show Susan was prompter (the thought of performing on stage was much too scary) so she didn't even have any learning to do; she just had to turn up for the rehearsals. She would go into school later on for the dress rehearsal before the show tomorrow. But right now there was no rush. Next week she resumed working in the café, so leisure time like this would be far less.

From her window she could see a fleet of little clouds festooning the sky. As she watched them she once again went over the conversation she had had yesterday with Wanda, which had started off being about the upcoming wedding at the beginning of September. It was to be a church wedding. They had found a vicar who was willing to marry them, despite Wanda having Katya. Susan had plucked up courage to ask Wanda about Katya's father, and Wanda had told her. It was a, how do you say, a one night thing, she had said. I was foolish, so foolish. By the time I had realised what was happening, it was too late. We had gone out on a date. I knew only his first name, and nothing of where he lived. That's awful, Susan had whispered. They sat in silence, and Wanda once more had the look of sad composure that she had had when they first knew her.

Promise me, she had said to Susan, promise me that the same won't happen to you. You should carry some contraceptives with you and make sure the boy uses them. Susan had been shocked, and told her that she didn't even have a boyfriend. But you will, Wanda had replied. When you go to university you will meet all sorts of new people.

University. It was there, black smoke on the horizon. The wedding was to be at the beginning of September and Susan would start reading English at Burlingham University at the end of September, lodging with Aunty Pat. The whole thing frightened her to think about, so she turned her thought instead to the plans about the wedding. She and Katya were to be bridesmaids, much to Katya's excitement, and yesterday she and Wanda were talking about how she was going to do her hair. Wanda wanted her to wear it pinned up into a neat French pleat. Susan had never worn her hair up in her life. Her long hair hung from a centre parting into two light brown curtains either side of her face, so that when she leaned forward her hair protected her from the probing gaze of the world. The only times she did anything with it was when school rules had dictated that long hair should be neat tied back, and in the cafe, for hygiene reasons.

She got off the bed and sat at her dressing table mirror, examining how she looked when she swept her hair up. She didn't know herself. Still, it was Wanda's day, and she would do it if that's what Wanda wanted. And Dad. Dad didn't really care about the wedding plans, he left all that to Wanda. Nowadays he went round with a permanent big grin on his face, as if his happiness was so great that it needed to burst out of his face. Susan let her hair fall back down and scrutinised her own solemn reflection. I wonder if I'll ever be that happy, she thought.

There was a soft knock on the door. It was Wanda, telling her that there was a telephone call for her, and it was from Richard. Susan rushed down to the hall, dismayed. They were due to meet at the end of term and all she could think was that he was going to call it off.

'Hello, is that Susan?' The soft Welsh lilt to his voice was more noticeable on the phone.

'Yes, it's Susan.' She was breathless.

'You know we are going to meet on Friday evening? Well, I propose a change of plan. I would be delighted to take you out for dinner, to celebrate and mark your leaving school and your full transition into adult life. I know a nice restaurant I can drive you to, a few miles out of town. Shall I pick you up at seven?'

***

Susan gazed down at the menu. There was so much to choose from! She decided that she would have prawn cocktail to start with and then gammon. She'd never had a prawn cocktail before. Richard was having the soup followed by a sirloin steak, cooked medium rare. Susan thought that having a steak not completely cooked was a bit peculiar, but probably very sophisticated.

Richard had suggested a bottle of red wine. After the waiter had glided away with their dinner order Richard smiled across the table and raised his glass in a toast.

'To you, Susan. To your future success in life.'

She raised her glass and took a sip; she wasn't used to drinking wine and she tried not to wince at the slightly sour taste.

'This is so exciting!' she whispered. 'I feel so grown up.'

'You *are* grown up. You are officially an adult and can run your own life. And, you are no longer at school.'

She took another sip and it seemed rather less sour. She looked at Richard over her glass as she sipped again. He was wearing a suit, but a different one to the slightly shabby ones that he wore for school. This was perhaps his Sunday best; a navy blue with a light blue thread shot through it and matched with a cream shirt and blue tie. The colours set

69

off his dark curling hair and dark eyes.

'You look very smart. Not like a teacher at all.'

He threw his head back and laughed. 'Are teachers really a race apart? Well, now I'm *not* your teacher, so you can just see me like a person. And if, you would like to, we could do some walking together, and perhaps go to some museums. But only if you would like to.' He looked at her steadily.

She nodded. 'Oh, I'd love to. I have to work some days in the café, but not every day. And I think I'm going to take a week off, to get a proper break before university. I don't know what I'm going to do.'

'I'm going on a walking holiday to Pembrokeshire, just for a week. I'm staying in Youth Hostels,' said Richard.

'That sounds lovely. Perhaps I should do something like that.'

Just then the food arrived and Susan started eating appreciatively, and drank more wine. She felt a warm uncurling in her stomach. She cleared her plate and sat back, replete, and gazed round the restaurant. It was quite busy, mostly with couples who sat facing each other across the white tableclothed tables. Susan felt the hum of their low conversation flowing around her.

Richard reached into his pocket and brought out a small package neatly wrapped in silver paper, which he put in front of Susan. When she didn't move, he told her to open it.

Inside was a thin gold bangle, plain and elegant. She gasped. 'It's lovely... I... I don't know what to say.'

'Put it on,' he said. 'And very belated happy birthday.'

She slipped it onto her wrist and stared at it. The waiter bustled up to them flourishing pudding menus. Richard waved him away.

Eventually she said, 'I feel like a princess in a fairy tale.'

'I couldn't give it to you on your birthday, of course, but reaching the age of majority deserves recognition.'

She turned her wrist, admiring it. 'There's a little of piece of gold that's darker than the rest. Look, here in the middle.'

'Ah, that's a piece of rare Welsh gold. That's what makes it extra special.'

'Richard...' Her voice was wobbly. 'Thank you. Thank you so much. You are very kind to me.' She reached over the table and gripped

70

his hand. 'I won't forget this evening. Ever. We will stay in touch, won't we? I mean after you've gone to your new school and I'm at university.'

He returned the squeeze of her hand and then let it go. 'I sincerely hope so. We can write to each other, and sometimes meet up in the holidays. Of course, you may not always want to. You're going to make new friends, you know.'

'No friend could possibly be like you.' The future now seemed slightly less daunting. There would be letters from Richard to look forward to, and the knowledge that she would be seeing him again.

***

One spare pair of socks or two? Susan held the woolly socks, a pair in each hand, as if willing them to make the decision for her. Apart from that she was all packed up and ready to go. She had her rucksack containing her spare clothes, a book, her notepad, water bottle and plasters. Richard had said bring plenty of plasters because walkers, especially those who weren't used to it, invariably got blisters. She checked her watch. He would be here in about ten minutes. Just time to make a packed lunch for both of them. She took her things down to the kitchen and opened the fridge to get out some cheese.

Susan heard a car pulling up outside. He was early. She opened the door. 'Hello,' she said, butter knife in hand, 'I'm just making some sandwiches then I'm ready to go.' He was wearing a cagoule and knee length shorts with sandals. He brushed her cheek with his lips.

'It will take some hours to drive to Pembrokeshire,' he said. 'Even though there's not much traffic on a Saturday morning. We'll go straight to tonight's Youth Hostel and then we can have a look round the local area before we meet the others tonight. You've got your waterproofs, haven't you? It looks like it's going to be wet for walking tomorrow.'

Just then she heard the sound of hurried footsteps coming down the stairs. 'Hello, Richard,' Dad said, heartily, rubbing his hands together. 'You two are just off, are you?'

'Hello, John. Yes, in a few minutes. Because it's her first walking holiday, I'm checking that Susan has all the appropriate things.'

No-one spoke. Susan paused in cutting the sandwiches, and looked from one man to the other. Dad was usually fairly relaxed with Richard and, although they didn't have much in common, when he came to the house they would chat together politely for a few minutes. They were even on first name terms now, albeit a bit awkwardly.

'Susan says it's Youth Hostels you're staying in,' said Dad, continuing to smile.

'Yes. It's arranged by a walking club that I belong to,' replied Richard pleasantly. 'I've been on several holidays with them. It's lucky that they were able to fit Susan in at short notice.'

'Susan, Wanda wants to speak to you before you go,' said Dad. 'Something about the flowers for the wedding, or some such thing.' He waved his hand dismissively.

'Oh, we already talked about that earlier.'

'Well, perhaps it was something else. She's upstairs. Just run along and speak to her, will you?'

As she tramped up the stairs she could hear Dad's low voice from the kitchen. She knew perfectly well why Dad had sent her upstairs. How dare he not trust me? she thought. He's treating me like a child, and I'm not, I'm an adult. I'm eighteen and anyway, Richard says I can make my own decisions now. So I will.

***

9 August 1971

Dear Dad, Wanda and Katya

Pembrokeshire is absolutely beautiful – the sea, the beaches the hills! It rained a bit on the first day but after that the weather improved. Up to now we have done three days walking with the group, and each night we have stayed in a different Youth Hostel, and they have all been very comfortable. We sleep four people (women) to a room, which is a bit cramped, but not too bad because I spend hardly any time in there. Richard and I have had evening meals in some lovely old pubs. I

72

hope this postcard gets to you before I get home on the weekend.

Love, Susan xxx

***

'So this is where you've lived these last years.' Susan looked around the room, taking in the shabby armchairs, one each side of the gas fire, the floral curtains which jarred with the patterned carpet. A tiny kitchenette occupied one end of the room and there were two doors which she presumed led to a bedroom and a bathroom. Two boxes packed with books stood near the entrance to the flat. The room held a sense of imminent departure; no longer a home, now a repository of assembled belongings. There was a desk, empty now except for a lamp and a scattering of letters, and Susan could envision him sitting there, the pile of unmarked homework gradually getting smaller through the hours, while the 40 watt bulb burned in the lamp. The thought sorrowed her; she wanted to arrange flowers, to hang a brightly painted picture, to make steaming coffee in a cheerful mug.

'It's been pleasant enough,' said Richard, several books cradled in his arms. 'Close to the school, not much noise, reasonable rent.' He fed the books one by one into a half filled box. 'I think that's all the books. All that I have here, anyway.'

'You have *more* books?'

'Oh yes. They were at my parent's house, but then my brother and I sold the house after they died, so now they're taking up space in his attic, until I get a house of my own.' He took the boiling kettle off the gas. 'And anyway, by the time you're my age, missy, you'll have lots of books too.'

'By the time I'm your age,' she mimicked, sitting down in one of the armchairs. It was more comfortable than it looked. He sat down opposite her and handed her a cup of coffee. They sipped in unison, holding each other's gaze through the steam. He had grown his hair longer during the summer, until it tickled his collar, giving him a carefree, holiday look. By the time he started at the new school on Monday the curls would be lying like dark question marks on a barber's

73

shop floor in a Welsh village.

'This is like we're an old married couple,' she said.

'Yes. Except that we're neither old nor married.'

'Well one of us isn't. Old, that is.'

'Cheeky.'

Susan put down her cup on the hearth. The sun was coming in through the window and catching the dust in the air.

'You will write?'

He nodded. 'Of course. And we'll meet up in half term week, like we said.'

'Richard…'

'What is it?'

A fly was buzzing nasally in the window.

'When we were out having dinner last night, I felt that people were watching us. Like they didn't know what to make of us. I'm sure the couple on the next table were talking about us.' Their sly looks, muttered words, the tawdry, slightly uncomfortable feeling that she had felt then flitted across her mind again.

'Well, people like to talk.'

'But it made me wonder… Richard, what are we to each other? We've spent all this time together this summer and it's been wonderful. You've opened my eyes to all these new things and it's been the happiest time of my life.' She paused. 'So… does that mean I'm, sort of, your girlfriend? I'm a bit confused.'

He sat back in his chair, and carefully placed his coffee mug down on the hearth, in a space made by a missing tile. Then he placed his hands on his thighs.

'I'd like to think that we're friends. Special friends. I'd like to think we'll stay friends. But my girlfriend? No.'

Susan shifted in her chair. 'That's what I thought. It's just that… I don't know anyone else who has a relationship like we do.'

'Unlucky for them, then.'

'Yes.' Susan hesitated, her confusion still not quite banished. 'Do you have girlfriends though? After all, you're only mid-thirties.'

He laughed. 'Not quite over the hill yet, then. Yes, I have had a few relationships. No-one since I have been living here. Before that, I went out with someone for four years. The she broke it off. It was part of the reason why I moved here.'

'Oh. Oh, I'm sorry.'

'Don't be. When I look back now, we weren't really suited. My pride was hurt more than anything.'

The noise of traffic in the street filtered into the room.

'Anyway, let's get back to the present and the future shall we?' He stood up. 'I have to put the last few things in the car, see my landlord, and drive to Wales.'

'To your new home, your new job, your new life.'

'Yes, to the next phase of my life.' She could sense that he was ready to be off, eager for the new horizon. 'And you too, are soon starting the next phase of your life. I wish you all the luck in the world.' She stood up and he took her hands in his.

'You will write? And we'll meet at half term?' With those things to sustain her, she could accept the inevitable.

'I promise.' He gathered her into his arms, into a long hug that she could have dissolved in. His chest rose and fell steadily.

As she walked away down the street, a line of prose came into her head. Something about *'when I was a child, I spoke as a child... and now I have put away these childish things.'* What was that from? She turned round and waved once, waved goodbye to her childhood.

PART 2

Chapter 7

'How was your weekend away?' I asked Matthew. Out of the corner of my eye I could see the blinking of the cursor on the computer screen.

'I would say... successful.' He hesitated, as if turning the word over in his mind. 'We went to visit Paul's parents. Paul's my partner and his parents have been... well, a bit distant, shall we say. But this time they seemed more welcoming. So yes, it was good.'

'I'm glad.' I almost said, 'I missed you', but it didn't sound quite right. So I said, 'It must be difficult for parents sometimes.' That didn't sound quite right either.

'You have children, don't you?'

'Yes, three. All grown up, of course, and none of them married.' An awkward pause. I didn't know why I'd said that. 'But they're all happy in their chosen paths.'

'And that's the main thing.' He got up from his usual perch on the bed. 'Well, duty calls, I suppose. See you later.'

As he closed the door I turned back to the computer screen and in five minutes I had forgotten him.

The bus stop was only a couple of minutes' walk away from Aunty Pat's house, but even knowing that, Susan still arrived ten minutes early. Tendrils of Aunty Pat's scented hug, for good luck, still clung. The September day was mild; she had paused on the doorstep, her key in her hand, deciding whether or not to take her coat. She had eventually unlocked the door again and hung her coat on top of the muddled assortment of jackets, overcoats and scarves that were on the hallstand, checking her watch again.

The boys had left the house early to start their shift in the factory at 8am. Susan had stayed in bed and listened for the sequence of sounds which after three days she was recognising as the morning routine: the clomp of boots down the stairs, water being drawn for the kettle, the slam of the backdoor, the drone of Aunty Pat's radio, and running water in the bathroom. Then the lighter clicking of heels down the stairs and it was safe for Susan to emerge. She sat on the edge of the bed and drew on her dressing gown. The room was smaller than her own room at home, but they had managed, by shunting the dressing table up into a corner, to fit Susan's own desk in. Dad had transported it on Sunday, tied upside-down on the top of the car like a dead insect. The desk had one wobbly leg and a scratch across the top from her pair of compasses a few years back when she was doing her geometry homework. Her lamp was poised on top of the desk, ready to illuminate her studies with its familiar light. She could use the old chair that was already in the room, and she was all set. And, by virtue of having long spells with the window open, the miasma of Frank was nearly gone.

On Sunday when she arrived she had tried to tell Frank how grateful she was that he was giving up his room for her. He had shrugged. It was alright, he told her, his pale eyes sliding away from hers; Mum said he and Lionel could both pay a bit less rent, because she was going to chip in. More beer money, he had said.

Nevertheless, Susan had persevered. It's good of you not to mind sharing with Lionel, she had said. Once again, the shrug. 'Old Li misses having Norman to share with, since he went and moved out a couple of months ago. And what do I care, it's only a place to sleep.' He had smirked at her then in a way that she found not entirely comfortable.

She got up from the bed and sat at her desk, looking at the large envelope that she had placed there, ready to take with her today. In her own room at home the desk had been replaced by Mum's work table, complete with the sewing machine. Beneath it were boxes of Mum's sewing things, which Susan had been unable to part with when she had sifted through the contents of the sewing room in order to make a space for Katya's things, her bed and her clothes and toys. Dad had been too busy to help, and she had the time, didn't she, while she was waiting to go off to university. Katya had bounced on the bed accompanied by yelps of excitement while Susan opened drawers to reveal kaleidoscopes of coloured fabric remnants and rainbows of sewing cottons which had sat silent and patient for the past years. Susan had fingered a piece of blue flowered fabric and remembered exactly the dress Mum had made with it.

Susan sighed and refocused her mind on today. It wasn't so bad at Aunty Pat's, now she was actually here. And anyway, once Dad and Wanda had come back from the honeymoon, she knew it was inevitable. Meeting Wanda on the landing in the morning, tousled with sex, her thin dressing gown hardly covering the new bloom of her body, had been something that Susan could barely tolerate.

The bus was coming. It was on time. Not that it mattered this morning, because enrolment was from 10am. But other mornings she might have lectures at 9am and she would need to be early. Maybe she should look at the bus timetable again and see about earlier buses. She settled herself on a seat near the front and checked in her bag again to see that she had her enrolment paperwork. Her latest letter from Richard, writing a picture for her of his new life, was tucked into her pocket. She pulled it out and entered again into his world, the ivy-clad school with its conglomeration of grey-uniformed boys, the storybook village of Llanley, the green cliffs and wild sea. A world away from Burlingham.

Dad had driven her to the university on Sunday, so that she could get her bearings. Back then, it had had an air of serenity, of peaceful contemplation and academic study. Not so today. Today the corridors echoed with hundreds of raised voices, as students jostled each other, frowning at notice boards or greeting each other with hugs and whoops after a summer selling hotdogs or pulling pints in a bar. Outside, clumps of students gathered together were blocking entrances and causing chaos. Sometimes a harassed staff member, laden with sheaves of paper, would push himself or herself stoically through the crowd and disappear into the world beyond the engorged corridors.

Susan clutched her bag in the midst of the turmoil. The letter she had received told her that enrolment was in the Great Hall. She looked around, hoping for clues. Eventually a sign pointed the way for her. In the echoing splendour of the Great Hall the queues were endless snakes of young humanity. Here it was at least quieter, because the queue of new students were freshers like herself and mostly didn't know anyone else. There were a few tentative smiles, and the question 'where are you from'. Susan kept her eyes on the ground. When she was about six people from the front, she realised that she had joined the wrong line. She hadn't known the lines were alphabetical, and she was in the N-R line, rather than the S-Z line. With apologies to the people behind, she squeezed her way out and joined the end of the correct line.

At last. At last she had negotiated the enrolment desk and had the official document in her hand. Now she must find the Finance Office to see about her Grant money. More corridors, more waiting. This time she was careful to choose the correct line. At the desk she handed her completed form and enrolment certificate to the outstretched hand of the woman behind the desk. The red nails of the hand battled with the pink of her ruffled blouse.

'Where's your SEC?'

'Pardon?' said Susan.

'Your SEC. Subject Enrolment Certificate.'

'I... I don't know what you mean.'

The woman sighed. Even her sigh seemed to have a flat Midlands twang, to match her voice.

'What subject are you going to do?' she said. Susan told her. 'So you need to go to the English Department and get enrolled there. This,' she brandished the certificate that Susan had given her, 'is just your general university enrolment. See?'

Susan stammered her thanks but the outstretched hand was already reaching towards the person behind her in the queue.

***

In the Ladies toilet Susan ran cold water into her hands and splashed it onto her face. She dried off with a paper towel and scrutinised herself in the mirror. Apart from a slight redness in her eyes, the evidence of her tears behind the toilet door was washed away. After eventually finding the English Department and more queuing and confusion, she now had the precious SEC certificate safely in her bag. She felt as if she had entered a strange country which consisted of a crush of unknown people and unfathomable systems. And now she had to face Mrs Pink Ruffles in the Finance Office again. She sank down on the chair that was next to the sanitary towel machine and surveyed the wreckage of her confidence, so carefully constructed over the last weeks.

A toilet flushed and a girl emerged. She glanced at Susan. Susan dropped her eyes and took in the girl's tight jeans and red suede pixie boots. She could hear her washing her hands and then rummaging in her bag.

'Hey, excuse me?'

Susan looked up.

'You wouldn't have a comb, would you? I seem to have lost mine. Gee, I'm dumb.'

Susan joined her at the mirror and passed over her comb. The girl's hair was jaw length ripe-corn blonde, yellow almost, and when she drew the comb through it, it rippled like a swirl of wind passing through a meadow. The girl grinned into the mirror, unabashed by Susan's stare.

'Sorry, I didn't mean to stare. It's just... you have really beautiful hair.'

The girls smoothed down the waves and turned her head to examine her reflection.

'Thanks. If you're blonde, they think you're an airhead, though.' She examined Susan in the mirror. 'You must be a fresher. How are you getting on?'

'Not too well, actually. It's so difficult finding where you're supposed to go, and nobody seems very helpful.'

The blonde girl snorted. 'Still a drag then? I remember when I started two years ago I nearly gave up and went home! But don't worry, if you can get through today, then lectures are a blast.' She pulled a lipstick from her bag and gashed red across her mouth. 'What's your subject?'

She nodded her approval when Susan told her. 'Mine's Sociology. Hey, groovy skirt.' She picked a piece of Susan's long skirt and felt it between her fingers. 'Very West Coast. And the cheesecloth shirt. Cool.'

Susan felt herself flush. 'Oh, thanks. Thanks very much.' She looked down at the swirl of colours and prints which flowed down to her mid calves. 'I didn't, you know... I didn't really know what to wear.' She gave an embarrassed laugh.

The blonde pouted her lips into the mirror. 'Well you look fab. And, look, hang loose, you know? You're gonna do OK. Everybody's in the same boat.' She swung her bag onto her shoulder and flashed Susan a red smile. 'See you later!'

After she had gone Susan gazed at herself in the mirror. Groovy. That's what the girl had said. And cool. She smoothed her hands over her blouse and skirt. Just the Grant cheque to get now. She started to hum a Joan Baez song, and it was only when she reached into her bag to get her comb that she realised that the blonde girl had still got it.

***

2 November 1971

Dear Richard

Just a quick few lines before my next lecture to tell you that it was so, so wonderful to see you at half term. Thank you for coming to visit me. I hope Aunty Pat wasn't too annoying - she means well, and she's very kind to me but, well, you saw what she was like.

Don't go staying in a guest house, Aunty Pat had said to Richard. You can sleep on the settee here. And the floor boards on the landing don't creak too much. She had leered and winked, actually winked. Susan could have died. But Richard, he just looked her in the eye, thanked her politely but firmly, and said he had already made arrangements. Aunty Pat had looked from one to the other of them,

81

trying to work it out, eventually shrugging and saying she hoped they had a nice time anyway.

Today it's a lecture and a tutorial, then another lecture after lunch. It still seems odd to me that nobody takes a register at lectures. We don't have to go if we don't want to. Even so, I intend to always go. I'd be too afraid of missing something or getting behind not to. There are only five of us now in my tutorial group, because one person has dropped out of the course.

Susan paused again and looked up at the library clock. She could either finish the letter or go and get a coffee and a slice of cake in the refectory before the next lecture. Since it was going to be a lecture and a tutorial back-to-back, a two hour stint, some nourishment in the refectory was probably a good idea. She put away her writing pad and crept past the rows of students and the 'Silence please' notice. She looked over the rows of bent heads, like a field of cabbages, low over piles of books and notepads. Almost the only sounds were the crackle of pages turning or the occasional cough. The thick atmosphere of concentration was disturbed by one young man who was whispering urgently to the girl next to him, while she tucked a curl of hair behind her ear and whispered back, her giggles half caught behind her hand.

She found a table in the refectory with four other girls already sat at it, their heads together over the combining steam of their milky coffees. They didn't look up when Susan attached herself to the far end of their table. The high-ceilinged room echoed like a swimming baths with cutlery clatter and eager conversation. And then, there she was, two tables over. Susan put down the Eccles cake that she had been about to bite into and craned her neck to get a better view. The blonde wavy hair was an unmistakable beacon, and Susan caught a glimpse of her profile as she turned to say something to the man next to her, her hand on his shoulder. They both erupted with laughter, and the joke spread like a breeze down the long table to the other people in the group, and then they were all laughing together. Susan sat in her coffee aroma bubble, watching them. When the last dregs from her cup were gone she walked past their table, where the hilarity had subsided but they were still grinning as they chatted. She paused, a smile waiting at the corners of her mouth, adjusted her bag on her shoulder and looked back to catch the blonde's eye. *Remember me? We met in the Ladies' room on enrolment day.* For a second there might have been a glimmer of recognition, and then the girl's attention was caught by the guffaws of the man on her other side and the moment was washed away. Quickly Susan moved on, leaving them to their laughter at the next unknown and unknowable joke.

***

21 December 1971

Dear Susan

I write this to you on the eve of the last day of term. Tomorrow will be a busy day: the end of term concert, various items of administration to complete and a short staff reception with the Headmaster at the end of the day. The boys' excitement at the approach of Christmas is taking over the atmosphere of the school. On the whole this is good and stimulating, but it does however have the effect of fostering behaviour which is more unruly than usual. It recalls to me my own boyhood. Even after I had outgrown belief in Father Christmas, I still looked forward to Christmas with enthusiasm; the enormous tree in the hall, carol singers calling, the cinnamon scent of mulled wine, of which my brother and I were allowed a small taste. Then on the day itself, the Christmas stockings, church, a gargantuan turkey and various elderly (or so it seemed then) aunts and uncles around the table. As I write this, I realise how sentimental, mawkish even, my reminiscences sound. Has the lens of time distorted my emotions on the subject? I don't know. When we meet after Christmas you must tell me about your Yuletide memories from childhood.

I have been looking back on the last few weeks and I feel very satisfied about my transition into Llanley and the school, which is a few miles away from the village. When we make changes in our lives, a leap of faith is always required that it will be for the better; that we have made the right choice. Always there is the fear of stepping out into the unknown. I know how strong your doubts were about starting university and I am relieved that you are settling into the rhythm of academic study. I had probably not made plain to you my doubts about my own venture. My main reservation was that it would turn out that I had not, in fact, positioned myself more strategically for future promotion which, as you know, was my main motive for leaving my previous post. As secondary concerns, I had not taught in the private sector before nor previously lived in a village. The latter two doubts have proved to be groundless. The boys are a joy to teach, the school is well run and the village is charming, with beautiful cliff walks. As for promotion prospects, only time will tell, but I feel that I have made a favourable impression during my first term.

I was thinking of waiting until next summer before I begin to look around for a small house to buy. (I have just realised: previously I never wanted to buy a house or flat. An inner knowledge of impermanence, perhaps?). However, last weekend I was going for a walk in Llanley when by chance I saw a cottage for sale, standing empty and alone on the road that leads from the village to the beach. When I say alone, the village centre is actually only five minutes' walk away. I mean the cottage is not part of a housing estate. The cottage captured my interest, so I telephoned the Estate Agent and discovered that the price is favourable and within my means, that is, the legacy from my mother. I don't wish to be too hasty, because after all, purchasing a home is one of the most important decisions of life, so I will wait until after Christmas and, when I return from my visit to you over New Year, I will make further enquiries.

In two days' time I will leave to go for my usual Christmas sojourn with my brother and his family. Their Christmas festivities do not live up to my childhood memories, but nevertheless they make me welcome (even if over recent years I find it increasingly dull). The post at this time of the year will probably make it impractical for us to write to each other again before Christmas, so I shall close now by saying that I will telephone you at your home on Christmas morning to wish you a Merry Christmas, and I look forward to seeing you on 29th December. Please thank your father and Wanda for their kind invitation to put up on their sofa. However I have booked a room at a guest house just a short drive away.

With best wishes,

Richard

Dear Richard

Guess what – I got my results today for the assessments that I did before Christmas, and I was graded 58% overall. This puts me about in the middle of the class, which is better than I had hoped, and it's really cheered me up. I was feeling a bit blue, being back at uni. Over the Christmas holidays I'd got used to being home, and I'd got used to Wanda being there all the time. Now I've got to settle into being at Aunty Pat's again. And, of course, I miss seeing you. I loved the long walks and the conversations that we had over New Year. Already it seems ages ago.

I decided to do what you suggested and try one of the university activities. Only because you persuaded me though! I decided to go to the Folk And Blues club, FAB club for short. One of the girls in my tutorial group was talking about it. It sounded like the sort of music that I like to listen to. What really made me prick my ears up was that she was saying that the first one of the term was going to be a Woodstock night. Probably not your sort of music, and not all exactly folk either. Anyway, I said it sounded good so she said why didn't I go with her because she's been going every week in the first term and I said OK, I'd try it. It was last night. I was nervous, and I nearly changed my mind and didn't go. The trouble was I'd told Aunty Pat that I was going and she'd made a really big thing about it, as if I was going out on a date or something. If I didn't go, I wouldn't hear the last of it. (If I hadn't gone, I wouldn't be writing to you about it either!)

Anyway, I quite enjoyed it. It was in an upstairs room of a pub near to the university. In the first half they played records of musicians from the first day of the Woodstock festival. Then there was a break to get drinks, and then in the second half different people got up to play guitars or to sing, or both. It was really friendly too. Some of the students who run the club came over to say hello. They said it was free for me this week, so I could try it out, and they hoped I'd join. I think I might.

That's all for now. I have to do some reading and wash up the tea things. Frank and Lionel do make such a mess. Never mind, I'd rather be here than in Halls of Residence.

I hope your new term is going well. Write and tell me about it. Oh, and tell me if you look at the cottage and what you think.

Best wishes,

Susan

Dear Richard

I know this letter is probably going to cross with your reply, but I just had to write again. Yesterday Dad and Wanda phoned Aunty Pat's with some news. Wanda is pregnant. Apparently she was almost certain at Christmas but she wanted to get to three months before she told anyone. She and Dad – and Aunty Pat - were all in raptures. I had to pretend to be pleased as well, but frankly I was shocked. I've got used to them being married, but I never thought that they'd have a baby. Why, Dad will be old by the time it's grown up. And, I've always thought I was special to Dad. He used to call me his Princess (that's a point, he hasn't called me that since he married Wanda), but now I won't be. The new one will take my place. And then there's my room. I think babies sleep with their parents to start with, but that can't go on for ever and sooner or later they are going to want my room for it. I'm being pushed out. Pushed out of my own home, pushed out of their lives. Staying at Aunty Pat's is OK, but it's not my real home. I feel like I don't belong anywhere.

I've just read back what I've written and I know I sound like a child. I wish I was still a child. Please, Richard, write and say something nice to me.

Best wishes,

Susan

22 January 1972

Dear Susan

Oh Susan, my dear Susan. I expect that by now you have had more chance to think about the situation and to have calmed down somewhat. I can see why you are shocked and upset but, my dear, Wanda is a young woman and it is only natural that she should want more children. I am quite sure that your father will continue to love you as he always has done. Parental love is like that; no matter how many children there are, the love expands accordingly, rather like God's love for us. Rest assured, you are still special to your father. You are special.

Now, concerning your bedroom. The new child and stepsister Katya can surely share a room for the first three or four years. By that time, you will be a well-qualified young woman with a budding career, which could be anywhere in the country. Very few students return to the parental home after university. You will be taking the next step in your life and establishing your own home and by then you won't feel the need to keep a stake in your childhood home. Trust me, Susan. Once you have your own home, letting go of the past is natural.

Let me give you some news of my own to distract you, concerning the cottage that I mentioned. As you know I didn't wish to talk about it when I saw you at New Year. I felt it was better to put it out of my mind, in order to view it afresh when I returned. I have seen over the property twice now and had a survey carried out on it. It is a sound building, more than one hundred years old, and somewhat outdated in the interior. Rather than being detrimental, the old fashioned character greatly appeals to me. Downstairs it has a living room, dining room and kitchen, and a bathroom and conservatory which were added at a later date. Upstairs there are two quite large bedrooms, one of which would serve admirably as a study if I didn't care to put my desk in the living room. I have several items of my parents' furniture kept in store (which my brother and his wife rejected) which would suit admirably. From what I have written you can probably guess what I am going to say next: I have decided to make an offer for it. Believe it or not, this will be the first property that I have owned. I will keep you informed of progress.

Well, Susan, I hope you have recovered your normal sense of equilibrium now. Keep busy, get involved. Keep going to your FAB club. I think about you often. Not only are you special to your father, you are special to me.

With best wishes,

Richard

Dear Richard

Sorry my letter is a bit late, I've been very busy this last few days. We had a deadline yesterday to hand in an assignment, but now it's done, thank goodness. Overlapping with this we had to prepare a piece to read out in tutorial as part of the Literature of Chivalry module. I don't like having to read aloud, but at least the group is small so it's no too much of an ordeal.

Tonight I'm going to the FAB club. That will make the fifth time I've been. I really like the music, and the atmosphere is really groovy and hip. (Part of me would love to be a hippy, in the USA. But that's just the fantasy me). Did I mention, when I was there last week, a boy called Ian started chatting to me. It turns out that we both like Joan Baez. He's a year ahead of me and doing French. He said he would probably be at the club tonight, and that he'd look out for me.

Wanda phoned yesterday. Apparently she had just felt the baby move for the first time, and she was going on about that. I'm still not very happy about this new baby, but there isn't anything I can do about it. After she phoned, I re-read the letter you sent me after I was so upset, and it comforted me. You have the knack of saying just the right thing. And me, a 'well-qualified young woman with a budding career', you say! I can't imagine it. Maybe I'll be a teacher like you. Anyway, I don't want to think about that yet.

I'm disappointed not to have seen you this half term, but I understand that's the only time it was possible for you to move into your cottage. By now you should be living there! Do write soon and tell me what it's like.

Best wishes,

Susan

5 March 1972

Dear Susan

I write this letter to you from my very own new home. I must say, I had heard that moving house is a stressful thing to accomplish, and now I can understand this, *even though I was only moving from a rented bed-sitting room. It is only now, when all the paperwork is completed, all the solicitors' letters done, my parents' furniture moved in and unveiled, all my personal possessions safe upstairs (but not unpacked yet, I fear) that I can fully admit that it has been a strain. But now it is done, and I sit here at the old table from my childhood, which had been hidden away and quietly awaiting its release, drinking a well-earned whiskey and writing to you.*

The house, like any house that is old, has its foibles. This, for me, is part of the charm. The coal boiler in the scullery (such a lovely word, rolls better off the tongue than 'kitchen') is capricious, and it has not accepted my offer of friendship yet. I have had somewhat more success with the fireplaces in the dining room and sitting room. This is fortuitous because I have to admit that it is cold; after all the building has stood empty for several months. Although I want to keep the cottage's original features, I am coming round to the idea that it – and I - might benefit from the installation of central heating. There, I have said it. However last night I built a magnificent fire in the sitting room and, with the closed curtains and glow from the fire illuminating the old brocade sofa, chairs and footstool, it was cosy indeed.

Now that I am safely ensconced in my new home, I can turn my attention to thinking about the near future. Susan, I was wondering if you would like to pay me a visit in the Easter holidays. This part of the Welsh coast is beautiful and we could have some walks along the cliffs, and perhaps a day visiting Cardiff, if that would please you. My cottage is only a five minute walk from the village, and there is bed-and-breakfast accommodation available there. If you let me know that you can come, I will make enquiries. By the way, there is no telephone here in the cottage, which I consider to be in keeping with its character and I intend to keep it that way. (There is, however, a telephone box close by). Once you have a telephone, the precious art of letter writing withers. I do hope that you can come.

Best wishes,

Richard

Chapter 8

The village of Llanley unwound itself lazily. Susan, keen and eager to drink in everything through the smeared windows, braced herself against the jolting of the elderly bus, Already the village – quite large, but just escaping becoming a town - had introduced itself to her through the lines of Richard's letters, and she nodded at landmarks already imagined. There was the Black Lion pub, the General Stores on the corner, with a few Easter eggs on display for those who had left it to the last minute to buy them, the quaint Copper Kettle teashop, and the spire of the church presiding from a distance across the rooftops.

The bus turned into a small square edged with stone grey buildings and a War Memorial in the middle and hissed to a halt at the stop. Susan took her small suitcase and got off, along with most of the other people. She looked around her, while everyone else dispersed along their known tracks. Surely he would be waiting for her? He said he would be.

'Hello, Susan.'

She turned around and there he was. As she entered into his hug she thought how he looked the same, just Richard, yet subtly changed. It wasn't possible to capture the impression because he was enquiring about her journey, picking up her suitcase, leading her down a lane and suggesting that they went to the guest house first because it was on the way home. At the guest house she did little more than glance at the single bedded room, plain yet adequate, wash her hands at the basin and dry them on the little blue towel, all the time hearing the low murmur of Richard talking to the landlady downstairs in the hall. They politely escaped from her barely hidden curiosity and hurried down the lane, giggling like children, their steps getting lighter as they approached the cottage. I will warn you, Richard told her. You are in a Welsh village now and people are friendly and like to know your business.

The roadside houses trickled away until there was a just a field on both sides of the lane. Richard pointed. There it is, he told her. The house stood on its own, with a finger of smoke crawling out of the chimney and blending with the grey sky. The house too was grey, with uniform windows that quietly guarded its secrets. In his letters Richard had not described the exterior of the house, and Susan felt with a shock the dissonance between her gingerbread rose-and-ivy covered imaginings and the reality of this austere silent block.

He approached the heavy wooden front door, key in hand. She observed, with a flare of interest, that the fanlight above the door was inlaid with a mosaic of green and yellow stained glass, and she grasped onto this first clue that maybe the house held its treasures within rather than announcing them gaudily on the outside.

The hallway was quite dark, but the wood panelling and pictures on the wall of Richard's parents blossomed into view when he switched the light on.

'Welcome to my home.' A moment of awkwardness vibrated between them as he hung her coat up on the hall stand. 'Let me show you around.'

He led her through the house, and she absorbed every room, her gaze drinking in everything from the skirting boards to the vintage glass lampshades. They first went into the dining room where the large oak table and matching Welsh dresser took up much of the space. Susan ran her hands over the smooth curves and ornate carvings of the dresser.

'Richard, it's beautiful! It only needs to be filled with equally beautiful crockery.'

'I haven't had a chance yet. My mother's dinner service is in a box somewhere.'

'I could help you. I'd love to.' Eventually, reluctantly, she dropped her hands from the polished wood.

The small kitchen led off from the dining room. There a coal boiler sulked in the corner, with a stove and an incongruously painted daffodil yellow cupboard crowded next to it. A sink and wooden draining board under the window, and a fridge that purred noisily, completed the kitchen area.

'Sorry about the yellow. I knew I needed a cupboard and a worktop in there, and I thought the colour would brighten it up.'

Susan nodded, absorbed in her critical assessment of the kitchen.

'Well, it's small, but it's adequate. A few shelves would be useful.'

'Shelves. Yes, I could get shelves.'

Next was the sitting room, where the glow of the fire lit up the walls, the cabinet, the piano, and exuded a languorous heat, making the armchairs and sofa beckon. Richard had propped a large calendar on the mantelpiece; a picture of a spring woodland brimming with daffodils.

'I was so busy, I forgot that it's the first of the month.' He picked up the calendar and turned the page over to a view of a grassy scene studded with primroses and violets. He paused and grinned at her. 'I could have left it and made it into an April Fool joke.'

'Ah, but it's after midday. That would make *you* the April Fool.'

The back of the hallway led to a bathroom, white and plain but serviceable, and a conservatory.

'This would be perfect for plants, or growing tomatoes. Oh and look! Is that an apple tree in the garden? Can we see?'

He opened the door and they stepped out into the spring day. The garden was not extensive, but there was room for a washing line and the two outhouses, which were a toilet and a coalhouse. A path up the middle divided the lawn in two, and a collection of bushes and trees flourished round the edges. A few late daffodils nodded here and there.

Susan twirled around on the grass, her arms outstretched. 'What a beautiful place!'

'Really? I thought it was rather wild and unkempt. It needs some work done in it.'

Susan shook her head. 'It's just right, all raggle-taggle like this. It's natural. Do you know, something my mother always wanted was a garden, but of course at the garage she couldn't have one, only a few pots by the door. So I've never lived anywhere with a garden either. Do you think birds nest in that hedge?'

Finally they went upstairs and Richard showed her the two identical bedrooms, one containing the high double bed and solid furniture of his inheritance, the other containing a single bed, a desk and a tumble of half unpacked boxes.

'There's something else. I wanted to save this until last.' He led her to the window in his bedroom. 'Look.'

92

Susan put her face close to the glass. She looked down the lane, across fields, trees, to a silvery smudge on the horizon.

'The sea!' she gasped. 'You can actually see the sea.'

His voice was close to her ear. 'It's only half a mile away. I knew you'd be impressed.'

***

The house tour complete, Susan sat in the armchair, her hands loose on its worn arms and her feet curled under her, watching Richard kneeling by the fire and spearing a tea cake onto a toasting fork. His face was rosy from the heat of the fire. A cheerful rotund teapot sat by him on the hearth.

'This house is magical. Stepping inside is like stepping into a fairy tale.'

He sat back on his heels and wiped the sprinkle of sweat on his brow with a handkerchief.

'A fairy tale, eh. Which one? Little Red Riding Hood? Surely you don't think I'm the wicked woodcutter?'

'Alright, not a fairy tale exactly, but you know what I mean. It's got a warm, old fashioned, slightly whimsical feeling.' She looked around. 'Not the sort of place I thought you'd buy.'

'Oh? Don't you think I'm warm, old fashioned and whimsical?'

She rested her head back on white antimacassar and grinned. 'Well, maybe old fashioned.'

'Someone isn't going to get a teacake if they're not careful.'

'OK, I take it back. But I thought you'd buy somewhere more simple and practical.'

'This is a village, so I liked the idea of a village cottage. And I liked the idea of part isolation, but with the village centre only a short stroll away.' He handed her a buttered teacake. 'So what's your view overall? Do you like it?'

'Like it? I *love* it!' She put her teacake down and gazed into the embers. 'It's the sort of place I would dream of living. I think that's what I meant when I said it was like a fairy tale.'

Richard was concentrating on buttering his own teacake. He took it and sat down on the sofa.

'And you,' she continued. 'I think the place has cast a spell on you. You're different somehow.'

'Oh?'

'I know.' She snapped her fingers. 'You seem more… more relaxed. And you don't wear your glasses much now.'

'Interesting. I do wear my glasses all the time at school, and for driving, of course. Part of my teacher persona, shall we say. But I'm not very short-sighted, so I decided to leave them off when I could.' He stared past her into the hypnotic flames. 'And maybe I am more relaxed now, but I'm not sure that's because of the cottage. My new job is really working out well. There were lots of political and administrative problems before, which is why I left. It's in the past now, and it would be boring to go into it, so I won't. And village life is much slower paced, then there is the wonderful sea air and… I've come home to Wales. Yes, I *am* more relaxed.' He looked at her, keenly. 'How perspicacious of you to have realised that.'

'We know each other quite well now.'

They smiled in unison. 'Indeed we do. Now,' he continued briskly, putting down his plate on the coffee table, 'tell me about you. I receive your letters, but I want to hear you tell me: how are you finding university?'

Susan drank from her mug of tea. 'I've written and told you about what we're studying. I've told you pretty much everything important.'

'And are you embracing the whole university opportunity? Are you making friends, are you integrating? I try to read between the lines of your letters, to gauge if you are saying what you think I want to hear.'

Susan put her mug down on the hearth. It made a slight bang. 'Of course I haven't been saying what you want to hear. I go to the FAB club, and I've got some friends now. Quite a few, in fact.'

'I'm glad. University is a unique time in your life. A rite of passage into adulthood. I was a little worried that your innately shy nature would hold you back.'

Susan uncurled her legs and wriggled into another position in the chair. 'Well you don't have to worry about me.' She gazed at the calendar on the mantelpiece. 'There's Jeanette, Lucy, Paul and William from my tutor group, Ian, Beth and Diane from the FAB club. And there's April.'

Richard sipped his tea. It was starting to get dark and a street lamp lit up red outside, sending its glow in through the window. 'Tomorrow, because it's Easter Sunday, I thought we could go to church in the morning, then in the afternoon I'll show you round the village and some of the lovely walks by the beach. Oh, and I've bought a joint of lamb. I've only used the oven once, and I rather hoped that cooking it could be a joint effort.'

Susan raised her eyebrows and looked at his deadpan face. Then she burst out laughing. 'A *joint* effort? Is that the best you can do?' She jumped up. 'Come on, let's have a look at this old oven, and see what sort of a state it's in.'

***

On Tuesday evening they sat in the Lounge of the Black Lion, licking from their fingers the last of the chicken-in-the-basket that they had just eaten.

Susan sat back and took a sip of her cider. 'I'm full,' she said.

Richard nodded his agreement through the brown depths of his pint of bitter. 'They do very acceptable pub food here.'

Susan gazed around. There was a log fire in the grate, polished horse brasses gleamed on the wall, and the low melodious hum of conversation drifted in from the Bar. 'I like it here,' she announced. 'It's cosy, it's homely.' She studied the only other couple who were in the Lounge. They were sat several tables away from them, their heads inclined close and their fingers curling together under the table. The glow of the fire brought out inky depths in the woman's black hair.

'That reminds me,' said Susan, 'I don't think I said in a letter about Aunty Pat's latest boyfriend? He's American. She met him around Christmas time, and they've been going out ever since. It's the romance of the century, the way she talks about him. And I think he must have quite a bit of money, judging by the places he takes her to.' Out of the corner of the eye she could still see the couple. The man had sneaked a kiss on the side of her neck. 'I met him last week, when he called to

95

take her out. I can see what she sees in him; he *was* charming, but a bit, well… American. You know, sort of boastful. He called me honey.'

'What's his name?'

'Chuck.'

'Chuck?' Richard almost choked on his beer and had to hide his laughter behind his hand. '*Chuck!* I didn't think anyone really was called Chuck! Well, it just shows how little I know about the USA.'

Susan had to smile. 'And he called Frank 'sport'.'

'But of course. How did Frank like that?'

'He just glowered at him. But Frank does a lot of glowering.' They both watched as the barmaid bustled over to put another log onto the fire, her skirt tight across her behind as she bent over.

'We hardly talk now, Frank and me. And when we do, we argue. He jeers at me, saying aren't I too big to still be in school.' She sighed. 'It's best to just ignore him. I don't talk to Lionel much either, when he's at home, that is. I've never talked much to Lionel, though.' She stared at the yellow snake of flame that was caressing the new log on the fire. 'But with Frank it used to be different. When we were children we were really close, and I feel I've still got a soft spot for him even though he's so awkward nowadays. I told you, didn't I, that we used to be called 'the twins' because we were born on the same day?'

'Yes, you told me. When I met Frank at New Year I managed to draw him out a bit, and get him to talk about what he likes – football and darts it was, I think.'

'Well, you're good at that sort of thing.' Susan studied Richard's face.

He rubbed his cheek. 'What's the matter, have I got tomato sauce on my face?'

'No, I was just thinking…' She let her eyes trace his features, softened in the gentle glow of the firelight.

'You seem to be getting younger! Every time I see you you're a bit younger, and now, during this week…' She frowned at the audacity of her thoughts.

'I'm flattered! You don't think this is anything to do with you getting older? So in terms of proportion, the gap between our ages is less?'

'A bit. Maybe. But when I compare you now to how you were a few years back, you seem… lighter.'

'Ah, but I had to hide my inner self under my mantle of teacher. I had to maintain order, respect, discipline. And I admit it now, I was nervous about teaching in a girls' school. Things could have gone wrong. I had to maintain a distance. If you remember, I was very careful to be your teacher, not your friend, right up until you left school.'

The barmaid slid over to them and pointed to their empty glasses. 'All finished here? Shall I get these out of your way?' she sing-songed, her eyes trailing towards the clock.

They took their coats and emerged into the fresh night, the air cool as water on their cheeks after the heat of the fire. They let their eyes accustom to the darkness and walked side by side down the lane.

'What was it like, not being able to be yourself?' said Susan eventually.

'I wouldn't put it quite like that. A schoolteacher is *one* of my selves. I think we all have multiple personas, different masks that we put on for different occasions.'

'Do you think I have different selves?'

'Assuredly. There's the fun-loving impish Susan, there's the shy Susan, the one that doesn't have yet have the faith in herself that she should have, there's the childlike Susan who takes such joy in simple things, there's the very able academic Susan, and there's the kind Susan.' He paused. There was hardly any sound except their footsteps, softly teasing the quiet night. 'This Susan cares about other people, and struggles to understand. Like you were saying about your cousin Frank back there in the pub. And there are other Susans who are only just emerging.' His voice was soft.

They had reached the guest house and Richard swung the ill-fitting gate open for her. The scrape of the metal on the path was harsh.

Susan was silent. His comments had taken her unawares.

'Well, here we are,' he said. 'What would you like to do tomorrow? More exploring?'

'I don't know. Anything.'

'Let's wait and see what the weather is like. Goodnight.' He kissed her gently on the cheek.

From within the house the front room curtain shifted slightly, letting out a finger of light across the path.

***

The next day grey clouds had rolled in. In the cottage the conservatory roof amplified the monotonous drumming of rain on the roof. Richard said he had some preparation to do for lessons the following week and so could Susan amuse herself for the morning, perhaps reading? Would she mind awfully? Of course not, she had replied, and had settled herself at the kitchen table with a book while Richard went to his desk upstairs. Susan fidgeted, listening to the rain and turning pages idly. She looked around the room, at the expectant shelves of the Welsh dresser and at the boxes stacked in the corner. She closed her book with a snap and went upstairs.

'Richard?' she knocked gently on the door and went in. He was surrounded by books and making notes in a sturdy hard-backed notebook. A swift memory ran across her mind of Richard, when he was Mr Morgan, coming to classes with a similar book under his arm.

'Mmm?' he looked up but didn't put down his pen.

Susan put her hands behind her back and swallowed a giggle. She had an urge to say 'Please, Sir'.

'This is just an idea, and of course I don't mind if you say no, but would you like me to unpack some of your boxes? I know you're very busy at school, and you've been spending all your time with me these last few days, but things like china and stuff, I could get it out and put it on shelves and in cupboards. If you like. If it would help.'

'Are you sure you don't mind? It would be a great help.'

Susan clapped her hands in front of her and bounced up and down. 'I'd love to! I'll be very careful,' she called over her shoulder as she bounded downstairs.

The first box she unpacked contained less commonly used kitchen items. She delved into the crinkly newspaper wrapping and pulled out an ornate corkscrew, a mincer, and several other items. Last to emerge from that box were three bright red kitchen jars, labelled 'coffee' 'tea'

98

and 'sugar'. She took them to the kitchen and placed them on the yellow cupboard, standing back to appreciate the rainbow effect in the dull little room. She duly filled the containers with instant coffee, leaf tea and white sugar, humming while she worked. The other kitchen utensils she found space for in cupboards and drawers. A fat ceramic hen, to be used for storing eggs, she kept out, noting that when Richard had put up shelves, the hen would look perfect perched there. Perhaps with a plant.

Another box contained various framed photos, mostly sepia toned; severe looking people stood in stiff rows, an unsmiling woman holding a plump baby while a toddler stood shyly by her side. She wondered if the baby was Richard. She put the photos to one side and started on the final box. Her eyes rounded at the first thing she pulled out. It was a willow pattern plate, distinctive with its blue depictions of pagodas, trees, birds. Her gently probing fingers soon found five more. By the time she had laid everything reverently on the table there was a tea pot, jug, a lidded tureen, oval and rectangular platters, and several cups and saucers. When Richard came downstairs later she was hanging the last of the cups on the hooks of the Welsh dresser, so that it was decked like a dressed Christmas tree.

'What do you think?' she said, standing back, hands on hips.

'Susan, it's perfect! Just like I remember it from my parents' house.' He picked up one of the empty boxes. 'And you've unpacked all this in just one morning.'

She led him by the hand into the kitchen and living room, and pointed out where she had placed items, bobbing up and down with delight.

He nodded, gazing round at it all. 'It would have taken me weeks to get round to doing all this. Thank you.'

'Oh, it's nothing. I've really enjoyed it.'

'And, I've worked hard too. I've done all the preparation I needed to do this morning, so I think we both deserve some lunch, don't you?' He glanced at the clock on the mantelpiece. 'Goodness, it's one-thirty already.'

They sat at the kitchen table eating a ploughman's lunch – crusty bread which Susan had brought up from the bakery that morning, strong cheese and pickles. Richard said a ploughman's lunch didn't taste right without beer to go with it, so he had opened a bottle of brown ale for himself. He offered Susan some but she screwed her nose up at the first taste and shook her head, preferring to stick to lemonade.

They ate their meal to the accompaniment of the solemnly ticking clock.

'You're quiet,' said Richard, when they were left with the crumbs on their plates and down their fronts.

Susan picked at the crumbs with her fingers. 'I've had an idea,' she said slowly. 'It's totally crazy but...' She paused, 'Not crazy at all, really.'

Richard sat back and folded his arms, his smile indulgent and loosened by the beer. 'I have no idea what you're talking about. Do you want to enlighten me?'

Susan looked down at her plate. The idea that had wandered into her mind, first of all just a whispered wish, had in the space of a few minutes become so enormous, so audacious, that she didn't know how to take hold of it.

She took a deep breath. 'You're never going to have the time to look after this place properly, let alone look after yourself. You tell me you stay after school a lot of days, running clubs and other things, and that you spend time on weekends doing marking and preparing lessons. You're going to end up not eating properly, and going to school with your shirts not ironed.'

'I have been looking after myself for many years now, you know.'

'Ah yes, but only in a small bed-sitting room or a flat, not a house with a garden.'

He drained his glass, tipping his head back and allowing the drink to slide down his throat in one go. 'Ahhh,' he said appreciatively, gazing at the trickle of foam in the empty glass. 'So, what's your big idea to save me from this dreadful fate?'

'You need a housekeeper.'

'A housekeeper?' he laughed, 'That would be nice, but I can't afford it. Where would I find one who would work for a pittance?'

'You already have. Me.'

'What?'

'Oh Richard, it would be perfect.' She leaned forward and gazed into his face, her eyes wide. 'I just love it here. I could do all the housework and cooking, you know I'm used to that. You wouldn't need to pay me, I could have the single bed in the other bedroom, and you could bring your desk down into the conservatory or the sitting room - we'd sort that out - I could get a part time job…'

'My *housekeeper*?' he interrupted, his face aghast. 'Don't be so ridiculous. You can't possibly be my housekeeper. You're talking rubbish.'

Susan recoiled from his harsh tone. She reacted, defensive. 'It's not rubbish! It makes sense. And… and I thought you liked my company.'

'I do like your company. But have you forgotten you're nearly one year through a three year university course?'

Susan was silent and hung her head. 'Oh Richard, I haven't taken to it. I've tried to, but university's just not for me. I didn't want to let you down, because I know you've encouraged me. But I just don't… I just don't really fit in. I could give it up tomorrow, and not care.'

'Susan.' He voice was gentler now. 'I'm sorry that you're struggling to fit in. But just give it time. It will be worth it, believe me. And I'm delighted that you like it so much here. I hope you can visit again in the summer.'

Susan clutched at the opening he had offered her. 'I have three months off from uni in the summer. I could come then and we could give it a trial, me being your housekeeper…'

'*No!*' His chair scraped back across the stone floor and he strode into the kitchen and stood gripping the side of the sink with both hands, his back to her.

'Richard? Why are you so angry?' She approached him cautiously, as if he were an animal that had suddenly bared its teeth at her. 'I'm sorry.' Her throat was starting to block. 'I just… I just thought it was a good idea, that's all.' She gently put her hand on his arm.

He spun round, shaking off her hand.

'Do you really not know? We are spending these wonderful days together and are you telling me you don't *know*?'

She felt as if she had lost all her bearings. 'I don't know what? I have no idea what you mean! Please, please tell me!'

He took her by the shoulders and scanned her face. 'You really

101

don't, do you.' He dragged up a deep breath. 'I love you, Susan. I love you and I've been watching you, waiting for you to grow up.'

All she could do was to stare at him.

He groaned and let his arms drop. 'Oh, I never intended to tell you. Not yet. I wanted - I still want - you to have your chance to lead your own life, to become your own person, and then later on I had hoped, maybe... but you can see now why I couldn't possibly have you here as a housekeeper. If you come to live here, it won't be as my housekeeper.'

Still, she couldn't grasp what he was saying. She felt dizzy, as if the ground beneath her feet had become unstable.

They stood motionless, staring at each other, while the tap in the sink behind them dripped monotonously. Then he reached out and cupped her face in his hands, like a piece of fine china. Her soft fruit mouth opened without effort when he kissed her. His arms yawned round her and held her close, and she knew she had come home.

Chapter 9

When I get out of here, we could go on holiday. Somewhere with sunshine, winter sunshine. Gran Canaria, perhaps? We could go back to the same hotel that we went to a few years ago. I liked it there. I closed my eyes and I could almost feel the sunshine warming me through, reaching right down to my bones. Soon.

They sat on the sofa, encased in the glimmer of the firelight, Richard's arm lying around Susan's shoulders. Her legs were crossed over his and they held hands, their fingers twining and untwining.

'I still can't believe it,' said Susan, her voice half muffled against his chest.

'No more can I. I've wanted to hold you in my arms like this for so long.'

She lifted her head and looked at him. 'When did you first know? When did you know that you loved me?' The taste of the words in her mouth was unfamiliar.

He didn't answer straight away. 'I think I started to realise how special you were when you started coming to the Creative Writing group, in the Sixth form.'

She wriggled her toes. 'Special?'

'Yes. You seemed different from the others girls. You had this... depth. It came out in your writing. Yet in other ways you were so naïve, so childlike. It was only when we started having the sessions with just the two of us, that my feelings grew.' She studied his face, seeing as if for the first time the line of his jaw, the slight shadow of stubble. 'I started looking forward more and more to our sessions.'

'So did I. They were the high spot of my week.'

He acknowledged her with a faint smile. 'Then I can remember, quite clearly, driving away from your house one day and realising that I had fallen in love with you. I hadn't chosen to do so; it had chosen me. I stopped the car and just sat there. I was devastated.'

She stopped moving her toes. 'Devastated? What do you mean?'

'I mean, you were my pupil and I was your teacher. Falling in love wasn't supposed to happen. And, I didn't see how you could possibly return my feelings. I didn't know what to do, so I just allowed our friendship to continue.'

'And then,' she interrupted, 'As soon as I left school, you asked me out. Well, sort of. You said you never really were my boyfriend. I just thought we had this wonderful, special relationship.'

'We did, my darling, and we do.'

Then she frowned slightly. 'But why have you always encouraged me to go away to university? How could you want me to leave you if you loved me?'

'Because, little one, you have a lot of potential. I didn't want – still don't want – to stand in the way of your education and development. I thought that once you settled into your new life you would find other friends, maybe a romance, and that would be that. And it would probably be best for you. That's another reason I took the job here. To put some distance between us.'

'Oh, Richard.' She turned her face into his chest again. 'How could you bear that if you loved me?'

'I want what's best for you.'

For a while she didn't reply. A part-burned coal on the fire tumbled down and hissed into the space of their silence. 'Yet we met last autumn half term, New Year, and now this week.'

She felt rather than saw him smile. 'Well, we both obviously enjoy each other's company, and I did nurse this hope that if I waited a couple more years until I declared my intentions... then maybe, just maybe, the time would be right...'

She sat up. 'What do you mean, 'declared you intentions'?'

He shifted his position. 'I'm saying too much.'

Susan shifted her gaze onto the curtains, closed against the intrusion of the night. 'Do you mean,' she said, keeping her voice neutral, 'That your 'intentions are honourable'?'

'But of course.' He stopped abruptly and shook his head. 'This is too much, too soon. I know it's too soon, but the last couple of days with you have changed everything.' He took a deep breath. 'Oh, I'm going to have to say it now. Susan, one day, perhaps two years or so from now, I hope you might agree to marry me and come here to live with me as my wife. I don't expect you to answer me now but –'

'Yes.' She clutched her hands together to keep them still. 'Yes, I'll come here to live with you as your wife.'

'My dear, you say that now, and I'm happy to hear it, but you might change your mind when you get back into the swing of university and meet other people.'

'I won't change my mind.'

He took her hands. 'Susan, I want so much to marry you, but I want you to be absolutely sure. For instance, what about that young man that

105

you met at the music club? What is it... the FAB club?'

Susan stared at him blankly. Then she burst out laughing. 'Oh Richard, you haven't been jealous, have you?'

He withdrew his hands and looked away. 'It was the first time you had mentioned a man, and I couldn't help wondering.'

She stopped laughing and took his hands again. 'I did see Ian again, the next time I went to the club. He came over to my table, said hello, chatted a few minutes, went away again, and that was that. And anyway, how can you think I could possibly look at anyone else now?'

He scooped her up onto his lap and held her tight against him, kissing her cheeks and her mouth.

She lay resting against him, absorbing it all. Eventually she said, 'I know you think it's important that I finish my course, but I can come here in the summer can't I? Can I stay here?'

'No, my darling, you can't. I have a reputation to keep up. I don't want to threaten my prospects in any way if I'm going to be providing a secure future for you. Nor do I want to compromise you.'

'Then where will I stay? It will work out a bit expensive at the guest house.'

He thought for a moment. 'We'll find a solution. I believe one of the secretaries at the school has a spare room that she might allow you to use.'

'And she would know I was your... your girlfriend?'

'Yes. There's no need for secrecy.'

She hesitated. 'Wouldn't it look better – for you, I mean – if she knew the relationship was on a firmer footing than that? Rather than thinking I'm just some young girl that you've taken up with?'

He stroked her cheek thoughtfully. 'You may be right. You would still be free to change your mind if you wanted to, but perhaps we should get engaged in the summer.'

She allowed the words to melt inside her, like chocolate.

***

Through the window of the bus Susan watched the landmarks of Llanley rewind themselves. The pub, the shops, the church spire

106

scratching the sky, it all drifted past her. One week, she thought, one short week, and everything is changed. I am changed.

They had embraced in silence at the bus stop, both aware of the enormity of what had passed between them. Then Richard had whispered, only a few weeks and I will come to visit you. Susan had wanted to see him for the entire school half term week at the end of May, but he had pointed out that it would probably be just before her exams then. Susan was crestfallen, and eventually they compromised on Richard coming to Burlingham for a weekend to see her. It would have to be enough.

As the bus rumbled out on to the main road, the sea sweeping out on her right hand side, Susan sat back and closed her eyes so that she could more easily think about the last few days and everything it meant. The realisation that she now belonged somewhere, that she could see her future, warmed her inside like hot soup. She didn't even mind too much about going back to her studies, not now that she knew the cottage and Richard were waiting for her.

In the noise and smoke of Cardiff bus station, Susan changed onto the coach for Burlingham. She settled back as the coach glided through countryside and towns. She watched, dreamy and contented, as they passed fat smiling houses and trees that said hello to her with their waving branches. She hugged her secret to herself. They had agreed to keep it between the two of them until Richard had written to her father. You don't have to do that, she had said to him. I'm old enough to get married without permission. He had replied that he still considered it a courtesy to tell her father first, to explain that he was in a position to give Susan a secure home and that his prospects were good, and to formally say it would set the seal on their happiness to have his blessing.

'I wouldn't think he'd have any cause to withhold his blessing,' Richard had said, 'Even though some people might see the age gap as rather large.'

Susan had snorted. 'Don't worry. This is a gift to Dad and Wanda. Now they won't have to worry about keeping a bedroom for me. The new baby, when it comes, can have my room and welcome to it. I can always stay at Aunty Pat's. Oh yes, Dad will give us his blessing alright.'

'Aren't you being a little cynical? I'm sure your father wants your happiness.'

She shrugged. 'Maybe. As for the age gap...' She paused, thinking. 'Gosh, do you realise that the difference in our ages is the same as that between Dad and Wanda? It's never occurred to me before. What a coincidence! So he's hardly likely to object that you are older than me.'

'A coincidence... Yes.' He too was thoughtful. 'And what do *you* feel about me being older? Does it worry you at all?'

She laughed outright; a pure, uncomplicated sound. 'I don't think of you and me in terms of age. We're just us.'

The coach was slowing down now. She craned her neck to see what was going on. There were weekend roadworks so one lane of the motorway was closed, and various diggers and pieces of machinery sat there looking important but doing nothing. It didn't seem as if they would be held up for long. She went back to her reverie.

She remembered how, only the week before, the idea of not having a secure place in her family home had upset her. The thought moved uncomfortably in her now and she turned away from it. She thought instead of when Dad had given his blessing - Richard said he would write within the next week - and they could announce their plans to the world. I think I would like a diamond in my engagement ring, she thought. Nothing showy, just a single diamond. Like Mum's. She thought of her mother with a slow sadness and allowed herself a moment of regret that she would not be sharing her engagement plans with her. Mum, you would have been so happy for me, she said silently. You would have adored Richard. I know I haven't written to you for a while, but I do think about you.

But if she couldn't have Mum, Aunty Pat would be more than happy to share her plans. She could already hear her telling Susan that she had suspected it all along, suspected that that handsome Richard was more than a friend. Oh how romantic, she would say.

Susan wondered if Aunty Pat would be at home when she arrived. It would be about six o'clock, so she probably would be in. No doubt she would be going through the ritual of painting her nails and doing her hair before the Saturday night date with Chuck. She tended to see him one or two nights in the week, but Saturday night was their big night out when they would go to a restaurant with dancing afterwards. Susan would put her head under her pillow so she didn't have to listen to them coming in at two o'clock in the morning, and what followed.

Susan bit her lip. If Aunty Pat was there, she didn't see how she could possibly not tell her, even though it was supposed to be a secret. She'll get it out of me, Susan thought. She'll take one look at my face and know that something has happened. So maybe she would have to tell her – but she would impress on her that it had to be their secret until Richard had written to Dad.

The decision made, Susan sat back, gently fizzing with anticipation while she pictured them sitting side by side on the sofa, Aunty Pat's cigarette waving excitedly as she quizzed Susan for every delicious detail.

***

Something wasn't right. She knew it as soon as she opened the front door, struggling to get her suitcase over the step in the fading light. There was a staleness, a stillness. She wrinkled her nose at the smell and went into the sitting room, pulling her coat off as she did so. The stone cold remains of a fish and chip dinner lay in newspaper on the coffee table, along with several empty beer bottles, some upright, some scattered on their sides like skittles in a bowling alley. An ashtray was full of cigarette butts. Susan tightened her mouth and picked up the ashtray, holding it at arms' length, and gathered up the fish and chip paper with her other hand. Clearly the boys had had a session last night. Aunty Pat must have stayed out all night because there was no tell-tale lipstick on any of the cigarette stubs. Besides which, even she would never have left the ashtray full like that all day.

Susan took the rubbish into the kitchen to dispose of it. What she saw stopped her in her tracks, the newspaper and ashtray balanced one on each hand as if she were weighing them. The sink was overflowing with dirty crockery. On the table was a sliced loaf with the bag torn open and slices of bread tumbling out of the gap, along with a collection of dirty mugs, a bag of sugar that had spilt and a jaggedly open tin of baked beans with a spoon in it. Susan jolted out of her stillness and plunged the rubbish into the bin. Her instincts told her to check upstairs.

The door to Aunty Pat's bedroom was already standing open. Susan stared, unable to take in what she saw. Most of the drawers were open, jutting out at crazy angles. Some had been emptied completely, others still had a few clothes cowering inside them. Four or five outfits were strewn over the bed like lifeless dolls, and when Susan pulled open the wardrobe door she saw that only a couple of dresses remained. A memory twitched within her, a memory of another empty wardrobe that she had opened. She took a step back and felt something crunch under her heel. She picked it up; it was one of Aunty Pat's earrings, a big droplet of coloured beads and gold wires that used to swing exuberantly when she tossed her head. Now, it lay mangled in Susan's palm.

The police, thought Susan, I must get the police. Someone has been in the house. Burglars. Then she heard a door open across the landing followed by the thud of footsteps and she almost cried out.

'You're back, then,' said Frank from the bedroom door. He was pale and his clothes were rumpled.

Susan gasped in relief and stepped towards him; her hands outstretched. 'Oh, thank goodness it's you. Whatever has happened? The house has been ransacked! Oh, they haven't been in my room have they?' She started forward but he stood solid and unsmiling in the doorway, blocking her.

'Frank? Let me through!'

He ignored her. 'She's gone.' His voice was dull.

'What? What do you mean? Gone where?'

Frank sighed and sat down on the side of the bed, moving as if his body was too heavy for him.

Susan sat down beside him and shook his arm. 'Tell me.'

Frank explained. Apparently, *he* – you know who I mean, he had said – has been called back to Los Angeles, or wherever it is, out of the blue and he asked her to go with him. 'She told me about it on Monday,' he said. 'I tried to talk her out of it, but she was dead set on it. This is my big chance, she kept saying. I'm never going to get a chance like this again. And she kept going on about his wonderful flat –

apartment, she called it – with two bathrooms, showers and something that did the washing up, and all these palm trees and sunshine. I reckon he's having her on and she's been right taken in.'

So many questions were going round in Susan's head. 'Is she just going to live with him? Has he said anything about marrying her?'

Frank shrugged. 'He says he'll be able to get her a job in America.' He took in a slow breath, as if it hurt to breathe. 'Tuesday evening I came in from work and she'd already left that morning. She left a note to say goodbye. Just a note. She couldn't say it to my face.' His voice oozed with bitterness now.

'Oh Frank!' Susan put her arm around his stiff bulk, and felt him trembling. 'But... but surely she can't just *go*? What about her job? What about all... all the arrangements?' What about *me*? she wanted to say.

Frank picked up the sleeve of one of the discarded blouses on the bed and let it drop from his fingers. 'Well, she already had a passport, didn't she, from that trip she did to France last year. And she says they are getting a visa or whatever it is in London.' He shook his head slowly. 'She phoned me from London on Wednesday, but she wouldn't say where she was. I said, why don't you come home and perhaps go to America later, when you've had chance to weigh it all up and do things properly. But she wouldn't have any of it. I reckon she thought if he went back on his own he'd soon forget about her.'

Susan tended to agree, but she didn't say so.

'She said she left a note for you too. In your room,' he said. 'As if these notes make it alright.'

Susan jumped up and left him sitting on the bed.

The note was propped up on the dressing table, with 'To Susie' written on the envelope. She tore it open and devoured the words.

Dear Susie

By now I reckon Frank and Lionel will have told you. I was so upset when Chuck said he'd been called back to his central office in Los Angeles. Then you could have knocked me down with a feather when he asked me to go with him. I can't just leave, I said, not just like that. Why not? he said. Life is for living. You

111

have to grab your chances when they come. And the more he talked, the more it made sense.

Please, please try to understand. What is there for me here? Nearly twenty more years working in that boring job, that's what. I'm not stupid, I know I'm not a spring chicken any more. One look in the mirror tells me that. Who am I going to meet if I stay here? The men round here haven't got a clue. Not compared to Chuck.

Our Lionel and Frank tried to talk me out of it, of course. Wait, they said. Do it all properly. But if I wait, I know I'll lose my nerve. I'll get scared, and I'll let them persuade me to stay. So, I just packed my bags and upped and went. I'm going to Los Angeles! I'm really going! The sun shines there all the year round, Chuck says. Can you believe it?

I am ever so sorry this has happened when you were away. You know you are like a daughter to me, the daughter I never had. Even more so since your poor Mum died. You're so much like her, you know. I want you to know that you can stay in the house as long as you like. I told the boys to get the Council to put it in their names, and I told them, Susie gets to stay as long as she wants. You can sort everything else out, the bills and that, between you. It will do those boys good to take some responsibility for a change.

Chuck is such a wonderful man. I really can't believe my luck. I have to pinch myself to know I'm not dreaming. Susie, you're going to find your own wonderful man one day. When you do, hold on to him.

As soon as I get settled I'll write.

With all my love,

Aunty Pat xx

***

Susan stood at the sink, up to her elbows in hot soapy water while the pile of clean crockery on the draining board grew higher. On her instruction Frank trooped backwards and forwards to the dustbin outside, taking out the accumulated waste of the last week, one piece at a time. Susan had searched through the pantry and came up with a tin of minced beef in gravy, tinned peas and some potatoes which she had cooked for their tea. They had eaten with little conversation, Frank because he was never communicative at the best of times and Susan because her mind was spinning as she tried to grasp the truth: Aunty

112

Pat had gone. What was this going to mean? Her happiness of a few hours ago seemed distant now.

'You and Lionel are going to have to help more,' she said over her shoulder from the sink, raising her voice above the clatter of crockery. 'I can't run this house all on my own.' She frowned when he didn't reply. He was sitting at the table, starting moodily at its surface.

'Frank, are you listening to me?' He slowly lifted his eyes to her and mumbled something she didn't catch. 'Come and dry these dishes. Come on now, you can see the draining board's almost full.'

He took a tea towel and fumbled at the plates. 'I'm not used to this,' he complained.

Susan swallowed down her sharp reply and calmed herself with a long breath. 'I can see how upset you are,' she said, 'and I know you've never had to do this, but you'll soon learn. We'll make a plan together.' She let the greasy water gurgle down the plug hole then she picked up another tea towel and joined him in the wiping.

'Done,' she said a few minutes later, hanging the tea towel to dry. 'I don't know about you but I'm exhausted after all this shock.' She dragged her hands over her face and groaned. 'Look, I'm going to bed now, and we can talk more in the morning.' As an afterthought she said, 'Has anyone told my Dad?'

He stood by the door looking at her, his arms hung limply by his sides.

'I said, does my dad know?' Irritation sharpened her voice when he didn't reply. 'Did you hear me?'

He nodded, as if to himself. 'We'll be alright. You and me.' He didn't seem to have heard her question.

'Yes, we'll sort it out somehow.' Susan bent wearily to pick up her shoulder bag. She glanced at her suitcase where she had dumped it in the hall. That could wait until tomorrow. It could all wait until tomorrow. Suddenly she was so tired she could hardly stand.

'I'm going upstairs.' He was still standing by the doorway and didn't move to let her through.

He stood in half shadow. 'It was always going to come to this somehow, you know,' he said slowly. 'I always knew it.'

Susan had an ache in her neck and shoulders that was spreading down her back. 'I don't know what you're talking about,' she said. 'Tell me in the morning. And where's Lionel? I didn't make him any tea.'

'He's staying out at his mate's tonight.' He put his hand out and closed it over her arm.

She tried to pull her arm away and he tightened his grip. 'Let go, will you? I want to go to bed.'

Instead he took a step closer and put his other arm round her back, pinioning her arm down. He began to speak rapidly. 'I've been watching you and waiting, ever since you came here. Waiting for you to get all this nonsense about learning and university out of your head. It's supposed to be you and me together. Ever since we were kids. We're twins, remember?'

His breath was hot against her neck. She struggled, but he only pulled tighter. 'Frank! Have you gone crazy? Let me go!' His mouth was crawling on her neck now, and she twisted her head out of the way as he tried to get to her face. 'And anyway,' she gasped in desperation as panic started to spurt inside her. 'I already have a boyfriend. We're going to be married.'

His grip slackened for a moment and she took her chance, ripping herself away from him and heading for the stairs.

'I don't believe you,' he shouted as he lumbered after her. She had managed to stumble half way up the stairs before he caught up with her. She swung round with her shoulder bag and caught him across the head, sending him sprawling to the bottom of the stairs. She threw herself into her room and found the strength to push the chest of drawers across the door and under the door handle. She stood, trying to get her breath, and she heard him bellow from downstairs.

'Go on then, run away. First Dad, then Mum and now you. You all leave me in the end.' His voice ended in a sob.

***

It was just after dawn when Susan started to ease the chest of drawers away from the door. She had hardly slept. Not that she was too worried about Frank barging his way in, because not only was the chest firmly against the door, but when she had heard him come upstairs last

114

night, she had sat on the bed, her heart beating in thick strokes, watching for the door handle to start turning. However, he hadn't even stopped outside her door. But even if it had been possible for her to calm herself enough to sleep properly, she needed to be up as soon as it was light. Her alarm clock was in her suitcase downstairs, but anyway she would not have risked using it in case it woke Frank.

She eased the chest inch by inch away from the door. Frank's room was next to hers and she kept pausing to strain her ears for any sounds. Eventually she had unblocked the door and put her hand on the handle to open it. She held her breath as she slid it gently open. Even going as slowly as she could, the door still groaned, the sound enormous to her oversensitive nerves. She froze, every fibre in her body alert as she listened for movement from Frank's room.

Nothing. This was it. She sprang lightly across the landing and into the bathroom, sliding the bolt across with fingers that seemed to have grown fat and clumsy. A few minutes later she eased the door open, which thankfully didn't creak like her bedroom door. She concentrated her whole being on listening for sounds. Her plan now had been to creep slowly and carefully downstairs as quietly as she could, but when she looked downstairs and saw the enticement of the front door with her suitcase next to it, her nerve broke. She raced down the stairs, grabbed her suitcase and hurled herself through the front door. The fear was threatening to gobble her up as she dashed out of the garden, clumsy with her load, and struggled down the road. Only at the corner did she allow herself to stop briefly and look back at the house, as bland and silent as its neighbours. A paperboy went past on his bike, newspapers bulging from his saddle bag. Someone was out taking their dog for an early morning walk, and he called out a cheery 'Good morning'. Susan gulped at the fresh morning air and looked at her watch. She wondered what time the buses started on a Sunday morning.

Chapter 10

Susan floated out of a mist of sleep and lay blinking at the ceiling. There was enough daylight coming through the thin curtains to allow her to see a crack making its crazy route outwards across the ceiling from the bare light bulb in the centre of the room. Outside a car was revving its engine. For a few seconds she couldn't think where she was. Then she remembered.

What day was it? She had almost lost track, what with all the upheaval of the last few days. Thursday. Yes, it was Thursday. She turned over in bed to look at her clock. Quarter past seven. She didn't need to get up yet. Besides, she could hear someone in the bathroom, so she would wait. Today she was going back to Aunty Pat's house to collect her belongings. Before she went in the house she would check that Frank's bike was gone, which would mean he was at work. Richard had suggested that she got a taxi and asked the taxi driver to wait for her while she quickly packed up her things.

The bedroom was sparsely furnished – bare desk and chair, wardrobe, cupboard. So, this is to be my new home, she thought. It would look better when she had her personal things; her silver-framed picture of Mum and Dad's wedding, her jewellery box where the little ballerina spun round when you wound it up, her books. It struck her that maybe she should get a picture of Richard too, or a picture of them together. And anyway, she thought, this is not my home, it's just a temporary lodging. My real home is going to be with Richard in the cottage. I will be in Llanley in the summer, even if I'm not actually living in the cottage yet. It's only a few weeks away.

After her early morning escape from Aunty Pat's house she had got the first coach of the morning to Cardiff and then arrived at the cottage in the middle of the day. While she was on the coach it suddenly occurred to her that Richard might be out. No, she thought, he can't be out. He just can't be. It's Sunday, he'll go to church and then come home to have his lunch. I wish he had a phone. She had asked him last week why he didn't have one, and he had told her that he liked keeping the cottage slightly old-fashioned, as far as was practical. But isn't it practical to have a phone, Susan had asked. I can use a phone at school if I need to, he had said. And there's a phone box just a couple of minutes up the road. Yet, said an uncomfortable voice inside her head, if I had been able to phone him he might have told me not to come. He would have told me to go to Dad's.

When she got to the cottage and found Richard preparing his lessons she threw herself into his arms and sobbed with relief. Richard allowed her to tell the story in her own way, passing her his handkerchief to wipe her eyes and nose. She told him that she was going to miss Aunty Pat a lot, and that she didn't realise how close to her she'd become. Richard asked her what she intended to do about the incident with Frank.

She twisted the handkerchief between her fingers. 'Nothing. I was frightened at the time, but I don't think he really meant it. He was just shocked.' She was thoughtful for a moment. 'And I daresay he's scared of being on his own.'

Richard frowned. 'Do you think you're giving him too much benefit of the doubt? What if he really is dangerous?'

Susan shook her head. 'I don't think so. Remember, I've known him all my life. Literally. He's been left by both his parents and he just went a bit crazy. I feel sorry for him, Richard.'

He kissed her on her cheek, all red and blotchy from crying. 'And that's to your credit, my darling. But you need to think of your own safety.'

'I feel safe here. All I wanted to do was to get back to you.'

Richard sighed. 'Have you told your father?'

'Not yet. I'll phone him maybe tomorrow, when I'm a bit calmer. But I'm not going to tell him about Frank, only about Aunty Pat. It would just cause a big upset. Richard, I can stay here tonight, can't I? Please?'

He hesitated and she thought he was going to say no. Then he told her of course she could stay for a couple of nights, but then she needed to get back and sort out some accommodation before the summer term started next week. She bowed her head. He talked her through how she could contact the University Accommodation Office the next day, and that they were sure to have lists of available lodging places, although this late in the academic year there might not be a lot of choice. For the next academic year, she would be able to choose a place at leisure. Did she have enough money? Yes, because she had her grant, and out of that she had only been paying Aunty Pat a small amount to cover her food, so she had some savings.

The next day Susan spent a long time in the phone box, first handling Dad's shocked questions and then phoning the Accommodation Office and jotting down a few possible rooms. Then she rang landlords. They all sounded the same: the uninterested, take-it-or-leave-it, flat nasal twang. Eventually she arranged to see a room late on the Tuesday afternoon. She cried again when Richard came home. Just when the future seemed all set, now it's all unknown again, she had wailed, her voice buried in his shoulder as he cradled her in his arms. It's just a temporary setback, he had soothed. Think of it as one of life's bumps.

And so she had ended up here, lying in bed listening to the sounds of water gurgling in the bathroom next door, in a rented room in a student house. When she heard the bathroom door close she swung her legs out of bed and reached for her dressing gown. Of the five lodgers only she and another girl were in the house at present. The other three were coming back at the weekend, ready for the start of term on Monday. She picked up her towel and went into the bathroom. The tiles were a pasty cream colour, some fringed with grey mould. She turned on the shower and wiped the steam off the mirror with her hand. Her reflection emerged, palely. She scraped her fringe back off her face and studied herself. Her eyes were dark and shadowed, the brows bushy. Mournful eyes, she had always thought. How can Richard possibly love me? Yet he does. He does. The mirror Susan smiled at her.

When she turned to the shower and drew back the plastic curtain, she discovered that the water was barely lukewarm.

***

118

Dear Richard

I'm writing this in the library at uni. It's quieter than where I'm lodging. When I wrote to you after my first day and night there it didn't seem too bad. A little shabby, but quiet enough. And it's only for a few weeks, I told myself. But on the weekend the others came back, so now there are five of us — two men and three girls. Oh Richard, they are so untidy, and SO noisy! After only a few days the kitchen is a complete mess. They just leave food lying around and nobody seems to clean up. When I want to make something to eat I have to move all their dirty dishes — I'm not washing them — out of the way before I can even start. And they stay up so late! Up to midnight there will be music blaring and them shouting and laughing. They all seem to know each other quite well. The two men are doing Civil Engineering and the girls are doing Biology, all first year. There was another girl doing Biology, but she got pregnant and had to go home. So I've got her room now. They've asked me to join them in the evenings, but I've said no. At least they don't get up very early so I've learned to get to have the first shower while there's still some hot water.

On the weekend I went to see Dad and Wanda. He was stunned, of course, about Aunty Pat and, I think, quite angry with her. I found myself sticking up for her a bit, which was strange. In fact the whole weekend was strange, because I had to be careful that I didn't let anything slip about Frank, or about you and me, so I didn't really relax. Dad didn't ask why I had moved out. Probably he thought I would not want to stay anyway with Aunty Pat gone. Wanda looked really well, waddling round with her big tummy, and Katya is excited about the baby coming.

My lectures and tutorials in uni are OK. Everything is geared towards exams now. I can't wait to see you at half term. How long are you coming for? Have you written to Dad yet? It's only thinking about you and the cottage that keeps me hanging on here.

Write soon,

All my love, Susan xxxxxxxxx

Dear Susan

Oh dear, I'm sorry that your lodging is disappointing. Keep telling yourself that it's not for long. It's not unreasonable to ask your fellow tenants to be more respectful in their behaviour, but I recognise that this is difficult. Your best course of action is probably to smile bravely, like I know you can, and make the best of it. Perhaps you should get some earplugs (that is a serious suggestion).

As for next year, in my second and third years at university I stayed as a single lodger in the spare room of a charming middle-aged couple's house. That's the sort of thing that would suit you — quiet and civilised. The university will have such places on their list. When I come at half term I could help you, if you wish. It's a good idea to find somewhere and pay your deposit early.

At half term I will come for four nights, but I will need to bring some preparation work with me. I can do this while you are revising. I hope that this visit won't clash with any of your exams. With luck they will be in the following week. I have written to your father, asking for his blessing on our plans. I explained that I will cherish and take care of you always. As indeed I will, my darling. When I come to see you in May, I hope that we will be able to call on your father and Wanda.

I think about you every day. I cannot believe my good fortune that you are in my life. You are my sweet rose, my cool water, my blue sky.

Be patient. This difficult time will pass, as difficult times always do.

With all my love,

Richard xx

***

Susan stood outside the examination hall with ranks of other students. Some were chattering to their friends, some were leafing through textbooks or pages of notes, their faces drawn with anxiety. She watched some of them as their lips moved in time to their fingers trailing across the words, in an eleventh-hour attempt to imprint the facts on their brains. The late May afternoon weather was pleasant; a springtime mix of sunshine, fluffy clouds and breeze that made you think of lambs and daisies, but not the sort of afternoon to be sitting for two hours in an exam hall.

The big doors opened to admit them. A tremor of anticipation spread through the crowd, nervous laughter and calls of 'good luck'. They processed in, leaving their bags in a tumbled pile behind the invigilators' desk. The examination hall seemed massive after school exam rooms; about two hundred desks stood waiting in military rows, chairs pushed under, a face-down exam paper and book for writing answers waiting ominously on each desk. Conversation died down as each student found their desk and started arranging pens, pencils, rubbers and lucky mascots on the desk top.

Susan settled herself on her chair and got out her pen. She looked round with interest, taking in her first experience of a university examination room. Exams had never made her nervous. She had known girls at school who would be physically ill before exams, and then there were those who left all their revision until the last minute. Yet she herself, provided she had revised thoroughly – and she always had – found the whole experience quite exhilarating. She would read the questions and her brain would spring into action and spill onto the page through her pen. She had never been a brilliant pupil, but her marks were always good.

The invigilators at the front of the hall were checking their watches and peering over the room, watching for any student waving their hand in the air with a question. Susan sat back and folded her arms.

'You may turn your papers over and begin now,' came the solemn voice of the chief invigilator from the front.

There came the crackle of two hundred pages being turned in unison, while two hundred pairs of eyes looked down and swept hungrily over the words. At this point in an exam Susan would usually become oblivious to everything around her, the sighs and shuffles of others, the softly padding feet of the invigilators. Her focus became the paper in front of her and the transfer of what was in her head onto the beckoning white page.

She read the question sheet. The instructions were to answer three questions from a choice of four. She read them all and decided that she could answer any of them; they were all challenging but fair. She picked up her pen and started on number two, making a few rough notes first, then crossing them out and writing a short paragraph. Then she started on a fresh page and wrote three lines as a start of the answer to question one. Then she put down her pen and looked at her watch. Nearly half an hour had passed. She looked around the room at the bent figures, some with pens flying across pages, some head in hands, some gazing into space as if seeking inspiration. Everyone was oblivious of her.

As quietly as she could, she turned her examination paper face down on her desk, packed up her pencil case and eased herself out of her chair. As she tiptoed past the front desk an invigilator raised an enquiring eyebrow at her. Susan half shook her head and crept out, allowing the door to close quietly but firmly behind her.

***

F for Fail. She knew that was what was going to be written on the Notice of Results document before she read it. The document had been pinned up on the appointed notice board at the appointed time. She arrived late, so that the main crush of students had already drifted off, many heading noisily for the bar in the Students' Union. Just a few students remained, some hugging each other, some crying, some jumping up and down. She found her name on the list. Next to the Fs on the list was an asterisk, and at the bottom of the page the additional information was appended: *Please see your personal tutor as soon as possible.* Her personal tutor was Miss White. Call me Veronica, she had said with an overstretched smile when Susan and the rest of the tutees had met her at the beginning of the academic year. Susan had only seen her once since then.

She supposed she had better get it over with, so she decided to see if Veronica was free.

The door was ajar. 'Come in,' called out a voice when Susan tapped on the door.

They looked at each other as Susan stood on the threshold. Veronica was in her late thirties, Susan would have guessed, with short untidy hair that stood up in strange peaks around her head. In her hand she held a bunch of papers, extracted from the mountain of documents on her desk. She stared at Susan blankly, obviously with no idea of who she was. Susan explained why she was there.

'Ah, yes, yes. Come and sit down over here.' She moved a couple of books off a chair and gestured to it. Veronica rummaged among the papers on her desk and eventually came up with what she had been looking for.

They both sat on the edge of their chairs, facing each other. Veronica leafed through the pages in front of her, presumably to find Susan's name. She frowned as she scanned across the page.

'So Susan, whatever happened? We would have expected a much better mark than this from you. And you didn't even turn up for the last exam.' She was managing to keep the exasperation out of her voice.

Susan kept her head bowed so her hair fell over her face, partially obscuring it. 'I just couldn't do it,' she said. 'I went to pieces.'

'But why? Presumably this didn't happen in your A-levels.'

Susan briefly told her about Aunty Pat leaving. She said it had upset her, and how unsettled she was her new lodgings.

Veronica gave a gusty sigh, closed her eyes and drew her hands over her hair. 'Susan, don't you remember when you first came here, I told you all, if you have any personal problems, please, please come and see me. If you had done that, I could maybe have pleaded extenuating circumstances for you at the meeting of the Exam Board. But now it's too late. I can't do anything.' She spread her hands.

She asked Susan more questions about what had happened. Susan answered as briefly as she could. She kept her eyes on Veronica's flat black shoes, which were scuffed at the toes and in need of some polish.

Having exhausted her pastoral care role, Veronica then said briskly, 'Look, I'm afraid there is no option now for you to proceed to year two, Susan. You will have to repeat the whole of year one. Unfortunately you won't get your grant money again. But if you want to complete your degree, it's what you will have to do.'

Susan shook her head slowly, allowing her hair to fall down further over her face. 'I can't afford to do the year again,' she muttered. 'It's just not possible.'

In her mind she was reviewing the coach timetable to Cardiff.

***

Susan Smith and Richard Morgan were married a few weeks later.

Chapter 11

'You haven't eaten your lunch,' said Matthew. 'And it's our best shoe-leather gammon and soggy apple pie with lumpy custard.'

I paused, my hands lurking over the keyboard. 'I'm getting to it. I just needed to finish this bit.' I contritely picked up my knife and fork and shovelled up a forkful of mash and peas. 'Sorry. Look, I'm eating it now.'

'It'll be getting cold,' he fretted.

Actually, the food wasn't bad, as institution food goes. A little lacking in imagination, taste, consistency and colour, but apart from that it was fine.

Matthew watched me eat, arms folded like a vigilant nanny. He nodded towards the computer. 'Going well today?'

'Very well,' I said through a mouthful of gammon. 'I'm really hitting my stride.'

'How's it going to end?' he said.

'I don't know,' I said. 'I really don't know.'

The pie that Susan had made for the evening meal was reposing in the fridge alongside the peeled potatoes resting in cold water. From the dining room drifted the fragrance of polish that she had lavished on the table and dresser. She flexed her shoulders, savouring the slight ache from her efforts, and went into the living room. She checked the soil of the potted spider plant with her fingers, and finding it still damp, moved it from the mantelpiece to a new place in the centre of the coffee table. Then she straightened the cushions on the sofa, arranging them so that their edges sat obediently parallel. What time was it? Half-past two. Through the window she saw an afternoon of grey quietness, and she felt a signature chill of autumn. The first cardigan day, she thought, doing her buttons up. She peered again outside, as if she were hoping she had been mistaken the first time. No, she thought, I won't go for a walk, it looks like rain. And anyway, I went to the village this morning.

She ambled back to the dining room and glided her hand over the table, caressing the shine that she had coaxed from the old wood with her patient polishing. She turned the radio on and sat listening to a T. Rex song. Her fingers drummed idly to the insistent rhythm. After a few minutes she went upstairs and opened the bottom drawer in her dressing table, where she kept her notebook, writing materials and recent letters together in a box. She brought the box downstairs and got out her notebook and a pen. For a while she stared at the blank page, tapping her teeth with the pen. Then she stared to write.

9 October 1972

Dear April

Surprise surprise! It's been a while. In fact, the last time I saw you was during exams. How have you been? I have such exciting news: 'Reader, I married him'. Yes, Richard and I were married in August. I am Mrs Richard Morgan! I look at the ring on my finger and I still have to pinch myself. Here's how it all happened. I failed my exams, completely, disastrously failed, so I had to leave uni. Let's just say that university wasn't really for me. There was no longer any reason for us to wait to get married, so that's what we did!

It was a very quiet wedding, which was what we wanted. But Richard was adamant that we should be married in church, so that we could say our vows before God. And I must admit, the words and the cadence of the wedding service are so emotional, all that 'to have and to hold, in sickness and in health…' etc etc. We decided, because I wasn't affiliated to any particular church, why not have the wedding in the little church in Llanley, where we were going to live? Richard (and now me too) go there every week and sometimes he stands in to play the organ for the Sunday service, when the regular organist is away. April, our wedding was so beautiful. People talk about it being the happiest day of your life, and for me it was. We chose it to be intimate, rather than inviting lots of relatives that we never really see now. So our only guests were my Dad, Wanda, Katya as a bridesmaid and Richard's brother (the best man) and his wife. But then people from Richard's school and various people who go to that church turned up to see us married and to wish us well. Oh, and there was also my new half-brother, Marek, who was less than a month old, and a darling. Luckily he slept throughout the service.

Let me tell you about what I wore. Dad said Mum's wedding dress was still up in the loft, and he would be happy if I wanted to wear that. I got it out, and it was still in beautiful condition even after all these years. It was creamy white lace with long sleeves and cut so it sort of flowed over your hips into a short train. I tried it on, and I just knew that was what I was meant to wear. I could hardly recognise myself in the mirror. Dad was quite overcome when I showed him. He said I looked so much like Mum. I needed to have it altered just a little bit. The dressmaker was able to let out the seams a bit over the bust to make it more comfortable – Mum was always quite petite. The veil had got ripped so I didn't bother with that, I just wore the headdress. To go with it, I carried a bunch of white roses and wore my pearl necklace, which had been Mum's. I truly felt like a princess.

After the wedding service we sat down to a roast dinner at a nearby hotel. There weren't really speeches as such, but we followed tradition by Dad saying a few words, then Richard, then his brother. And Dad had insisted on buying a couple of bottles of real champagne! It was lovely. And of course we had to have a wedding cake to cut, to finish things off.

Then Richard and I went off on our honeymoon to London. London was so exciting. I've only been there twice before, and then only on day trips. We were there for five nights, and we saw all the main sights, some museums and a show. I had to keep looking at the gold ring on my hand to remind myself that I wasn't dreaming. Then we came home – home! – and decided to go camping and walking for a week in Mid Wales. Quite a contrast – a smart hotel in London and then under canvas!

127

It rained a bit, which was a shame, but we didn't really care.

Then Richard started back to school in September and I started tackling our cottage. It's in a beautiful spot, about half a mile from the sea, in a village called Llanley. It's a labour of love getting it all straight and homely, and unpacking all my things. It's starting to look really pretty now. I've just made new cushion covers and next I'm going to tackle replacing the curtains. I'll take a bus into Cardiff to buy the fabric. I can spend the whole day there, browsing round.

The private school where Richard teaches is about three miles away, so I had expected that he would be back each day before four o'clock, but he does a lot of things after school such as clubs and supervising detention, so it's usually more like half past five when he gets in. Then he still often has marking and preparation. He tries not to work the weekend though and we do things together then.

So what are you doing? Did you get your degree? I bet you did, and a good one. Have you got a job? If you have, I imagine that you might not live with your parents any more, but I'm sure they will have forwarded this letter. Do write and tell me how you're getting on.

Love, Susan x

Susan read through what she had written, happy to conjure up again the memory of her wedding and honeymoon. Then she put it aside and picked out a letter that was at the front of the box, and had arrived on Saturday. Inside was a short note from Wanda and Dad, and two photographs. Not a lot of time for writing letters nowadays, Wanda apologised, but everything was good with them and she hoped Susan was enjoying married life. Susan picked up the photos, one in each hand, and gazed at them. One was of herself standing by the side of Wanda's hospital bed with the shawled parcel that comprised her new half-brother laid in her arms. She was looking down with a tight smile at his walnut face. I've never held a baby before, she had confessed as Dad had placed Marek's head in the crook of her elbow and she had clasped him and felt his warm solidity. He won't break, you know, Wanda had said. She was propped up in bed looking as frail and beautiful as a lily. Dad sat beside her, his hand laid on hers.

The other photograph was of Dad, Wanda, Katya and Marek and had been taken more recently in a studio. They were decked out in their best clothes. Dad, in a suit, stood behind his wife with a hand on her shoulder. Wanda, in a floor length flowered dress, was seated with Marek on her lap, his blue romper suit matching the tiny blue bootees. Katya stood alongside her mother, her arms stiff to her sides. A large aspidistra in a pot completed the group. This would have been Dad's idea, Susan thought. A vague memory came back to her of the three of them – her, Mum and Dad – posing for a similar photo. She must have been Katya's age, perhaps a little older. It had been a hot day, even hotter in the studio, and they had gone for ice cream afterwards. What had happened to the photos? She remembered the studio, but she didn't remember ever seeing the resulting photos. How strange memory is.

She carried the two photos into the living room and propped them up on the mantelpiece. I must get a frame for the family one, the thought. She stared into it. Even allowing for the ridiculous poses, they looked happy, and she was glad. The few weeks that she had spent living with them before she got married had been a holding time for them all; she had been waiting to marry and start her new life, and they had been waiting for the new life, the baby. Wanda had been very tired in the last month of her pregnancy and Susan had slipped easily into the role of looking after the house. She had shopped, cleaned and played with Katya. I don't know what I would do without you, Wanda would say from the sofa, her legs propped on a stool and her great belly undulating gently with her breathing. And they talked, the two young women, sharing their excitement about their futures.

But best of all were the evenings when Wanda, weary from her load, would go to bed early and Susan and Dad would sit up talking. These times were particularly poignant because they both sensed the ending of an era. An ending and a beginning. Soon they would both have a new chapter in their lives, and they would live many miles apart. They talked a lot about old times and about Mum, and how pleased she would have been to see that they had both found happiness. Dad was delighted, genuinely delighted, about Susan's forthcoming marriage. I should have spotted it, he said. I should have spotted what was happening between you two. So should I, said Susan.

When Marek was born the rhythm changed. There were no more

cosy chats. Instead the days were punctuated by endless washing of nappies and tiny garments, and Marek's evening colic. Wanda had chosen to breastfeed him so Susan didn't help directly with his care (she shied away from changing his nappy), but as ever she took care of other household chores. It was strange to see Dad holding his son, and she imagined how he had held her nearly twenty years ago.

The time came for her to sleep for the last time in her old room. By the time she came to visit again, the room would no longer be hers, it would be Katya's, because Katya would have moved there from Mum's old sewing room to make way for Marek, hence completing the cycle of change. Besides, by the next time she visited her old home she would probably have her husband with her. She looked around her at the familiar furnishings. There was a vague, nostalgic sadness, but no regrets, only a bubbling excitement as she thought about her forthcoming wedding day...

A knocking at the front door intruded on Susan's memories. For a second the sound disoriented her with its unfamiliarity. She went to open the door.

'Hello, I hoped I'd catch you in,' the woman on the step beamed at her out of a face that was ruddy and weather-beaten, like a storybook farmer's wife.

'Hello,' replied Susan. She knew the woman from the local church. Susan had been to three Sunday morning services so far and she had discovered that it was usual for the congregation to come and introduce themselves after the service. She also realised that she was a novelty - the young bride. She had clung to Richard's arm as various people had shaken her hand and asked her questions, leaving her feeling dissected and exposed. It's just their way of being friendly, Richard had said afterwards. You'll get used to it. She remembered this particular woman, who now stood on her front doorstep. In church she had had a rumbustious family of two boys and a girl with her, who had fidgeted and shoved each other throughout the service.

'I bought you a bara brith.' The woman proffered the item in a paper bag at Susan, and she realised from the shape and the delicious smell that it was some sort of fruit loaf.

'Oh... thank you.' A pause. 'Well, do come in.' Susan stepped back, clutching the warm loaf. The woman followed her in and peeled off her anorak.

'In here, is it?' she said and without waiting for a reply went into the dining room. 'Ooh what a lovely dresser! You can't beat a good Welsh dresser, I always say.' She put her anorak over the back of a chair and rubbed her hands together, looking around her.

'I'm really sorry,' said Susan, 'but I can't quite remember your name…'

'It's Mary. I remember yours because I heard your husband – well, he wasn't your husband then – saying it during your wedding service. And then of course he introduced us proper after church the other Sunday. But you were meeting so many people, bless you, it's no wonder you didn't remember.'

Susan invited Mary into the living room to sit down. Her voice babbled on merrily. Merry Mary, thought Susan. I won't forget again. In the living room Mary again took everything in – not at all covertly, but openly and with bright-eyed interest – exclaiming here and there over décor and furniture. It might have been intrusive, but this stocky little woman was exuding so much friendliness it was impossible to take offence.

'That bara brith is straight out of the oven, baked specially. It's best eaten warm, you know.'

Susan took the hint and went to make tea and slice up the fruit loaf. When she came back with the tray she half expected to find Mary going through the books in the bookcase. Instead, she was examining the new photographs on the mantelpiece.

'Who's this little baby? And these others?'

Susan told her.

'Well. So your stepmother is young, not much older than you by the looks of her. Just like you and Richard, in fact. I was ever so pleased, you know, when Richard told me he was going to be married. He's been coming to the church ever since he moved here last year and we'd started to get to know him. He's a fine man.'

Susan poured the tea and they munched on the bara brith, which was excellent.

Mary brushed some crumbs off her chest, gave a contented sigh and sat back with her cup. 'So, tell me all about yourself, Susan. How did you come to meet Richard?'

'I've known him since I was fourteen. You see, he was my teacher to start with…' Susan was surprised that, once she started, the words flowed out of her. Normally she was reticent with strangers, but Mary, with her twinkly brown eyes, was the perfect audience, asking questions here and there and nodding encouragement. Susan even talked about Mum's death and her childhood.

They drank more tea. 'Sorry, I've been doing all the talking, and I've hardly given you a chance,' said Susan. 'I'm not usually like that.'

Mary waved the apology away. 'Oh, not much interesting about me. My husband's Bill. He works hard but likes to drink hard too. He's a good man though. Then there's the three kids, always fighting and growing like weeds. Anyway, speaking of the kids, I'd better be going. They'll be back from school and be looking for food, as usual.'

To her surprise Susan realised that Mary had been there more than an hour and a half.

'Thank you so much for coming,' she said. 'And for bringing that delicious fruit loaf.'

'I'll give you the recipe. Now, you must come round to my house one day. If you can stand the mess, that is.' She pulled on her anorak and gave Susan a warm hug before she left.

Susan stood with her back against the closed front door. What an unexpected afternoon. Both April and Mary. An afternoon of friends.

***

Dear Susan

It was so fab to get your letter. And you're MARRIED! Far out! I can't imagine being married. Me, I've never been out with someone for more than a few weeks. It starts off well but then I just get bored and want to try someone else. And there's plenty to choose from!

Where shall I start? I got my degree. I got a 2.2, so not brilliant but I was lucky to get that. I didn't exactly do a lot of work for it. After all, university is mainly about having fun, in my opinion. In fact, life is mainly about having fun!!! I would have liked to go for a year travelling again, but my parents said, woah, we already paid for you to go off to Australia after your A-levels, so now you've got to work, young woman. So I looked at what was on offer on the lists at uni, and guess what, I only applied for four jobs, two I had interviews for, and one made me an offer! They said they liked my 'get up and go' attitude. Well, if I say so myself I do know how to put the act on. I'm part of the Marketing Team for a company that sells — well, all sorts of things, really. You don't want to know much about that, it's far too boring. So far, it's not too hard and I get on well with my boss. I've survived my first month anyway!

The office where I work from is west of London, so I've had to take a bedsit there. My God, Susan, it's SO expensive, even though it's tiny. Luckily, my parents help me out. I've made friends with a couple of girls at work and we go out some evenings. There's good pubs round here and at the weekend we've been to a nightclub that plays really great music. And there's lots of men! I haven't been out on a date yet but one is really good looking and he kept on pestering me, so I'm going out with him tomorrow night.

Do keep me posted about married life in the wilds of Wales. It was so great to hear from you.

Write soon,

love, April xxxx

***

'It's nearly our very first Christmas together in our very own home. Doesn't the tree look beautiful?'

Susan stood back to admire it, where they had made space for it on the sideboard. It was a Saturday, and they had gone together earlier that day to the Christmas shop in the forest to pick out the perfect tree — not too big, but bushy and healthily compact. Once they had selected the tree then they had to buy a box of baubles to hang on it and a fairy to go on the top. We'll keep these for years, Susan had said, and every year when we get them out we'll remember our first Christmas.

Richard stood up from in front of the fireplace, where he had been carefully placing coals on scrunched up balls of lighted newspaper to get the fire going. He brushed the coal dust off his hands and came up behind Susan, enfolding her in his arms. 'It's just right,' he said. 'And the smell of pine needles is divine. Or maybe it's you that smells so good?' He burrowed his nose into her hair and inhaled.

Susan giggled and turned round so that they could kiss. 'Are you happy, my darling?' he murmured as they stood clasped in each other's arms in front of the fire, which was starting to crackle and waft out heat.

'Yes. Oh yes! And I'm so excited about Christmas. It's going to be magical. Just like when I was a child.' She eased out of his arms and inspected the tree again. 'Do you think we should get some fairy lights too? To go on the tree?'

Richard considered. 'Well, we already have paper garlands, angels and the nativity scene from when I was a boy. Maybe that's enough for now, do you think?'

Susan clapped her hands. 'And we can build up our collection year by year.'

Richard smiled. 'If that's what you want. I love to see you like this. Like a happy little girl.'

They sat down together on the sofa, Richard at the one end and Susan curled up next to him. This was how they often spent much of their evenings. They would watch television or read or chat. Sometimes Richard played the piano or they listened to music, but not often because their tastes were different.

The tranquillity of the room settled over them. The warmth from the fire was stretching its fingers out to them and they sat silent, cocooned in the harmony.

After a while Richard said, 'Do you remember I told you about the Headmaster's Christmas soirée, at his house on the evening of the last day of term? I have to reply formally to the invitation.'

When Susan didn't reply he stroked her cheek. 'You haven't dozed off, have you?'

Susan sat up and shook her head. 'No.'

'So… can I reply and tell him that we will both be pleased to accept his kind invitation?'

Susan picked up one of the cushions off the sofa and hugged it to her. A thread was dangling from where she'd sewn the seam, and she pulled at it, trying to break it off.

'Susan?'

She turned her head towards the fire. 'I've told you how I feel. It's going to be a grand occasion, and they'll all be looking at me and wondering why you married me. I won't know what to say to them and I'll let you down.'

Richard sighed. 'We've been through this before. Just allow yourself to be natural. I will be immensely proud to have you by my side as my wife. It won't be an ordeal. All the other teachers are perfectly nice people and they will just talk to you normally. And I will be there.' His voice was calm and gentle.

She knew he was looking at her, even though her eyes were downcast. She bowed her head so that her hair fell forwards and he wouldn't be able to see her face.

He covered her hand with his. 'I would really like to take you to this party. Do this for me. Please.'

She swallowed. 'Alright. I'll do it for you.'

***

11 December 1972

Dear April

Well I'm starting to feel Christmassy, are you? We had a lovely time on the weekend getting a real fir tree and decorating the house with garlands and some holly we picked in the woods. And I've already made my Christmas cake and Christmas pudding. There's just one thing that's spoiling it all. Richard's Headmaster is giving his annual Christmas party – soirée, he calls it - for his staff and their wives at his house and I have to go and I'm dreading it. I'll be just an ignorant kid compared to them and they'll all be looking at me and chattering among themselves but I won't know what to talk to them about. I know what they'll be thinking: why on earth did Richard marry someone like that?

Richard is being very sweet, as he always is. Just be yourself, he says. But 'myself' is quiet and shy. You know that about me. Then he says, just smile graciously and answer their questions politely until you feel more settled. He says he won't leave my side and he will help me. He really is a wonderful man. Oh, and he also says for me to take the bus into Cardiff one day and treat myself to a new dress for the occasion, to make me feel special. I haven't had a new dress for a long time, so I suppose I will.

You probably think I'm just being silly. I know you wouldn't be like this, you'd go and be the belle of the ball, but then I'm not like you. I imagine you've got lots of parties and fun lined up for the Christmas season. Write soon and tell me about it.

Love,

Susan xx

Dear Susan

Yes, you're right I already have lots of Christmas fun planned. It's going to be a blast. The girls from work and me are going out for a shopping spree next Saturday to buy new outfits for the Christmas festivities. Something black and slinky, I thought, so I can be a 'femme fatale.' Then that same evening one of them is having a pyjama party, just us girls. So I'll have to wait to wear my new dress! The main Christmas event, apart from some hectic nights in the pub, is the company's Christmas meal and party. It's all paid for by the bosses! There's going to be a turkey dinner with all the trimmings and, so the others tell me, plenty of mistletoe about. I did go out on a date last night with a man called Andy who chatted me up in the pub last week. He's nice enough, and I'm seeing him again on Friday, but I can't see it lasting. He's a bit quiet for me. So, I'll be ready for the mistletoe! I already know one or two men at work who I wouldn't mind exchanging a Christmas kiss with!

And as for your Headmaster's soirée, yes I would love to go. It wouldn't be stuffy with me there! I'd dress to kill, for a start. (I hope you're going to get yourself something nice to wear too. It will boost your confidence. I can see you in something green - it would suit your colouring.) I'd wear my highest platform shoes, or perhaps my vinyl platform boots, and paint my fingernails holly berry red. Then I'd make sure I charmed all the men, even your stuffy old Headmaster. I'd drink the wine and nibble delicately at the sausage rolls and mince pies on the buffet (I take it there will be food?). But I'd still remain a lady, and keep them guessing. Who is that woman

of mystery, they would say?!
I hope I've cheered you up a bit, Sue. You sounded a bit down.

With love,

April xx

***

Susan went to Cardiff and bought herself a dress. It was a green maxi dress with little flowers on a green background and puffed lacy sleeves. But then she never got to wear it because on the day of the party she came down with a terrible headache and had to stay in bed. So Richard went to the soirée alone.

Chapter 12

12 February 1973

Dear April

Oh the weather is miserable here! It's been cold and wet for days, with a biting wind. All the footpaths where I like to walk are muddy and unpleasant. It would be better if it was really freezing cold and snowed, but apparently here on the coast it doesn't snow very much. And the cottage is cold, especially when the wind blows. It seems to get into the house. I try to keep the coal stove in the kitchen burning well, which should heat the radiator in the dining room, but I'm not very good at looking after it, and anyway, the stove is ancient. I said to Richard that we should have central heating fitted and double glazing. He said that would be a big expense all at once, but maybe we should have one of them in the summer. Meanwhile, I'm swathed up in jumpers and sitting in front of a puny electric fire. Later I'll try to light the fire for when Richard comes home.

So, I'm doing a lot of reading. Luckily there's a small library in the village and they are very good at reserving and getting books from bigger libraries. It's only a couple of weeks to half term and I'm really looking forward to Richard being home and having more free time. He takes his job so seriously. He spends a lot of time preparing work, marking homework and reading anything and everything that the boys write. Of course I can remember, from when he used to be my teacher, how he was always willing to look at and comment on pieces that us girls had written, and how he used to run a Creative Writing group. So I should have known.

Anyway, how are you? Last time you wrote you told me about a promotion at work (that seems soon – clever you!) which would mean you were going to have a company car and do some travelling around. Has that happened? It sounds so exciting! And are you still seeing Alan? He sounded fun. In fact your whole life sounds exciting and fun.

Write soon and tell me your news.

Love, Susan xx

Dear Susan

If you think it's cold in Wales, it's probably colder here in London! I don't really notice it though because the office is warm and my bedsit is only small so it's easy to heat. And to keep warm I've bought myself a fab new faux fur leopard skin coat, which is quite outrageous! Then I needed some boots to set it off so I've bought some platform ones, up to the knee and white, which make me about five inches taller! Of course, I can't wear those for work. For work I wear a suit – skirt not too short, I don't want clients having a heart attack - with some modest court shoes and sheer tights. I do jazz it up a bit though with a selection of blouses in bright colours. I've just bought a nice pink and purple one tied with a big bow at the neck.

Yes I have my company car! I had it last week. It's a Mini so it's small, but it's so, so fab. Last week I had to go and see a client on the south coast. They let me stay overnight because I had arranged to see another client the next day. I stayed in a hotel, and Sue, you should have seen the room! You could have put my entire bedsit into it! The bed was enormous (pity I was on my own!!) with mounds of pillows and crisp white sheets. There was a kettle, tea, coffee, biscuits, and you could ring down to reception to get anything you want. And the bathroom! Huge bath, bath salts, lashings of hot water and fluffy towels. I had a good soak before I went down for dinner. I ate prawn cocktail and then sirloin steak with chips and peas. With a glass of wine. All on expenses, of course.

I'm not going out with Alan any more. Yes, he was fun (and very sexy, may I say) but I seem to get fed up with men very quickly, and I want to move on to new adventures. That's just me.

With love, April xx

***

When the harsh trill of the alarm clock at 7am woke Susan the first thing she was aware of was how bright the morning was, even through the curtains. She lay with Richard's arms folded around her, her unfocused gaze on the fingers of sunlight reaching tentatively underneath the curtains. When she got out of bed and looked outside, she blinked at the pearly sky, clear and crisp, and a thin film of ice on the car windscreen which was just starting to melt as the late spring sunshine gathered strength. She went downstairs and put the kettle on. Then she went outside, shivering in her thin dressing gown and slippers, and breathed in the cold, sweet air.

'Richard, wake up, it's such a lovely morning,' she said, putting a cup of tea down on his bedside table.

'Is it?' replied Richard without opening his eyes. Susan jumped on the bed and peeled the blankets off him.

'You have to come and see,' she said. 'and anyway, it's ten past seven.'

Richard sat up and fumbled for his glasses. 'You're very cheerful this morning.'

Susan danced around the bedroom, floating her dressing gown out behind her. 'I'm dancing round the maypole,' she said.

She went downstairs to start the breakfast, which on a school morning was usually buttered toast for both of them. Sometimes Richard fancied a boiled egg, or there were cornflakes, or porridge in the winter. When Richard came down he was washed and dressed, his tie knotted neatly.

'You're right,' he said, 'there's not a cloud in the sky.' He sat down and bit into his toast. 'What are you going to do today?' It was their usual morning conversation. Susan might reply 'shopping, cleaning, cooking, going to the library, reading, writing letters.' Increasingly lately she shrugged and said 'not much...'

'Well,' said Susan picking up the teapot to pour for them both, 'First I'm doing the washing. Then...' she put the teapot down and looked outside the window, considering. 'I could go for a walk. To the beach, perhaps. I could take a picnic!' Her voice gathered enthusiasm; the crystal morning had woken in her a desire to be out and part of nature. She reached across the table to Richard, sorry that he had to spend the day indoors. 'I wish you were coming with me,' she said.

'So do I.' He smiled and returned the clasp of her hand. 'But I'm happy to know that you'll be enjoying the spring weather.' He sighed theatrically. 'Think of me trying to engage the Lower Fourth with Shakespeare while you're smelling the bluebells. And then marking a batch of essays from the Fifth form.' His eyes twinkled at her.

140

'You know you love it,' Susan replied.

'Yes,' he said, still holding her hand. 'I'm very lucky. In every way.'

Susan smiled back at him across the table. 'That's a nice thing to say. Anyway, if I'm going to go out later, I must make a start on the washing.' She jumped up from the table and pulled out the twin-tub washing machine from where it was stowed under the draining board. After waving Richard off to work she ran upstairs and stripped the white sheets off the bed, still warm from their bodies, and bundled them into the machine with plenty of powder. Then she sat down to finish her tea and toast while the water heated up. The twin-tub washing machine was the latest model and she was pleased with it, recollecting how Mum had laboured with a tub and mangle. She drew on her rubber gloves and lifted the steaming washing into the adjoining spin drier. She hummed while she worked, the domestic chores pleasing her; it was satisfying when dirty, soiled washing became clean and sweet-smelling.

As she pegged the sheets onto the washing line she checked on the sky. It was so blue it pinched her eyes. She had listened to the weather forecast on the radio and it seemed that there was a high pressure settling over them and they were to experience 'an early taste of summer', unusually warm and sunny for early May.

She made herself a small picnic consisting of a cheese sandwich, a drink of Barley Water in a plastic container and an apple. Excitement twirled within her; today she was going out to do something different. She hesitated about whether it was going to be warm enough for shorts, but eventually settled for a skirt, top and cardigan, although she did feel bold enough to rummage at the back of the wardrobe for her sandals, where they had been since last September. A towel and a book in her duffel bag along with the picnic and she was ready.

The brightness of the day unfolded its welcome to her as she headed down the lane towards the beach. The sight of the sea always thrilled her, but today she felt a particular gladness and vigour surging through her body. When she got to the beach she hesitated; she had the urge to venture further, to stretch her awakened body more. So she took the footpath west, up the cliffs and over the headland. The stony path meandered alongside the coast, past fields of grazing sheep on one side and pebbly beach on the other, and eventually into trees and past Trelissan, that everyone seemed to just call 'the Big House'. The house itself was just visible through the trees. She hadn't been this way since the previous autumn, when she and Richard had taken one of their Sunday afternoon rambles. She noticed that since then a new dry stone wall was being laid around the estate, replacing the previous dilapidated one. The small gate which led from the coast path into the grounds of Trelissan had also been replaced with a new wooden one with a 'Private' sign on it. Next to the gate there was a bench, where she and Richard had eaten a picnic once.

On the other side of the path Susan noticed a rough descent to the rocky coast. She had never been down there, and since she felt in an adventurous mood, she left the footpath to explore. She walked across the pebbles, and after a few minutes the beach became increasingly rocky and she was wondering how far she would be able to go before it became impassable. But then she climbed over some large rocks and gasped in pleasure at the surprise of a tiny crescent of pale sand, sugar fine and backed by trees. The little beach was terminated on the other side by rocks too big to climb over. It was a perfect spot, secluded and pristine. She spread her towel on the small sandy patch and sat down, delighted by her discovery of this magical place and also how warm the day had become as the sun climbed. In just her thin cotton top and skirt she enjoyed the delicious caress of the sun on her skin. She started on her sandwiches and shaded her eyes to squint at the sea.

Something was moving in the water, a shape getting bigger. At first glimpse she thought with excitement that it was a seal. Then she saw the flash of lifted arms and she realised it was a person, a man, coming out of the sea and jogging up the shingle in her direction. She stiffened, her half-eaten sandwich clutched in her hands. As he got closer she could see the water droplets glistening on his upper body. He was young, probably not much older than she was, with dark hair matted to his head and all over his body. He smiled and nodded at her as he passed close by, then reached behind a rock just a few feet away to pull out a towel from a bag.

'Oh, I'm sorry,' she said, in embarrassment. 'I didn't think anyone was here. I didn't see your bag.'

He was towelling his body vigorously. 'No need to be sorry. I don't own the beach. Beautiful spot, eh?' He had an accent, but she knew it wasn't local.

She nodded, feeling uncomfortable and deflated now that her perfect day had been invaded. She lowered her head and nibbled delicately at her sandwich as he wrapped his towel around his middle. She glanced discreetly at him. He was wiry, his body lean with economical muscles. She looked away quickly as he started dressing underneath the towel and put on workman's overalls. She was disconcerted that he then sat down near to her, although in truth the sandy area was small. He pulled out a pork pie from his bag and began to eat with large bites.

'Are you from round here?' he said. 'You don't seem Welsh.'

'No,' she replied. Then, not wanting to appear rude, she added 'I've lived here for nearly a year now.'

He grunted through his pork pie. 'I've been here a few weeks, and this is the first chance I've had to swim in the sea. Are you going in?' He talked while he was eating but she could make out the words.

'No, I haven't been in the sea since...' she paused. How long had it been? Richard couldn't swim and didn't care to go in the water. Before she came here, there hadn't been the opportunity for a long time. When? She realised she hadn't actually been in the sea, apart from just paddling, since that last holiday with Mum and Dad. A memory bloomed of squealing in the waves while Dad splashed her. That would have been the day Mum died.

She swallowed. 'I haven't been in the sea since I was a child.'

He laughed. 'That's much too long. You can't live near the sea and not go in it.'

'Isn't it awfully cold?'

'It's cold when you first get in, but then you splash around and it feels wonderful. The secret is, this time of the year, not to stay in too long and to get dried off quickly when you come out.'

She gazed at the water, absorbing the hypnotic slurp of the wavelets on the shingle. They both ate in silence, and she forgot about the stranger at her side as images of those happy holidays slid into her mind, running in and out of the sea, playing in the waves. She got to

143

her feet.

The sea, when it hit her ankles, bit savagely. She tucked her skirt into her knickers and gingerly stepped a little further in. It was cold, freezing cold, but in a clean, austere way. One wave reared itself up and threatened to crash into her legs so she quickly backed away to the shore and stood with the water nibbling her pale toes like curious fish. The tang of salt and seaweed flooded her nostrils.

When she turned around he had gone. She could just see him picking his way over the stones, the way she had come.

***

The next morning after Richard had gone to work Susan searched through drawers until she located her swimming costume, unpacked and thrust away when she had moved in and then forgotten. It was her school costume which she must have had when she was about fifteen; regulation black and with her name still sewn in the back. She had learned to swim when she was quite young. Dad used to take her to the town baths and had taught her. She held the costume up. It was fine and would still fit. The question was, would she be brave enough to go in the sea? And, surely it would unsafe on her own?

The tiny beach was deserted when she got there. She felt a flicker of disappointment; the day was even warmer than the previous one and she thought that he would have been there, given that he had been so enthusiastic about sea bathing. She changed into her swimming costume, pinned up her hair and approached the water. The waves splashed her ankles and she hesitated. Really it would be safer to go back to the main beach in Llanley, where there were other people. Then she looked back over her shoulder and there he was, balancing his way over the stones. Now she would be safe. Impulsively she waved and he waved back. She started to walk back up the beach towards him but then she saw he had thrown his bag down and was peeling his clothes off, so she turned back to the sea again and waited, looking out to the horizon.

'Hello,' he said when he joined her at the water's edge, 'You're going to brave it, then?'

Susan hadn't realised yesterday how curly his hair was, because it had been wet. Curly and dark, like a longer version of the hair on his chest.

'I think so. Do you mind if you come in with me? I can swim, but I'm a bit nervous.'

He grinned. 'Just stay in your depth and you'll be fine. Come on then, let's go!' He strode his way through the waves until he was waist deep, then he dived in head first and bobbed up sleek as a seal. Susan followed more slowly. Even though the waves were small today, hardly more than ripples, each one as it moved up her body made her gasp. It was icy. Inch by inch she got up nearly to her waist, holding her hands and arms up out of the water.

He swam up to her side. 'Slow is the worst way to do it! Just duck down now.' Still Susan hesitated. Then she did it. She squatted down in the water right up to her neck. The cold shrank her lungs and drove the breath from her body. She kicked her feet out and started to swim frantically, desperate to get warm. Her breathing eased as her body adjusted to the temperature. She felt herself lifted and held by the waves and she relaxed, slowing her flailing limbs down until they were just keeping her afloat. The horizon was now at her eye level, both far away and close, as if she and it were one. She turned around. The shore and trees, where her belongings waited, were part of a different world, a smaller world when viewed from the sea. She turned over on her back, opening herself to the limitless sky, and laughed out loud with the wondrous joy of the moment.

***

9 May 1973

Dear April

I have had such an exciting couple of days! We are having some glorious weather (hope you are too) and so on Tuesday I decided I would go for a walk and take a picnic. We have lovely coast here, and I ended up walking to a remote part where I hadn't been before. It was absolutely beautiful, like a beach in miniature, almost cut off (you have to scramble over rocks to get to this bit) and with the sea right close by. Well, I thought I was all on my own when what should happen but a young man emerges from the sea, looking rather like a Greek god! I felt embarrassed and to tell the truth a little bit worried, because it was a very lonely spot. But he seemed friendly enough and we talked a bit, including about bathing in the sea. I realised that it had been years since I had been properly in the sea. I used to love it when I was a child. (Do you like the sea?). I went down to the shore and paddled a bit, wishing (or half wishing) that I could go for a dip. When I turned round he had gone.

The next day (yesterday) I decided that I would be brave and so I went again to the same beach, this time with my swimming costume. I hoped he would be there because I didn't know if I would go in all on my own. He was! We both went in together (brrr!) and I swam around a bit, just staying in my depth and, oh April, it was just wonderful. I felt I was in a special magical place that you can't get to by standing on the shore and looking, only from actually being in the sea. Does that sound bonkers?

We didn't stay in too long, because it was so cold, and then we ran up the beach and dried ourselves vigorously and got dressed. My body was just glowing. Then we sat down on the sand to eat our lunches, which we had both brought. By now things were feeling quite surreal. Here I was with a stranger, feeling quite relaxed – me who is usually so shy! And he told me all about himself…

His name is Phil and he came here two weeks ago to work at Trelissan, which is a big house with huge grounds just at the back of where we were on the beach. He is from the north of England and he works with his father and brother at 'dry stone walling' – not something I know anything about. He is also a carpenter and general odd job man. They have employed him at the Big House (That's what we call it here) to redo all their stone walls and to do some carpentry (he told me some details but it was a bit much to take in). His father and brother are doing another job so it's just him this time. He is staying in a caravan in the grounds of the Big House. He was so easy to listen to, and he seemed to have a permanent smile on his face.

I haven't actually told Richard about Phil. On Tuesday evening when I said I had walked along the coast and that I had a longing to go in the sea, he frowned and said that I should be careful. Richard isn't a swimmer. So how could I tell him yesterday that I had gone into the sea with a stranger – and a good looking young man at that? It just seemed easier to say nothing. It was all innocent, after all. Is that what you would have done?

It's now ten o'clock in the morning and it's another glorious day. So I'm writing

146

this before I head off to the beach again. I wonder if Phil will be there?

Love, Susan

***

He was already there, sitting on the sand wearing shorts and crew neck T-shirt. Susan was surprised because it was only midday.

'Hello,' she said. 'You're here early today.'

'I'm between jobs,' he replied, leaning back and stretching his legs out. 'And the nights are so light that I can carry on working into the evening.'

'I wanted to go in the sea again,' she said, simply.

'Me too,' he said, jumping up and grabbing his towel. 'Come on, let's go.'

The shock of the water was no less, and even though she had told herself that she would run straight in, she couldn't do it, and instead moved forward inches at a time. Once submerged and used to the shock of the cold, she felt the same expansive wonderment as the water encased her body and she looked back at the land. Phil swam off, and Susan floated on her back, allowing the sea to lift her in its embrace. She had a brief moment of panic when she tried to stand up and her feet didn't reach the bottom. She gulped water and flailed wildly for a second, looking round for Phil, but then realised that she only had to swim a few strokes and she was back with the firm assurance of stones under her feet.

Phil swam back with powerful strokes, spurting out water as he came next to her. She wished she were that confident in the water.

'You're a strong swimmer,' she said.

'We used to live on the East coast and I learned there,' he said. 'Now *that's* cold water. I've always loved being near the sea. I'm always glad when jobs take me there.'

'I've never lived by the sea before,' she replied. They floated companionably side by side. 'The land appears to be further away than it is. I feel like I'm in a different world. A world between worlds.' She stopped, embarrassed to have spoken her thoughts.

147

'The sea does that to you,' he said.

They stayed in the water longer today. After they had run up the beach Susan dried herself briskly and huddled under her towel to wriggle into her blouse and skirt.

'I'm cold,' she said, trying to stop the chattering of her teeth. 'Yesterday I wasn't cold at all, so I didn't bring my cardigan today. I wish I had now.' She wrapped her arms around herself.

'There's more breeze come up today,' he said, as his head popped out of his tee shirt. 'And we stayed in the water longer. Too long for you, probably. Sit down on the sand and wrap your towel round you.'

Susan did as he suggested. She was starting to shiver uncontrollably.

'You really are cold, aren't you?' He sat down next to her and wrapped his own towel around her too. Then he put his arms right around her and chafed her arms.

Susan felt her blood flowing again and her shivering stopped as the warmth of the towels and his arms penetrated her body. His face was so close to hers she could feel his breath on her cheek.

'That better?'

'Yes. I'm getting warmer.' He stopped rubbing her arms but remained with his arms wrapped round her. She could feel the rise and fall of his breathing, ebbing and flowing like the waves.

'I don't want you to go home with frostbite.' His voice was low and teasing in her ear. She laughed and turned her face to him in acknowledgment. The kiss happened without warning. His tongue flowed into her mouth and she allowed it, caught unawares as she was. He fumbled under the towels and his hand burrowed under her blouse.

'No,' she gasped, wrenching herself away. She grabbed her towel, sandals, duffel bag and stumbled away, half running and clasping her belongings to her, her nipple still tingling from the brief touch. He made no attempt to stop her. She wasn't sure, but she thought she heard him laughing.

***

The warm sunny weather continued the next day, although the weather forecast foretold of an ending soon. The walk to the little beach was now familiar; down the lane to Llanley beach, up onto the cliffs and along to where the woods started, where the new stone wall – the wall he had built - marked the grounds of the Big House, then the abrupt turn down onto the rocky shore and along over the rocks to the patch of sand at the end. Susan hadn't slept well. The kiss had replayed over and over in her head, and she was in turmoil. She knew she had done the right thing by running away yesterday. Yet here she was again, treading the same path. This is probably the last day of sunshine for who knows how long, she told herself. It would be a shame to miss the chance to swim. And anyway, he might not be there…

Once down on the rocks she could see him on the crescent beach, already in his swimming trunks.

'Hello,' he said. The inscrutable smile. Was he mocking her, or was he pleased to see her? 'I didn't expect to see you.'

'They say it's the last nice day for a while,' she said primly. 'I wanted one last swim in the sunshine.'

'Is that what they say?' His eyes were dancing.

She turned away, anxious to be in the water. She ran ahead of him, and this time she managed to plunge straight into the waves. Phil swam off as usual and Susan drifted around, even going a little way out of her depth. The otherworldliness of the previous two days was suspended today because she was aware of him at the edge of her vision, splashing through the waves.

He swam back up to her. 'Don't stay in too long,' he said. 'Remember you got cold yesterday.'

'I brought a cardigan today and an extra towel.' The swell lifted them gently up and down.

After they had dried off and dressed they sat down side by side on the sand to eat their lunch. Phil had a packet of cheese and onion crisps and he offered her some. She in return asked if he would like some of her corned beef and tomato sandwiches. He accepted readily and complimented her on how good they were. She gave him some more; she herself wasn't hungry. Phil chatted lightly about this and that, while they looked out at the sea, glinting silver with the sunshine. She listened to his voice, answering when he asked her something as if she were reciting lines in a play.

They finished eating and drinking and fell silent. The day breathed.

Phil gently took her chin and turned her face towards him. 'Are you going to run off again if I kiss you?' The smile was now just at the corners of his mouth.

When Susan didn't reply he kissed her, this time softly, carefully. He slid his arms round her and gently laid her down. She sighed and lifted her arms round his neck. She closed her eyes and her mind emptied of everything except the unfolding of the moment.

Later they lay side by side. He propped himself up on one elbow to look at her. 'Well, now,' he grinned. 'You're a dark horse.'

She looked at him and said nothing.

He sat up. 'Come and sit in front of me. Right here.' He opened his knees and patted the ground in front of him. Dreamlike, she did as he asked and he folded his arms around her and breathed in the scent of her neck. 'Look at those waves,' he said, softly in her ear. 'Where has each wave come from? Where does it go? Do you ever think about that?'

'I think,' said Susan after a moment of feeling the waves' pulse, 'I think they've come from afar, from deep within the belly of the ocean. They collapse onto the shore and soak into the earth, which carries them back to start all over again.'

Instead of answering, he started humming a tune. She could feel the vibrations transferring through his chest into her body. Then he softly started to sing. Afterwards she could only vaguely remember the words; it was something about silver coins, a gypsy and tasting wine. But the sweet tune stayed with her.

He stirred and kissed her hair. 'I have to go. There's a lot of work to do this afternoon.' He quickly gathered his things.

She watched him swing his bag onto his shoulder and flash her a cheeky grin. 'Cheerio, then,' he said.

''Bye.' said Susan. She watched him striding jauntily up the beach. Then she lay back in the sun and stared up at the mocking sky until it was time to go home.

***

The weather forecast was right. Friday morning was dull and cooler than it had been for days, with a distinct threat of rain. The little summer had gone. Last night she had cooked dinner and chatted with Richard, then she had curled up in his arms in bed and made breakfast when they woke. As normal, as if nothing out of the ordinary had happened. And now she sat at the kitchen table listening to the solemn ticking of the clock. Suddenly she jumped up and put her bakestone on the stove to heat. She got out flour, currants, margarine, spices, sugar, eggs and milk. The familiar actions of measuring, mixing, rolling and dropping the little cakes onto the hot pan grounded and focussed her as it always did. The pile of cooked cakes grew. She put half a dozen into a bag and looked at the clock.

Today was not a day for sandals. She needed her sturdy shoes and a waterproof in case it should rain. The now-familiar path along the coast looked different today, muted and sombre now that it was without the enchantment of the sun. She came to the Big House with the low stone wall and the new gate that said 'Private' on it. She opened the gate and followed the path through the trees. He had described the caravan as being 'just down the path a short way'. And there it was. A small, rather dilapidated caravan next to some outhouses which looked disused. She looked around and listened. There was no-one.

Now that she was here, her courage all but drained away. It was lunch time, but still maybe he wouldn't be there. She knew nothing about his habits on a normal day, a day without sunshine and sparkling waves. Go home, whispered the voice in her head. There's still time.

She took a breath, walked up to the caravan door and knocked on it. Straightaway she heard movement inside and her heart lurched. He opened the door and, after the initial second of surprise, there was that mocking smile again.

'I brought Welsh cakes,' she said. 'They're still warm.'

Chapter 13

14 May 1973

Dear April

You'll never guess what's happened. I can't believe it myself.

I am having an affair with Phil. Last Wednesday, after we'd been in the sea and I was cold, he put his arms around me to warm me up and then he suddenly kissed me. It was totally unexpected and I was frightened and I ran off. It was like an electric shock running through me. Not that I've ever had an electric shock, but I expect you know what I mean. I agonised over whether to go back the next day. I so much wanted to see him and I wanted him to kiss me again but... I knew I shouldn't. I didn't know where it would lead. No, that's not true – I knew exactly where it would lead. And it did, right there on the sand on our own little beach.

I went home in a dream. In fact, it seemed like I'd dreamed it. The next day the weather had turned, and I didn't know what to do. He hadn't said anything about seeing me again, but I knew where his caravan was, and I guessed he'd probably be there around lunchtime, having his break, so I just turned up. It was like I couldn't help myself. He was surprised but not displeased to see me. It's always hard to guess what he's really thinking. He was just eating his lunch and he said I could join him if I wanted. We ate and talked just like nothing had happened. I admired his caravan (It's cosy but very messy. He has a guitar and lots of music tapes and all sorts of books, including a lot of poetry). I began to think what happened yesterday had just been a one-time thing, and I felt like a fool. Then, when he had finished eating he said, come and see the bedroom. He had a wicked sort of glint in his eye. Once in the bedroom he undid my blouse very slowly and unhooked my bra. I knew then it was going to happen. I was so excited and relieved and, April, it was like nothing I've ever known. Making love with Richard is nice, but this was different. Almost straight afterwards he said he had to go back to work. He didn't suggest meeting again, but perhaps that's because he just takes it for granted that I will come again. I'm going again today.

Of course, Richard knows nothing. The strange thing is that over the weekend it was easy to behave normally. We did our usual things – going for a walk, talking, going to church, reading the papers, doing odd jobs, etc. It didn't seem unnatural. It's as if I have split into two people. There's the normal me, who loves Richard (yes, I do love him) and this other person, who does outrageous things.

There isn't any way that Richard could find out. Phil's caravan is hidden in the woods, and no-one goes there. Richard is used to me going out for a walk in the middle of the day, and I'm back well before he comes in from school. I'm not hurting him, or anyone else. And, it just doesn't seem possible that something that feels so amazing could be wrong. I am right, aren't I? What do you think?

It's only you I can tell about this, April. I know you'll understand. It's usually you writing to me about your adventures and your exciting life, and now look! I'm having my own adventure!! I feel ALIVE!!

Love, Susan

***

The days took on a pattern. Monday, Tuesday, Wednesday Susan trod the cliff path to Phil's caravan in the middle of the day. She took something for them to share – apples, cakes, chocolate. They talked a little while they ate, he seeming to be taking his time, Susan trying not to show her impatience, watching the way his hands moved as he picked up his food, imagining the heat of them on her body. Then they moved to the bedroom. She did what he wanted and found that she wanted it too. Now they lay, tangled limbs in the soiled sheets. It was raining, and the sound of its drumming was magnified on the roof. Because of the weather, Phil was in no hurry to get back to work.

'Do you fancy a cup of tea?' he said as he wound his fingers into her hair. 'Have you got time?'

'Yes, I've got time,' she replied, pleased that he wanted her to stay longer. 'Why don't I get it?' She got out of bed and reached for her clothes.

'If you like.' He reached out and took her dress out of her hands. 'But don't get dressed.' She looked at him questioningly. 'There's no need to put clothes on. There's nobody around here. I often walk around naked.'

Susan laughed uncertainly. 'That would feel strange.'

'Well it shouldn't. We've all got a body. And yours is a particularly beautiful one. Especially with your clothes off.' He linked his hands behind his head and stared her up and down. Susan dropped her head and instinctively covered her breasts with her arms.

'Don't do that,' he said. It wasn't said quite as a command, but none the less she hesitantly dropped her arms. 'You have the most amazing tits. Don't you know that? They're round and firm and juicy. Like fruit. Fruit that's just ripening.' He rolled the words round his mouth.

'They've always been quite big,' she said. 'I used to be embarrassed about them when I was younger.'

'Don't be. Be proud.' He pushed the bedclothes back and she saw he was aroused again. To her surprise, so was she. Although, nothing really surprised her anymore. He reached out for her and pulled her down so she was straddling him and he moulded her breasts in his hands. Instinctively she began to move up and down on top of him, matching her rhythm with his, her hands clawing the hair on his chest. It was euphoric, this feeling of being in control, being able to set the pace and lift herself up or grind her body down on top of his. She was unaware that she cried out when she orgasmed.

Afterwards she lay with her head on his shoulder, listening to his breathing. Or was it her own breathing? Or were the two the same?

'So you didn't want a cup of tea, then?' he teased. She was about to say let's have it now, when she remembered the time. She groped for her wristwatch on the floor and frowned when she looked at it.

'It's nearly three o'clock. I must get back.' She sorted through the tumbled pile of her clothes to find her underwear. 'I don't think I'll be able to come tomorrow,' she said as she struggled to do up her bra. 'I usually go out on the bus to Cardiff on a Thursday and I didn't go last week because I came to the beach. It would look a bit strange if I didn't go two weeks in row,' she finished awkwardly. It was the first time she had alluded to her situation at home, and he hadn't asked. He hadn't even commented on her wedding ring. Maybe he hadn't noticed.

'OK,' he said with a slight shrug. He was also pulling on his clothes.

Susan moved towards the door, smoothing her hair as she went. She paused for him to say something more, to ask when he was going to see her again, but he didn't.

'But I could come Friday. Shall I come Friday?'

'If you want. You know where to find me.' He was pulling on his boots.

They kissed briefly and Susan set off through the woods at a brisk pace. *You know where to find me.* It would have to be enough.

***

Dear Susan

Gosh this is so exciting! You have a LOVER! And here was I thinking you were leading a quiet life in a sleepy little village. He sounds so dashing, your Phil. And mysterious and, most importantly, good in bed. Of course you must enjoy it for as long as it lasts. You didn't ask for it to happen, it just happened. What a sheer coincidence that you two should meet on a beach like that. It has to be fate. Oh, it's so romantic!

Women (and men of course) have taken lovers all over the centuries. I think it's perfectly acceptable as long as Richard doesn't find out, and you say he can't possibly find out. You have the best of both worlds now, Susan. Lucky you!

Well, I don't have anything exciting to write about compared to your life. I'm not seeing anyone at present, so it's just work and going out with friends. Quite boring compared to you!

Love, April.

17 May 1973

Dear April

It's still going on and it's still as incredible. Since I wrote to you last I have seen Phil Friday, Monday, Tuesday, and yesterday (Wednesday). Today I thought I should keep up appearances by making my usual trip to Cardiff and buying a few things. I didn't stay long though because I needed to get back and catch up on some chores. Nowadays I rush round in the morning to do them before I slip out about midday, but I'd still got behind, and I don't want Richard to notice anything

155

different. I'm scribbling this before he comes home.

Anyway, enough about chores and home. Every time Phil and I make love it's different. Honestly, some of the things I've done with him I could never have imagined doing. I'm too shy to write them down, even! But my body just seems to be at his command and I love everything he teaches me.

We've had a few interesting conversations too, even though there's not a lot of time. He quite a deep person, very much a loner. He knows a lot of stuff about things like nature and music. He's a bit of a hippy type really, although he does have a job. I asked him if he gets lonely, living on his own in the middle of the woods. He says he's used to it, he's done several jobs like this. He goes out to the White Rose pub some evenings (I must make sure Richard and I never go there; luckily we don't go to pubs in the evening very much). Oh, and one day he played his guitar for me, and sang a Bob Dylan song, and even played the mouth organ just like Dylan. I could have stayed all day and listened.

He doesn't ask me anything about myself, which under the circumstances is a good thing. He knows that I live locally, that I've been here since last summer, and some of my likes and dislikes. But that's about it. He doesn't seem curious about me at all. That's OK though because I love listening to him.

And guess what, when I left yesterday and said I wouldn't be coming today, he asked if I was going to come on Friday! This is a first!! Usually he doesn't seem to care one way or another, although I think he is pleased to see me when I arrive. He just seems to live each moment as it comes. What a way to be.

You know, April, I've always admired and envied you. You live your life adventurously. You do what you want to do. I thought I wasn't like you, but now I realise I am. I am! I can have adventures too!

Love, Susan.

PS – I wish now I'd invented a false name to tell him, then it would really seem like I had two lives. What should it have been? Suzette? Lucetta? Carlotta?

***

Susan and Richard were eating a leisurely Saturday morning breakfast when Susan heard the post arrive and plop onto the doormat. Richard had the newspaper folded and propped up against the tea pot.

'I'll go,' said Susan, getting up from the table.

'Mmm?' said Richard, engrossed in what he was reading.

The writing on the envelope was familiar. 'It's a letter from Dad and Wanda,' she said, carrying it to the table. 'Maybe there'll be a photo of Marek.' But as she opened the envelope, she realised it wasn't bulky enough for a photo. She opened the letter and began to read it to herself.

Richard glanced at her. 'Are they all well?' he said after a moment when she didn't speak.

'Yes, yes,' said Susan, frowning at the letter.

Richard put down his toast. 'Is something else wrong?' he said after a moment when she still remained silent.

Susan swallowed. 'They're coming to stay, with their new caravan. On Monday.'

'Monday? You mean the day after tomorrow? It's a bit short notice, but it will be nice to see them, especially for you.' He touched her hand when she didn't respond. 'Don't you think?'

Susan felt panic rising up inside her. 'It's too soon. I − I can't get everything ready by then!'

'It'll be alright. I'll help you. What do they actually say?'

Susan read the letter out:

Dear Susan and Richard

I hope this letter is finding you well. We here are perfectly in fine health. Marek grows in each day and now has two teeth in the top of his gums to match the ones in the bottom gums. He has just started to try for crawling around on the floor too, so soon nothing will be safe. Katya is so loving with him, like a second little mother. It is good to see them together. As for your father, he adores Marek. The garage has been busy lately and as usual he has been working too hard, but you know well what he is like.

So, I come to why I write. You remember I told you we have bought a small caravan? Your father bought this vehicle some weeks ago and as yet we do not find the time to take a trip with it. Next week there is less work in the garage and I say, it is time we take a little holiday. In truth I had to insist. We can take Katya from school and your men can look after things in the garage for one week, surely. Why

157

did we buy caravan if we do not use it?

Where to go on our little holiday, we thought. It is very wonderful if we could come to see you. I know you are by seaside and Katya would love it. We see you and Richard too so it is perfect. We put the caravan by your house, and there we sleep, cook, wash. We will not trouble you. But, it will be nice if we can see you and if you can show us the beautiful places of where you live.

I am sorry that we don't tell you so long before. We leave early Monday morning, 21 May, and will be at your home about midday. Perhaps to stay up to the weekend. I am posting this letter now so I hope you will get it on Thursday. If we are not able to come, then please telephone. Otherwise, we will see you on Monday.

With much kisses, Wanda

There was a scribbled postscript below, in a different handwriting:

Look what she's talked me into! But it will be good to see you. Dad xx

Richard took the envelope and studied the postmark. 'She did post it on Wednesday, but with only a second class stamp. That's probably why it took so long to get to us. I expect she thought it had gone first class.'

Susan put her hands up to her hot face. 'They can't come Monday. They can't. I'll phone and ask them to come later on.'

'Darling, they obviously have it all arranged. It must have taken some effort to get cover in your Dad's business. They will be so disappointed. I would have thought you'd want to see them. You seem to get on well with Wanda, and you like the children.'

Susan got up abruptly from the table and carried the empty plates out, clattering them into the sink. She heard the puzzlement in Richard's voice and she made an effort to pull herself together. She came back to the table, mustering a smile. 'You're right, of course.' She took a deep breath. 'It's just that it's the first time they will have seen our home, and I want everything to be perfect. And I'd like to cook some evening meals for us all, so I need to think about that.'

Richard folded away his paper. 'I can help you. We can get some extra shopping this afternoon. And don't worry about the house; it's

158

perfect as it is. Just like you.' He touched her cheek gently.

She studied his face and saw only love there. The carefully constructed barrier between her two lives trembled and she felt a qualm of guilt. 'I don't know what I've done to deserve you,' she said.

'That feeling is mutual, my dear. We'd better get started, now that we have extra things to do.' He gathered up the teapot and remaining breakfast things and deposited them in the kitchen.

'Oh,' he said, putting his head round the kitchen entrance, 'They said they want to see the area. You could show them some of the walks you've been doing lately.'

***

The next morning they were eating their customary bacon and egg Sunday breakfast when Richard said 'By the way, I forgot to mention, I need to stay behind after church today for a meeting. I'm going to stand in to play the organ for the next few weeks, and I need to sort out the music selection.'

Susan was listlessly stirring her tea. 'Alright. Will it take long?'

'An hour or so, I expect. It's probably best if you walk home on your own rather than wait.'

She dropped her head over her plate, to hide her expression. The church service was normally an hour, but now she would have an extra hour. The idea that was half-formulating in her mind, if only she dared, took more shape. She put her knife and fork down and pushed the half-eaten food away. 'I feel a bit strange. Sort of queasy, and I've got stomach ache.'

Richard looked at her in concern. 'Has it just come on?'

'Yes. Well, no, not really. I was feeling a bit funny when I got up, but I thought breakfast would settle it. But it hasn't and I feel worse now.' She put her head into her hands.

He stroked her hair. 'Do you think it's something you ate? That would be odd because we both ate the same things yesterday. Or do you think perhaps you're getting a bit anxious about the visit tomorrow?'

Susan nodded, her face still in her hands. 'You could be right,' she said through her fingers. 'I think I'd better not go to church. I'll just stay here and rest.'

***

It took about twenty minutes each way to walk to the caravan. It must be fate, she told herself as she hurried along the cliff path, Richard having to stay after church. She now had an extra hour. Just enough time.

When she got to the caravan it was a ten past eleven. All the curtains, saggy cotton affairs with faded prints of flowers on them, were still closed. She knocked on the door and waited. No reply. She knocked again. It seemed odd that he should have gone out without opening the curtains. She was just taking out the paper and pen she had brought with her to write a note saying that she wouldn't be able to come for the next week, when she heard a noise from inside and Phil opened the door. He was fully dressed apart from his shoes. His hair was tousled and his eyes were bleary.

'Oh, it's you,' He said. He turned away and ran himself a cup of water at the sink, leaving the door open, presumably for her to come in. She stepped in, uncertainly.

'I'm sorry to turn up unexpectedly like this, on a Sunday.'

He grunted and put the kettle on the gas, fumbling to light the match and cursing under his breath when he dropped the first one and had to light another. Without looking at her he went back into the bedroom. Then a moment later Susan could hear sounds of him using the toilet. She realised he must have slept in his clothes.

Susan drew back the curtains. The inside of the caravan looked even more dismal with the light that flooded in. On the table were the remains of a fish and chip meal, still in the newspaper, and a half empty bottle of whisky and a mug. The sink and draining board were littered with dirty crockery, and a bag of sugar had spilled over next to the draining board. The whole place smelt; a stale, sour smell. Susan opened a window and let in a swirl of earthy fresh air from the woods.

He came back, rubbing his hand over his face.

'You look terrible. Are you ill?' she said.

160

He blinked at her vaguely before answering. 'Hangover,' he mumbled. 'There was a late night session at the White Rose last night.' He picked up the whisky bottle from the table and frowned at it. 'Then I must have had a couple of nightcaps when I got back.' He groaned and slumped down on a chair. 'I can't remember much. God, I feel awful.'

Susan sat down cautiously to join him, not knowing what to say or do. She had never seen anyone with a hangover before. Not like this, anyway. In morning tutorials at university sometimes students would come in complaining, but really almost boasting, of a hangover. But they were cheerful and still functioning, ready to brag about the previous night.

He stumbled up again and went to the bedroom. She heard him rooting through the bedside drawers. More cursing. 'Got any aspirin?' he said when he came back.

'No, sorry.'

He opened the kitchen drawer and rummaged through it. He pulled out a glass jar of tablets, shook out three and swallowed them. 'Make some tea, will you,' he said, still not looking at her.

Susan did as she was told, putting three sugars in the mug. She knew by now that was how he liked it.

They sat in silence drinking their tea. Birdsong drifted in through the open window; a blackbird maybe. It was sweet and pure to Susan's ears. Eventually she said, 'I came to give you a message. I won't be able to come the whole of this week. I have family coming to visit.' It was a stiff, formal announcement.

Phil nodded without interest. He poured himself another mug of tea from the pot. Then he said, 'It was a great night last night, though. What I can remember of it. It was somebody's birthday, and they were buying drinks. Then some bloke started a singsong and that was it. We were there for the night.' He looked around him and outside into the woods. 'I was lucky to find my way home.'

'Shall I make you some breakfast?' Susan said. 'And I could clear up a bit if you like.'

'I could eat a couple of pieces of toast.'

Susan got up and lit the grill, clearing the table while the bread toasted.

By the time Phil had finished his toast he was becoming more animated. He pushed his plate away and sat back, arms folded, and focussed on her.

'This is a surprise,' he said, as if seeing her for the first time that morning. There was even a hint of the old smile around his mouth.

Susan started to relax. This dishevelled, grumpy person had disoriented and unsettled her. The return of the usual Phil was reassuring.

She smiled in relief. 'I hope you don't mind me just turning up like this.'

He cocked his head onto one side. 'Why should I mind? You made breakfast and you cleared up,' he said. This was definitely the normal Phil.

'I can't stay very long...' She let the words trail.

He stretched, but made no attempt to move.

The clock ticked inside Susan's head. There was so little time. She stood up and slowly started removing her clothes. First her trousers, then a slow unbuttoning of her blouse, followed by sliding out of her pants and last of all she turned her back and took off her bra. Then she turned to face him.

He raised his eyebrows at her and wolf whistled.

***

The coastal path was slightly muddy and slippery from overnight rain, but Susan picked her way as fast as she could along it. Usually when she had left the caravan she was flushed and glowing with exhilaration, but not today. She was shaken not only by seeing another side of Phil, but by seeing another side of herself. Straight after they had made love she had had to dress and hurry away, leaving Phil sprawled in the fusty bed. The whole episode had been tawdry and she knew it.

As she left the cliffs and turned up the lane to the cottage she checked her watch; a quarter to one. It was fine. She should have at least a quarter of an hour at home before Richard got back from

162

church. From church. Her conscience rippled within her. That's where I should have been, she thought. But what could I do? I had to let Phil know I wasn't going to be coming for a week. You could have gone first thing tomorrow morning and put a note through the door, a voice said in her head. But you knew he would be out working then…

She slowed her pace and started to get her breath back as the cottage came into sight. She got to the gate and was reaching in her pocket for her keys when she stopped dead. Someone was on the doorstep calling through the letterbox. The person must have heard the gate swing open because she turned around. It was Mary.

'Thank goodness you're alright!' cried Mary, her round face full of concern. She rushed to Susan. 'I was worried about you when I got no reply at the door.' Susan felt her frank stare taking her in. Mary wouldn't miss anything. 'Richard said at church that you were feeling poorly so I thought I'd pop round.' She reached out and touched Susan's arm. 'Has anything happened?'

Susan realised how aghast she must be looking and struggled to compose herself. 'It's fine,' she said, managing to smile. 'I started to feel a bit better so I thought a little walk would do me good. Clear my head.'

'Oh. Richard said you were feeling sick and had tummy ache.'

'Yes. Yes, that's right. I *was* feeling sick but then I started to feel bit headachy too. You know, hot and feverish. Then what I really needed was some fresh air.' Susan felt the sweat forming on the back of her neck from the brisk walk.

Mary studied her face with a frown of concentration and felt her brow. 'You certainly do look a bit peculiar. And you are a bit hot. Why don't I make you a nice drink?'

'No, no, it's fine. Really, Mary.'

'Well, I'll just come in and stay until Richard gets back.'

'No!' said Susan, just managing not to shout. She took a breath. 'It's really kind of you, but I feel much better now. What I need to do is freshen up in the bathroom. I've got all hot. And Richard will soon be back.' As she said the words agitation rose up in her. She virtually pushed past Mary and put her key in the door.

'Well if you're sure…' Mary was still looking doubtful. She suddenly brightened 'Oh, by the way, Richard told me about your Dad and his family coming to stay tomorrow. How lovely for you.'

'Yes,' said Susan, into the house now and speaking from round the door. 'I'm looking forward to it. There's a lot to do, and I am a bit nervous about having proper guests. I think that's what's been the matter with me today. Just nerves. Well, goodbye Mary, and thanks again.' Susan tried to shut the door, but Mary took her cue.

'I can help you! Why ever didn't you ask? I could come over to help with anything, and I'd love to meet them! You told me all about them, remember?'

Susan clenched her teeth. 'If I need help, I promise I'll ask. Now I really have to go.' She shut the door firmly, practically in Mary's face. She dashed upstairs, ran water into the sink and strip washed frantically, flannelling herself with soap and cold water. She hastily yanked on some fresh clothes and, as she sat down at the dressing table to brush her hair, she heard Richard's car pulling up outside. She took a deep breath and stared at the wild-eyed person in the mirror. A person she didn't recognise.

Chapter 14

Dear April

Oh what a weekend I've had. I had to make a surprise visit to see Phil yesterday, while Richard was in church. I had to do it because on Saturday morning I got a letter from Dad and Wanda saying they were coming to visit on Monday – that's today - and staying until Friday. You can imagine how I was feeling when I got the letter – I wouldn't see Phil for a whole week and I needed to let him know. I just didn't know what to do. Anyway, fate played into my hands and on Sunday morning Richard announced that he had to go to a meeting after church. That meant, if I didn't go to church I would have time to go to see Phil. So I did. I pretended to Richard to be ill and I went. But I was rushing home afterwards when who should be on my doorstep but Mary (do you remember? She's a friendly woman who lives nearby, heart of gold, but a bit overwhelming). She was concerned because Richard had said at church that I was sick. I had to tell her that I had been out for a walk to clear my head, then I couldn't get rid of her, and I only just had time to wash and make myself presentable before Richard came home. By the skin of my teeth, I just got away with it.

I've been lying awake thinking about it. The whole episode scared me. Really scared me. I was so close to being discovered. And, I had to tell a lot of lies. Before, I hadn't actually lied at all. I had said to Richard I had been walking in the days, which is true, I walk to the caravan and back. I hadn't actually TOLD him about Phil, but I hadn't lied about it either. That's different. The lying made me feel awful.

At the caravan it was different too. Phil had a hangover so he was grumpy, and the place was a total mess. I was in turmoil because I knew I couldn't stay long. I didn't think he wanted to make love but then I persuaded him. I did a sort of striptease. I've never done anything like that before, but then, there are so many things I've never done before. I feel sort of proud of it now! (Have you ever done a striptease?) I had to jump out of bed and rush away straight after. At the time I was quite upset about how Phil was, but now I've thought about it a bit, I realise it was my fault for turning up out of the blue.

Still, soon it will be all back to normal. I will go to the caravan while Richard is in work, and Phil will be expecting me. That's how I want it to be — a separate time, a separate me that doesn't involve any lying and problems. It's made me think, though, that I mustn't take any chances again. So far I've being going four days a week. Maybe it should be three? What do you think?

My busy life recently has made me very efficient with my chores! I got my washing done in record time this morning, it's all hanging on the line and I've got time to write to you before the visitors arrive. Now that I've accepted that I won't be seeing Phil this week, I'm quite looking forward to seeing everyone

There was a sudden knock on the door. Twenty-five to eleven, it said on the clock. They were early! Hastily she stowed the letter in her writing-case and went to answer the door. Her father's bulky silhouette loomed through the glass.

She opened the door to see Wanda unloading the children from the car, and Dad on the doorstep with a huge smile on his face.

'Hello princess. How's my big girl?' His voice was warm and jolly. As ever.

'Dad,' she cried, muffled in his bear hug. 'I'm so pleased to see you.' And she was.

***

28 May 1973

Dear April

This is getting to be quite a habit, writing to you on a Monday morning, after I've done my washing! I ended up having a lovely few days with my family. I do think of them all as 'my family' now, not just my Dad. They were so impressed with our home, and gave me a lot of compliments. I felt very proud. They were so lucky with the weather - not especially warm but nice and bright so they could get out and about. I showed them Llanley beach, and Katya just loved playing and making sandcastles — just like I used to do. Marek sat on a blanket mostly. When he did crawl onto the sand, he tried to eat it! He's funny. He's a very cheerful little chap and laughs a lot. I've never had much to do with babies (have you?), but I like him,

166

and I was getting more confidence with him by the end of the visit. I even fed him his lunch one day.

On the first two evenings I made a meal for everyone. We felt like a real family. Richard goes out of his way to be pleasant to my Dad, and you can see Dad appreciates it. They are still a bit wary of each other, but getting more relaxed all the time. Wanda seems like a big sister to me now. The big sister I never had. It seems incredible looking back, that I was so jealous when she and Dad first got together. But of course I didn't have Richard and my own home then. On the last two nights they were here we suggested that Dad and Wanda go out on their own while I babysat. They really appreciated that because they don't get the chance to go out much. They settled Marek down for sleep before they went, then I sat in the caravan with Katya until they came back. Katya and I played games, snakes and ladders and snap, for a while until it was her bedtime. It was nice being just me and her. She's a sweet little girl. Then I just stayed in the caravan until they came back. They went home after lunch on Friday. The house seemed very quiet then. I had enjoyed having the company, and Richard enjoyed it too.

Surprisingly, I didn't think about Phil much last week. It was like I put that other life away in a box in my mind. But now I'm excited about seeing him today. Everything will be back to normal this time, I'm sure. Perhaps having a break was a good thing. It's Spring Bank Holiday and half term, but Richard left this morning to take some boys on a trip to London for a couple of days. I feel a bit guilty saying that I'm glad, because otherwise I wouldn't be seeing Phil for two whole weeks.

Nowadays I seem to have so much to tell you, but look at the time – I must get ready and go.

Love, Susan xx

***

Susan was smiling as she stepped up to the caravan door and knocked. She waited; nothing. She knocked again, louder and harder this time. Still nothing. She checked her watch; he was usually here by this time. She tried the door and discovered it was locked. Deflated after her eagerness, she sat down on the step to wait. But maybe he had gone somewhere because it was the Bank Holiday? In her eagerness she had not thought of that.

After some minutes had passed, she disconsolately got up and walked up and down, pausing to peep in through one of the windows. The window was high, so she couldn't see right down to the floor, but straight away she saw that something was different. There was no crockery on the table or near the sink as there usually was, and the packet of tea, the coffee jar, the usual loaf of bread and transistor radio were missing. In fact, the area was quite bare. Susan stepped back from the window in confusion, then she went to all the other windows and looked in. It was the same story. In the bedroom the bed had been stripped and the alarm clock and other miscellaneous things from the bedside table were gone, along with the clothes that were usually strewn around. She went round the back of the caravan to look in through the windows from that side, her brain refusing to take in what her eyes were telling her. Finally she looked in the last window to see an empty space where his guitar case had been, and bare shelves where his books had been. Phil had gone.

She sat down in the grass and tried to think what could possibly have happened. Perhaps he had been called away urgently. Perhaps someone in his family was ill. Yes, that could be it. Maybe he had left her a note. She searched around the area, picking up stones, but there was nothing. Well, perhaps he'd been in a rush and maybe upset, she reasoned. She peered back into the caravan again, as if she might have been mistaken. But *everything* was gone. If you were just going for a few days visit and coming back, you wouldn't take everything... The realisation seeped in. He was gone. She sat on under the trees, not knowing what to do with herself. Eventually she got up and retraced her steps home. There she trudged upstairs and lay down on the bed and let the tears of self-pity ooze out onto the pillow.

***

On Tuesday she trailed down to the caravan again, hoping that the previous day had somehow been a mistake, and that he would be there with his lazy smile and dark hair curling down onto his collar. Also, she didn't know what else to do with herself; this had become the pattern of her days. But the caravan was the same empty shell that it had been the day before. By Wednesday she had formulated a plan. Instead of setting off down the lane to the beach and cliffs, she turned left from her cottage and walked up the lane towards the village, but turned off before she reached it, and instead took a small side lane to the left, which wound down towards the coast, ending up eventually at the Big House. Susan had followed this with her finger on the map before she had set off.

The wrought iron gates of the Big House were open, and the drive wound through the spring greenery. The walls were newly maintained, and the realisation that this was Phil's work shot her through with pain. Her pace slowed when the Big House, grey and dignified, came into view. It was not of stately home proportions, but it was big enough to be an imposing edifice. She was almost overcome with nerves as she approached the enormous double front door, and nearly gave up on her mission.

With a deep breath she pulled on the doorbell, and heard it ring within the house. Her heart was pounding and she wanted to run away. She was just about to do so when the door opened. Susan had imagined that some sort of servant would be standing there, but this was obviously no servant. She was a middle-aged handsome woman wearing a tweed skirt and a plain jumper with a double string of pearls at her neck. She looked at Susan impassively; one barely perceptible downward flick of her eyes was enough to take her all in at a glance. It hadn't occurred to Susan to put smart clothes on, her church clothes, and to tie her hair up neatly in order to make an impression.

'Can I help you?' The voice was cultured. Polite but cool.

Susan licked her lips. This was it. 'Yes, um... it's about someone who I think was working here until... until recently...'

The woman raised her eyebrows but said nothing.

'You see, I saw him one day sitting on the bench on the coast path, just outside your grounds. He was reading this...' Susan reached into her bag and brought out a paperback book of twentieth century poets. It was one that she had seen on his shelf, and she had exclaimed in delight that she owned the very same volume. She pressed on, emboldened by desperation and because the lady of the house had not turned her away. 'We fell into conversation, because I know this book, and he told me that he worked here. When I walked that way the next day, I found that he had left the book there, on the bench, and I wanted to return it to him.' Susan wondered if the story sounded as implausible to the listener as it did to herself.

'Not possible, I'm afraid. He no longer is in our employ.' Her voice was neutral.

Susan feigned surprise. 'Oh. I see. Well, if you could kindly give me a forwarding address, I'd be glad to return it to him. It seemed to mean a lot to him.' She was gaining confidence.

The woman's eyes narrowed and Susan felt herself being assessed more keenly. 'The man in question ended his contract with us last week, and I am not in the habit of giving out personal information about employees.'

'What do you mean, ended his contract? Did it end suddenly? Do you mean he was sacked?' Susan abandoned her rehearsed part and her anguish leaked into her voice.

The woman's tone sharpened. 'Certainly not. He had a contract with us for five weeks' work, he completed the contract, and now he has left.' She began to close the door. 'I'm sorry, I can't help you any further. Good day.'

Susan stood staring at the closed door in front of her. He *knew*. All the time he knew exactly when he would be leaving, and he hadn't told her.

***

Life crawled on. Susan no longer walked the cliff paths, she simply went about her daily business, cleaning the house and cooking meals for Richard. She tried to re-normalise her world, but she felt marked and soiled by what seemed now an unbearably tawdry episode. She scrawled incoherent pages to April, bemoaning how she could have been so stupid, venting her hurt, going over and over why she hadn't asked more questions. There was no reply from April. What was there to say, after all? 'It's not your fault?' Well it was. 'You've still got Richard and thank heavens he didn't find out?' True, he didn't find out,

170

but she felt withdrawn from him, which was strange, since she hadn't felt that way during the fevered weeks when she had been seeing Phil. If there had been a reply from April, it would probably have said 'What did you expect? Men will be men. I wouldn't have let it upset *me* for long.'

It was the end of the week and Susan was making corned beef hash for their tea. Richard had suggested that they go out to one of the local pubs and treat themselves to steak and chips, but Susan said she didn't feel like it.

Richard was relaxing on the sofa, his tie removed and a glass of sherry by his side, which was his custom on Fridays. 'Oh, do let's go,' he called to Susan, who was in the kitchen. 'It will be a nice change for you. For us both.'

Susan heard but didn't reply. The potatoes and onions were boiling steadily and she picked up the can of corned beef and inserted the little metal key in the side to open the can. It opened about three quarters of the way and then broke off. She grunted in irritation and put her thumbs inside the gaping can to ease it open. Then she yelped in pain. Her left thumb had slipped, and she had gashed her thumb on the sharp edge of the can. Blood oozed out and she automatically grabbed her thumb with her other hand and watched the blood well up between her fingers.

'Richard,' she called, but he was already on his way. His experience with years of scraped knees and other misdemeanours came to the fore. 'Let me see,' he commanded briskly. 'Under the tap.' He led her to the cold tap and plunged her thumb under the stream of water. 'Ow,' she moaned. 'It really hurts.'

'Clean tea towel, please.'

Susan reached with her free hand into the drawer. Tears were clutching at her throat. Richard inspected her thumb, frowning with concentration.

'I don't think it needs stitches,' he pronounced. 'I'll just clean it up a bit and dress it.'

She sat silent at the kitchen table while he gently bandaged her thumb. 'There,' he said, smiling at her. 'Give it a few days and it will be good as new.'

His gentleness, following on from the shock of ripping her thumb, tipped her over the edge and she dropped her head down onto her arms and broke into noisy sobs. Richard stroked her head. 'It's all right. It will soon heal.'

Susan shook her head. 'I'm sorry,' she managed eventually, wiping her tears away with her un-bandaged hand. 'I... I don't know why I overreacted like that. I've just felt a bit low lately.'

'I've noticed.' Richard touched her cheek where the tears had wet it. 'What's wrong, my darling? It distresses me to see you upset.'

Susan dropped her gaze from the confusion and loving concern in Richard's eyes. She shrugged. 'I don't know,' she whispered. 'I just feel... I feel... unsettled.'

'It seems to be since your family visited. Is that what's upset you? Do you miss them? We could see them more if it would help.'

'No,' Susan shook her head in an anguish of frustration and remorse. 'Well, partly,' she corrected herself cautiously. I can't go on like this, she thought. I don't know what to do, and Richard doesn't deserve this.

'Why don't you go and visit them? Go for a week.'

'It's not very convenient for them. I'd have to sleep in with Katya. It wouldn't work,' she finished listlessly. She knew that both her Dad and Wanda would see that there was something wrong. 'The potatoes,' she said suddenly, getting up to turn off the gas.

Richard got up and gently moved her back from the stove. 'No you don't,' he said. 'You could easily drop it with your awkward thumb. He removed the pan and drained the potatoes over the sink. Susan sat back down and let him take charge.

When he re-joined her at the table, he looked at her thoughtfully. 'I really think you need a break. A change. If not with your family, then somewhere else. Is there somewhere you'd like to go? Or someone you could stay with?'

'I don't know,' said Susan. 'I haven't thought about it.' Her thumb was throbbing and she touched the dressing cautiously.

There was silence. Then Richard said, 'What about your friend from university? The one you write to.'

Susan stopped touching her thumb. 'You mean April?'

172

'Yes, April. Could you go and stay with her? I believe you said she has a flat.'

Susan looked at him. He was looking down at the table, tracing his finger along the wavy pattern in the Formica table top.

Her mind jolted. It was the last thing she had expected him to say. The letters are well hidden, she thought. He doesn't know anything. It's the one blessing, he doesn't know.

She considered what he'd said. Now he was looking at her steadily, waiting for her reply.

'It's an idea,' she said eventually, her thoughts whirring. 'It hadn't occurred to me, but I don't think April would mind.'

He got up and went to the stove before he replied. 'That's settled, then. You get in touch with her and see what you can arrange. Now,' he continued briskly, 'I'll get the corned beef out of this dangerous can and you can instruct me on what to do next.'

Chapter 15

The train is pulling into the station, past houses with conservatories bulging from their living rooms and rockeries in their back gardens. Tenway is a small seaside town, quiet in the winter but swelled by holidaymakers in summer. In June, the full rush of visitors has yet to happen. That would be the end of July and August, when the schools have broken up.

Susan puts her suitcase down on the street outside the railway station. A bus is exuding fumes and loading up with passengers. A taxi driver, lounging against the side of his taxi reading the *Daily Mirror*, gives her an enquiring glance. When she doesn't move, he calls across 'Taxi, love?' She shakes her head, picks up her suitcase and walks away. There is only one main street, so she walks down that. She has no map, so when she comes to a crossroads, she picks the direction where most people seem to be going and continues walking. Ahead a church with a very tall spire points towards the sky, so she aims for it. The street is lined with shops, a post office, a couple of pubs, a small library and a café. Any town, anywhere. A sign on the other side of the street catches Susan's eye: '*To the seafront*' it reads, and it points to a small alley between Boots the Chemist and Timothy White's. She goes through it.

She emerges to a harbour studded with fishing boats at anchor, a few cottages and a small pub clustered on the quayside. Around the corner from the harbour a path leads through a stone arch down to a beach, a tract of gold laid bare by the receding tide. The beach, Susan sees as she walks along it, is backed by grey cliffs, and atop the cliffs elegant, aloof houses keep watch. It is a pleasant scene, and it makes a small gesture towards soothing the misery that lies on her like a heavy blanket.

What to do. It had taken the whole morning and part of the afternoon to travel to Tenway from Llanley, first by bus and then the second leg of the journey by train. She must find somewhere to stay. She knocks on the doors of several guest houses near the seafront, each

174

one bedecked cheerily with hanging baskets of flowers and with spanking clean paintwork. Most have vacancies, but she finds that the price is more than she wants to pay. She wanders back towards the station where she finds several small places offering accommodation. She finds one which has a single room without bathroom. It is shabby and plain compared to its manicured seafront cousins, but it is cheap so she takes it. It doesn't really matter.

She unpacks her clothes and then goes out to explore the town. The coast, with its powdery sand and gentle sea disappearing into the horizon, draws her and so she returns there. She takes off her shoes and feels the support of the warm sand under her feet and allows it to soothe her as she walks and, leaving the town behind, wanders into undulating sand dunes. By the time she walks back she is tired and hungry. She finds a café and orders fish and chips with peas for her tea. She sits alone, whereas the other tables are occupied by couples and families. This is how it would be, she says to herself. This is how it would be.

After her meal she goes back to the boarding house. The midsummer evening is long and, even after she has read her book for a while, it is still not completely dark when she draws her curtains and gets into the narrow bed. This is how it would be.

***

The next morning the weather was still fine so Susan decided to take her time exploring the town and coast, and to make a plan. She shopped for bread, cheese, an apple and a bottle of Tizer and made herself a picnic to take to the sand dunes. Already as she had walked through the town she had noticed the Labour Exchange, and she had looked away quickly and walked on. Then her steps had slowed and she turned round to look again at the impassive building. She had crossed the road and peered in through the window. A couple of people were scanning boards containing small cards, and others were waiting in a queue to talk to staff behind desks. An employee, a man, turned away from the board, a card in his hand, and Susan quickly stepped away from the window so that he didn't see her.

There was a newsagent's on the corner, where she discovered that the weekly local newspaper came out that day, so she bought a copy. She sat in a secluded dip in the sand dunes and slowly scanned the pages, skipping over happy wedding photos and reports of local events, chewing her lunch as she did so. Brushing the crumbs off the page, she traced her finger down the column labelled 'for rent'. One item caught her eye: 'Room to rent in owner's house, town centre, shared facilities, very homely'. Susan ringed it with her pen.

Then she gathered up her things and walked back to the town. *Very homely...* She had only intended to look through the paper for information but the words continued to murmur in her mind. It took her some time to actually go into the phone box and to dial the number. The woman who answered did indeed sound homely; her husband had died recently, she explained, and she wanted to rent out her spare room both for a bit of extra money and for a bit of company. Would Susan like to come and see the room? It had recently been redecorated. And so it was that Susan arranged to view it late the following afternoon.

Outside the phone box she was oblivious to the rumble of the traffic but heard only the dull thump from inside her chest. Feeling slightly lightheaded, she decided to get a cup of coffee. The café was across the road from the Labour Exchange and over the rim of her cup she watched the steady flow of people in and out. By the time the hot drink had warmed her stomach she had gathered her courage and made her decision.

In the event it all turned out to be remarkably easy. She had waited in the queue for her turn to talk to a bored-looking woman with bad skin. What were her skills and qualifications, the woman wanted to know, her eyes flickering with lack of interest across the desk. Susan thought for a moment and listed her O-levels and A-levels. The woman's face remained impassive as she scribbled on a form. I need some kind of a job as soon as possible, Susan told her, trying to keep her voice steady. As an afterthought, she mentioned that she could cook and had good housekeeping skills. Well, they are desperate for some extra help in the bakery... And so an interview was arranged for the next afternoon, two hours before she had agreed to view the room that was for rent. It all fitted perfectly. Susan went back to her room and spent the evening lying on the bed trying to concentrate on her book, but actually spending more time gazing at the ceiling. This is how it would be. This is how it will be.

***

Next morning Susan awoke feeling stale and listless after a fitful night. She picked at her breakfast and then took her notepad and pen with her to head for the beach again, but dark clouds were rolling in threatening rain so instead she found a park and sat on a bench. She took out her pad and wrote *Dear April.* But the words would not form themselves. The way that her thoughts and feelings usually spilled out onto the page when she wrote to April just didn't happen today. She recalled April's early letters, recounting how she had effortlessly moved to another part of the country where she knew no-one, and had settled into a job, and then even got promoted. Susan tried to get some of April's confidence to rub off onto her. I could go to night school, she thought, study to get a better job, make friends. I could be like her.

A young mother approached and asked if she could sit on the bench too; Susan nodded her permission. The woman, who was pregnant and had a toddler in a pushchair, didn't look very much older than Susan. She leaned over clumsily and released the child, a little girl, who clambered out and took a few paces on her short jelly legs. She picked up a stone and carried it back, waved it triumphantly and presented it to Mummy. The child then smiled shyly at Susan, from the safety of Mummy's side. Susan made her lips smile back. A ball of misery was solid in her chest.

'On holiday, are you?' said the woman.

'Yes. Well, sort of,' Susan replied.

'With your husband?'

Susan twisted her wedding ring. 'No… it's… it's just a short break on my own.'

And then a picture of Richard slid into her mind. This woman was going home with her child to cook a meal for her husband, to talk and laugh with him, to spend a quiet evening watching television together.

Abruptly Susan got up and walked out of the park.

**

Susan let her feet carry her through the streets. It had begun to rain now, fat dark blobs speckling the pavement. It eventually penetrated through the depths of her misery that she was getting wet and should seek shelter. A café, was her automatic response, but she was out of the town centre now and there were none to be seen. Then she saw a small church with its door ajar and she went inside.

The interior was cool and quiet, cave-like, with the faintest linger of polish and incense. She sat down in one of the carved pews and turned her eyes up towards the stained glass window. Being in the church made her think even more about Richard; how she had sat beside him during the Sunday services and how he would sometimes covertly hold her hand within the folds of her dress, his touch warm and reassuring. How some Sundays he would play the organ, and she would sit alone in the pew and watch with pride. And then there was their wedding day, when they had stood before the altar and made their vows. Vows I have broken. Oh, Richard, I miss you so much already. She whispered the words and started to cry quietly, the tears not soothing her pain but rather inflaming it.

She didn't know how long she had sat there when she heard a voice next to her. She looked up, startled, and saw a man, a man dressed in priest's robes looking at her with concern.

'Are you alright?' His voice was low.

She gulped and smeared at her wet face with her fingers, unable to speak.

'Here,' he said, sitting down beside her and passing her a clean handkerchief. 'Take this.'

After a brief hesitation Susan took it and dabbed at her face. She glanced at him. He was ugly, with a big nose and lank hair. Only his eyes were beautiful, and they glowed with a soft compassion.

She covered her eyes with his handkerchief, aware that he was observing her intently. 'I'm sorry,' she gulped.

'No need to be. You're not the first and you won't be the last to come in here and pour out your heart to God.'

'I only came in to get out of the rain.'

He said nothing but sat back against the pew, so that they were both facing the altar. He placed his hands on his knees, one palm on each. Susan could hear the slight rasp of his breathing.

'I don't know what to do,' said Susan. He didn't reply or move. She continued, 'I've made such a mess of everything.' There was a faint hum of traffic outside, and the muted swish of tyres on wet roads.

'Do you want to tell me about it?'

And so she told him. She told him about her marriage, her home, her unfaithfulness, her lover's rejection of her. She spoke of her shame, her guilt, her remorse. She finished with the agony of her dilemma now, unable to continue her married life but terrified of starting a new life on her own.

After she had fallen silent he said, 'So your husband knew nothing?' She agreed. 'And would you ever take a lover again?'

She shook her head violently. 'No, never! I don't know whatever came over me.' She paused. 'I think more than anything, I was bored. But that's no excuse. I can't forgive myself.'

He flexed his hands on his knees. His hands were pale and smooth, hands of a man unused to any manual work. 'What you did was wrong. You acknowledge that yourself. But you are truly sorry and I think you have suffered enough. You can let it go now, and return to your husband, where you belong.'

In a strange way he reminded her of Richard. Perhaps it was in the eyes, the kind eyes. Her mind fingered its way around his words. It couldn't be that simple. 'But what about the truth?'

'Ah, the truth.'

'I mean,' she groped, 'doesn't Richard deserve to be told the truth? But... but then he might not want me anymore.'

'Judging from what you've said about his character, I doubt that. But why hurt him unnecessarily?' Outside the rain had stopped and the sun was coming out, waking up the colours in the stained glass window.

***

179

The bus pulled into Llanley and Susan got off to begin the familiar walk down the lane to the cottage. The light midsummer's day was eventually drawing to a close, to the accompaniment of an evening chorus of songbirds. Susan was weary, totally drained by the emotions of the day. Her suitcase felt heavy but she kept going because soon, very soon now, she would be home. The words played like music in her head: I am going home to Richard where I belong.

After she had left the church earlier in the day it was all she had wanted to do: go home. However there was a frustrating hour's wait at the boarding house for the landlady, who was out. Susan needed to pay her and explain that she was now not staying the week, but had to leave straightaway. She took the next train out of town but then found that she had just missed a bus connection to Llanley, so there was more tedious waiting. When she was on the train she remembered that she hadn't cancelled the job interview or the room viewing, but it was too late now.

Dusk had settled by the time she got to the cottage, its grey bulk familiar and reassuring. She searched through her bag for her key and then realised that she had left the cottage without it. So she knocked on the door, and her ears strained to hear Richard's tread in the hall. But it didn't come. She knocked again, more urgently this time, and peered through the letterbox into the empty hallway. No reply. Her heartbeat began to quicken. She left her suitcase and went round to the back door, noticing that his car was there. The back door was locked; she rattled it and knocked on it hard. Nothing. As she ran back to the front door sheer panic overtook her. He wasn't going to let her in! He knew, he knew everything and he wasn't going to let her in! She banged on the door with both her fists, unaware that she was whimpering. She lifted the letterbox again and cried through it, 'Richard, please, please open the door!'

Then through the letterbox she saw his bare feet descending the stairs, and relief flooded her. He was fastening his bathrobe. He opened the door and she collapsed into his arms.

'Susan, my darling girl, whatever has happened?'

She could hardly get the words out. 'I thought you weren't going to let me in. I'm sorry! I'm so, so sorry that I went away.'

He held her and soothed her. 'Ssh… everything's going to be alright. You're home now. I was upstairs running a bath, and I didn't hear you. That's all.'

She started to calm down but still kept her face pressed into his neck. He smelt like biscuits. Eventually she pulled herself away and took a breath. 'I don't know what came over me,' she said. 'I just felt… unsettled. But it's over now and I'm home. For good.'

To her dismay she saw his eyes fill with tears and he gathered her to him again. They stood clasped in each other's arms.

'I thought I might have lost you.' His voice was muffled in her hair.

'You haven't lost me. I lost myself for a while, but you haven't lost me.'

He kissed her face, her eyelids, her lips. It was as sweet as sunshine. 'Let's go to bed,' he said.

***

9 July 1973

Dear April

I have exciting news: I am going to learn to drive and my first lesson is booked for next week! I'm a bit nervous, but I'm telling myself it will be fine. Then when I have passed my test Richard says I can have the car some days, drive him to school, and then either pick him up or he will get a lift home. Imagine me, driving around the lanes, or going to Cardiff without having to take a long bus ride. Or even going to visit Dad and Wanda for a couple of days. So many possibilities open up!

Since I came back we have talked and talked and everything is alright now. More than alright, it's wonderful. All the bad things that happened, that sordid affair with Phil, now seem like a nightmare, or something that happened to someone else. How can I have been so stupid? And how can I have thought I could move to a new place and make a life for myself? I know you did it but you're so much braver and more outgoing than me. Richard believes (of course, he still knows NOTHING about what I did) that I found life here was too quiet and a bit lonely for me while he was at school. I suppose that's true; I was on my own a lot. So, we've talked about me getting a part-time job after the summer holidays. That's something else to be excited about! I don't really know what, but I'll see what's on offer in the village.

Maybe a shop, or the library? Or, when I can drive I could go further afield. Well, why not? Do you know, a few weeks ago I would have felt I couldn't have done that, but now, although it scares me, I feel I can handle it.

Other bit of exciting news: We are going away in the summer holidays for two weeks. Guess where? France! Ooh la la! It's only camping, but it will be fun. I'm really looking forward to it.

Must go now, I'm going to make something special for dinner tonight. Write soon and tell me your news.

Love, Susan

Dear Susan

What a lot is going on in your life! Good for you! I'm so glad that you and Richard are happy together again. You say I was brave to move to a new place, but remember - I wasn't leaving a husband, and I was starting a career with a good salary. Very, very different. You sound so happy now and I'm glad for you.

I'm planning a holiday too! Three friends and I are going to take one of those package deals to the Costa Brava in Spain. It makes it a lot cheaper, paying for the flight and hotel all in one. We're going for two weeks in October, when all the children are back at school. We plan to do nothing except lie on the beach and drink the Spanish wine. But if there are any nice Spanish men around, you never know...

Talking of men (which I sometimes do!) I met someone interesting a couple of days ago. I had had a week off work and gone to stay with my parents, which was lovely. Nice to be spoiled for a while and not have to do my own cooking. Not that I do much! I caught the train, because I'm not supposed to use the company car for personal use. On the way back I got chatting to a man, because I spilled coffee on the sleeve of his suit on my way past. Not on purpose, honestly!! I was mortified, but he dabbed it off with his handkerchief and said it was fine. Anyway, we started talking, and ended up talking all the way back to London. He'd been away to a meeting and was travelling home. We got off the train together, and he lifted my bag off for me. Then he hesitated and asked if I had time to go for a drink. Which I did. He's... I don't know, interesting. He's at least ten years older than me, I would say, and very smart and sophisticated. Not my usual type. He asked me if I'd like to have dinner with him tomorrow, and guess what... he's coming to pick me up in his sports car! I hope it doesn't rain, so that we can have the roof down. I'll let you know what happens.

Love, April.
PS – his name is Michael.

10 September 1973

Dear April

You'll never believe what's happened. I'm pregnant. I'm going to have a baby! I'm looking at the words I've just written and I don't quite believe it. When I first missed a period I thought it might be all the upset I'd gone through. I had missed a few days of the Pill when I went away, but I didn't think that would matter. Then when my second period didn't come and I started feeling sick in the morning, I knew what it must be. Yesterday I went to the doctor and she confirmed it. I haven't told anyone else yet, except Richard, of course. I don't know how I feel. It's just such a shock. Richard is delighted – already he's treating me as if I'm made of bone china. We had vaguely talked about having a family one day, but it was all some time in the future. After all, I'm only twenty so there is plenty of time. Richard says everything happens for a purpose, and it will all turn out alright. He says I'll make a wonderful Mum.

Oh, don't get me wrong, I don't hate the idea, and I don't hate babies. My little half-brother Marek is cute. It's just that this is happening to ME. A baby, a tiny person, is growing inside ME and it doesn't seem possible. Will I love it when it comes? Everybody seems to. Will I know how to look after it? I suppose I'll have to learn.

Well, my grand plans about getting a part time job won't be happening now. It would hardly be fair to start for just a few months. I'm continuing with the driving lessons, though. The instructor is very patient. Last lesson I had my first try at reversing. I thought it was awful but he said it was fine for my first attempt. As I said, he's very patient.

Richard has given in about us having a phone put in. Hurray! He says that he doesn't want me here alone with the baby and not able to get help if I need it. He also wants to look into getting central heating installed. He's much more organised and practical about all this than I am. I feel like I'm dreaming.

Anyway how's the new romance?

Love, Susan xx

Dear Susan

Get you, going to be a mum! Far out!! I must say, I'd rather you than me, but I think Richard's right and that you'll make a lovely mum. Congratulations!! Everything will fall into place when the little bundle of joy arrives. I've remembered something my Mum used to say: 'they bring their own love with them'. So, you see, you won't be able to help loving your baby. By now, I expect everyone will be congratulating you and you'll be getting used to the idea.

The new romance is going… now, what would I say – brilliant? Amazing? Fantastic? All of these and more??? We see each other several times a week now and I can't stop thinking about him. He's a true gentleman, he treats me like a lady, he's witty, he's smart –and yes, I know what you're thinking, he's a good lover. Oh Susan, I've never felt like this before. I think I'm in love. He could be the one. He could be Mr Right!! Me settling down – can you imagine??

Take care of yourself now you're pregnant. Lots of vitamins and milk and things.

Love, April xx

Chapter 16

The ticking of the clock on the mantelpiece was making Susan drowsy as she lay on the sofa under the blanket. Put the central heating on if you're cold, Richard always urged, but Susan kept it turned off in the day if she could. And they still liked to have a fire in the evening. In the grate the fire was already laid with paper, sticks and coal. Up until the last month Susan had laid the fire herself, but now that her expanded girth got in the way when she crouched down over the hearth, Richard insisted on doing the task himself before he left for school.

Rest for an hour or two in the afternoon with your feet up, the nurse at the antenatal clinic had instructed. And so Susan would lie on the sofa, sometimes reading or listening to the radio, sometimes dozing, but more often lately simply gazing at the ceiling or walls, aware of the soft sounds of the house and her own breathing, one hand resting lightly on her belly. Sometimes she would feel the undulation of a tiny limb under her hand, and inside herself she would feel him flexing his muscles. Today, however, he was quiet. Mary had asked her during one of their many cups of tea together why she had taken to saying 'he'. Did she have a feeling it was going to be a boy? Susan had thought about it and said no, not really; but she didn't want to call her baby 'it'; the baby was a person, a tiny person, not a thing. Sometimes she talked to him, murmuring softly, telling him about how his life would be, how she had bought the nappies, the pram, the carrycot, how they were all ready for him. Mary (who seemed to be an authority on all things to do with babies) insisted that the pram and cot should not be in their house before the birth, because it was bad luck. So they were stored at Mary's house.

Susan yawned, swung her legs over the side of the sofa, and awkwardly got herself upright. She went to the toilet – something she had to do frequently nowadays. In the hallway she passed her suitcase, all packed and ready for when she started labour. This was also according to instructions from the antenatal clinic: 'during the last two weeks of pregnancy have your bag all ready to go, in case you need to get to the hospital urgently'. The bag had sat there for ten days already. Susan looked at it and sighed. Now she just wanted to get the waiting over. She went to the window and looked out, her hand supporting her spine in the classic pregnancy posture. It was a dark afternoon and cold for March. In fact some snow was forecast, although not enough to settle. She peered out at the bloated, ugly sky, aware that she hadn't had any fresh air or exercise yet today, and decided to go for a short walk.

She walked down the lane, sedate as a sailing ship, to look at the beach. Richard's raincoat was enveloping her in its roomy folds, because her own coat wouldn't fasten any more. On the way back from the beach it started to snow gently, a few fat flakes that drifted down, squeezed out of the unwilling sky. Her footsteps slowed as she watched the flakes quietly reach the road and melt, gone forever. At the garden gate she paused and lifted her face to the sky to savour the whisper of the snow on her cheeks and forehead. She pulled her hands out from where they had been buried deep in the pockets of the raincoat, and held out her hands to watch the flakes disappear on her warm palms. And then the strangest feeling came. It was not the snowflakes that were melting but it was she, herself. It was as if she were dissolving. She stood still while the light snow shower faded away, but the sensation remained.

***

It was in the middle of that night that the first pain gripped her, and then retreated. It happened three more times before she awoke Richard in the early morning and told him that it was time.

***

Last time I was in the car it was so different, she thought. Just a few days ago, but now everything has changed. There had been tension then, even though Richard drove in his normal, steady fashion towards the hospital, calm like he always was. Had it been tension? More excitement really; excitement that at last it was happening.

186

'You're quiet, my darling,' said Richard, as he turned the car off the dual carriageway and down the road towards Llanley, taking extra care to drive smoothly. 'How are you feeling?'

'I'm fine. I was just musing.' She looked down at the shawled baby nestled in her arms. The little face was like the finest porcelain.

'Are you disappointed that we have a girl?' Richard asked.

Susan's arms tightened around the baby. 'Oh no. Of course not. And you?'

'How can I be? She's perfect.'

The cottage was warm inside and the carrycot and pram were waiting in the sitting room. The carrycot had been made up by Mary with flannelette sheets and a white blanket that Wanda had crocheted. When Susan pulled back the sheet she was touched to find that Mary had put a small hot water bottle there to take any remaining chill off the sheets. Richard watched while she lowered the baby carefully into the cot and tucked her in. Then he took Susan into his arms. She stood passive in his embrace.

'My darling, I am so glad to have you home again. Was it very awful?'

'Not so awful. And it's over now. Already it seems... distant.'

'Well, I think you were incredibly brave. Now,' he continued, 'how about a cup of tea?'

Susan extricated herself from his hug. 'Not just now, thank you. But I'll tell you what I would like.'

'What? Anything.'

'I would like a big bar of chocolate.'

Richard frowned. 'Oh dear, we don't have any. I'll go out and get you some later, after you're settled in.'

'Could you go now? Please?' When he hesitated she added, 'I'm really craving for some. It must be something to do with the breastfeeding. And maybe you could look round for some extra fruit while you're at the shop.'

Susan fixed her gaze on the cot while she listened to the sound of the car reversing out of the drive and fading away up the road. When she could no longer hear it she picked up her sleeping daughter, carried her upstairs, and laid her on their bed. 'At last,' she whispered, 'at last we're alone, little one.'

She carefully peeled back the shawl, like unzipping a banana. The baby was wearing a white babygro, and her legs were drawn up to her body, as if she hadn't yet realised she was no longer confined inside Susan's womb. When Susan moved her face closer to the baby's, she could make out the individual eyelashes lying on the gossamer cheeks. She put a finger into the baby's palm, and studied each nail individually as her tiny grip tightened reflexively. Her nails are like miniature seashells, she thought. She undid the babygro and slid out her legs, teasing each one out to its full length. She gently squeezed the plumpness of the thighs and dotted her finger over each toe. She picked up a foot and pressed her lips to the smooth sole of it, closing her eyes to concentrate better. Then she eased up the baby's vest and trailed her fingers over the velvety skin of her chest. She realised that she was holding her breath.

She leaned down and, avoiding the black withering stump of the umbilical cord, inhaled the scent of the baby's warm abdomen. The child, disturbed, had begun to writhe, her limbs waving like seaweed. Susan sat back and scrutinised her, drinking her in with her eyes. You are mine, she thought. You are an absolute miracle and you are mine. The baby had opened her pink mouth now and was moving her head from side to side, searching for nourishment, her face creasing like a walnut.

'Are you hungry, little one?' said Susan as she felt the milk prickle in her nipples. 'Little one without a name.'

***

She was vaguely aware of the sound of tyres on the drive and the front door opening and closing. She sat in a low chair in the living room, while the baby suckled with ecstatic concentration. When she could tear her eyes away from the baby's face, she looked up to see Richard standing quite still, framed in the doorway, as if he were too reticent to enter. Here, stood shyly on the threshold, was the man who had given her this most incredible gift, the man who loved her utterly. And, without warning, the huge wave of emotion that she felt for her daughter spilled over and caught him up too in the circle of its inexorableness. She looked at him as if seeing him truly for the first time.

'Richard,' she cried, holding out her free hand, 'don't stand over there. Come here with us.'

He moved to her slowly, almost reverently and she saw that his face was working with emotion. 'I think that is the most beautiful sight I have ever seen,' he whispered, kneeling down beside her and reaching out to lay his fingers on his daughter's head. Susan caught his other hand, kissed it and laid it against her cheek. They remained so while the baby suckled on obliviously.

'She is going to bring us such joy,' said Richard at last.

Susan raised her head. 'And that's what we must name her. Joy.'

***

Joy. Yes, we named her well. She has brought us nothing but joy, happiness and pride. She has never given us pain, and I suspect that there are not many parents who can say that about a daughter in her thirties. The years that she was growing up were blessed. We didn't realise how lucky we were.

***

Joy was a contented baby, not often fretful or ailing. Susan expanded into the world of motherhood as easily and naturally as breathing. After Richard had come home from work they would delight together in their growing child: her first tooth, her first words, her first tentative steps. For Susan, having Joy also unlocked the door into village life. She joined a mother and baby group, and she found increasingly that she was able to chat and make friends easily because of Joy's presence, that attracted people like sunshine.

A couple of years later she and Richard decided that there was room in their life for another child, and that Joy would benefit from having a little brother or sister. She was nearly three when Nicholas was born. They called him Nicky for short, although Nick, for 'Old Nick', would be better, Richard often lamented. It wasn't that Nicky was naughty

189

exactly, but after Joy's placidness it was a total contrast to experience her brother, who was loud, demanding, active and mischievous. Yet he was endearing too, with his impishness and his loving ways. Joy was a second little mother to him and, later on when they went to school, she looked out for him. Susan was in her element with her two complementary, growing children – one simple, open and kind, the other more complex and volatile. Her family and her home were her world.

Richard worked diligently, as he always had, with the goal, the hope, of becoming Headmaster one day. He rose to become Deputy Head and expected then to have to wait some years before progressing further. But unexpectedly the Head had to retire because of ill health and consequently Richard got his job, twelve years after starting at the school. Joy was coming up to ten and Nicky was seven. Susan couldn't have been more delighted for him, and then there was the realisation of a hefty salary rise, which meant they could move house. They had been aware for some time that they really should leave the cottage for a bigger family home. Even with the second bedroom recently split into two smaller ones for the children, the house was too small for a growing family, and although Richard put up with having his study out in the conservatory, it was far from ideal. But they all loved the quirky little place and so they had procrastinated.

Then something else happened which made their minds up for them. Susan discovered that she was pregnant again. What have I done to deserve to be so fortunate, she often thought. I have it all; a hardworking husband whom I love dearly, two healthy children, many friends and now this, this unlooked-for delight of new life, a new soft little body in my arms.

***

The cottage was bare and echoing with all the furniture gone, the very bones of it exposed palely. There were no toys littering the floors, no tottering piles of books and papers. The walls were blank and inscrutable, bearing outlines where pictures and mirrors had until recently looked out at them. Susan walked upstairs and surveyed each bedroom. The windows were standing open to let fresh air flow through and take away the disturbed dust and the slightly stale smell of the vacuum cleaning that she had done after the removal men had humped the beds and cupboards downstairs. The men had worked swiftly and efficiently, and had lifted each item between them as if it weighed almost nothing. Only their grunts and sweaty faces, and the mugs of sweet tea that they downed almost in one, told the full story. She closed the windows and took in for the last time the view down the lane to the sea. At the new house, just a mile away, there was no view of the sea.

She went downstairs to the dining room. It occurred to her that she had never seen this house without its furniture. A memory swam up to her of the first day that she had come here, her sheer delight in its charm, the feeling of safety and sanctuary. The feeling of coming home. Now the room seemed stark without the dining table and the splendid Welsh dresser that she had lovingly adorned with Richard's crockery all those years ago. This week she had carefully wrapped that same crockery in newspaper and stowed it in a box, writing 'dining room' on the side of it in big letters. Each plate, each cup that she packed had been a little acknowledgement of the goodbye that she would have to say to the cottage, and she had allowed her fingers to linger over the swirls and patterns.

But now, somewhat to her surprise and mild regret, she realised that the goodbyes had been said and that she no longer belonged here. She laid a hand against the wall and closed her eyes. She wondered if it were possible that some of their laughter and vitality, the Morgan family, had seeped into these walls to join with other generations of those who had lived out part of their lives here. And the new owners, a young couple who had been holding hands on the doorstep when Susan had first opened the door to them, would they breathe in these mingled vibrations too, and add their own? She hoped so.

Finally she went into the empty sitting room. There he was, laid upon his blue blanket on the carpet. He had woken up, but unlike most babies of four months old, he wasn't crying for attention, but instead he was looking up towards the window, fascinated by the squares of light. He was kicking his legs and making soft little sounds to himself. Susan smiled. In fact she smiled every time she saw her new son. He was even more placid than his big sister Joy had been, and to him the world was a kaleidoscope of wonder.

'Edward,' she called softly. 'Hello, sweetheart.'

The sound of her voice drew his eyes to find her and his face broke into a smile. Susan scooped him up into her arms and sat down cross-legged on the floor with him, their eyes locked together, looking into each other's souls. 'I'm glad you're awake. Now I can give you your feed before we go.' She knew she had time; the removal men had said they were going to get pie and chips for their dinner before going to the new house to unload, so they told her there was no need to rush round with the key. A car passed by outside, its exhaust blowing noisily. The sound distracted Edward, and he moved his gaze again to the window with a slight frown.

'Nothing wrong with your hearing, is there,' said Susan as she unfastened her blouse and started to feed him. 'Look at us,' she giggled, 'sitting on the floor like gypsies.'

'Do you know, Edward,' she continued, 'We're going to our big new home this afternoon. You're going to have a bedroom all for yourself. And so are Joy and Nicky. You're going to have a nice room, with blue walls and lots of light. And there's a proper study for Daddy, a lovely big modern kitchen for Mummy and a huge garden for you to play in when you get bigger.' She kissed his head. 'You're going to love it, just like your brother and sister are.'

Joy and Nicky were nearly beside themselves with excitement. They had marked out their territory in their bedrooms, planning where their beds and toys were going to go. 'It's so *big*, Mummy,' Joy had said, her eyes round with wonder, when they all went to look at the house, Edward just three weeks old in her arms. 'Will there be a room for the baby?' Nicky had wanted to know. 'I don't want him sharing with me. His nappies are *stinky*!' Privately Susan shared Joy's feelings about the size of the house. The place seemed so grand and elegant after the cottage, which she had to admit had become a bit ramshackle. 'Are you sure we can we really afford this house?' she had asked Richard. Richard had reassured her: 'You know me Susan, I don't take financial risks. With my Headmaster's salary it is entirely within our grasp. It will be our family home. We won't need to move again.'

Susan, from her place sitting on the floor, saw in her mind's eye the new house and, for the first time, her trepidation and doubts were replaced by elation. She pictured all the furniture and belongings making their way there in the van. She had hardly been able to get Joy and Nicky out through the door this morning because they were so thrilled that when they came out of school that afternoon they would be going to the new house. Richard was excited too. Although she was aware that he was preoccupied with getting to grips with his role as Head, which was still relatively new to him, she knew that he was quietly anticipating the move with pleasure. Tonight they would all sit down together in their new home.

Looking down again at Edward, Susan saw that he was drifting into a doze. She drew him away from her, wiped a dribble of milk from the side of his mouth, and tucked him in his blanket.

'Well, little one,' she said. 'It's time to go.'

PART 3

Chapter 17

Susan had her hands in a bowl of flour and margarine, which she was rubbing in to make an apple crumble, when she heard the ping of a text message coming into her phone from where it sat on the kitchen worktop. Having only recently acquired her first mobile phone, the sound of it actually doing something which required her input unnerved her. She looked at the phone sideways, not wanting to clean her hands to pick it and then have to go back to finishing the crumble afterwards. She hoped the message wasn't from Nicky saying that they were going to be late. The leg of lamb was already roasting in the oven and starting to waft out succulent smells, and lunch was scheduled for about one o'clock. But it was a long drive from London, and timekeeping wasn't one of Nicky's best points.

She rinsed the pasty mess off her hands and picked up the phone, holding it delicately. After some hesitation she pressed the right button and saw that the message was from Joy. *Will be there about 12. Do u need me to bring anything'* Frowning with concentration she texted back *'no thanks'.* The message disappeared from the screen and after staring at it for a minute she shrugged and assumed that it had been sent.

Eleven o'clock. She looked round the kitchen. Everything was under control: the vegetables were prepared, two bottles of champagne were in the fridge and the table was laid for six. Time for a coffee and then she would get changed. She made three mugs of coffee and took them on a tray into the living room. Glancing up she saw that the door to Richard's study was still closed.

'Coffee, you two,' she called. When there was no reply she took two of the mugs into the study. Richard and Edward were both seated at the computer screen, wearing identical frowns of total absorption. It struck her afresh, seeing their heads so close together, how alike they were. Although she hadn't known Richard when he was twenty-one, she had seen photos of him and he had looked exactly like Edward did now, with serious brown eyes and hair slightly curly and dark. And now even Richard's grey, thinning hair and the lines on his face compared to Edward's youth could not disguise the fact that they were father and son.

Edward glanced up briefly before his eyes returned to the screen. 'Thanks, Mum.'

'You're welcome.' She waited in case there was any more response. 'Going well, is it?' she prompted. Since Richard had retired five years ago he had been researching the history of their area. When Edward came home from university for the holidays he would help him. Susan had never really worked out if Edward was actually interested in the topic or if he just enjoyed the harmony of working with his father. Either way, it was heart-warming to see how comfortable they were, and had always been, in each other's company, despite the age gap. Although she valued the peacefulness of retired life that she shared with Richard, it was also such a pleasure when her younger son had arrived home yesterday for the holidays. And now today, on this special day, the whole family would be together.

'Yes,' said Richard, sitting back and easing his back out with a sigh. 'Ed's been showing me some other ways to search online. It's opened up a whole new avenue of investigation. You're an enormous help,' he said to his son.

Ed shrugged and took a sip from his coffee mug. 'Do you want any help, Mum? Dad says you've been a bit off colour lately.' She felt the quiet scrutiny of his gaze. Susan wondered what Richard had said to him. 'Oh, I'm fine, and it's all under control in the kitchen.' She beamed at him. 'Besides which, you're the birthday boy! You just enjoy your day.'

His eyes had returned to the screen. 'Well, you only have to ask, you know.'

'I know.' And she did know. He was a good boy, always had been. 'Joy will be here by midday, and Nicky and Amita… well, they'll be here

195

when they get here.'

'Oh yeah, he told me at Christmas he was going out with this girl,' said Ed. 'It must be serious then, if he's bringing her. Have you met her?'

'We have,' replied Susan. An image of Amita arose in her mind; long legs, subtle, expensive perfume and well-bred politeness. 'We met her in January when we went to London to see a show. She seems very nice.' She paused, aware of how inadequate that sounded. 'Remember you have to get changed, Richard. Why don't you put on your new shirt?' Richard muttered something non-committal, his hands busy on the keyboard again, and so she left them to it.

So there was time for her to sit down and enjoy her coffee properly. She went into the living room, but then changed her mind; the morning was bright enough to sit in the conservatory where she could see out to the garden and look at the daffodils nodding and primroses peeping out from under the hedges. A robin was perched on the edge of the birdbath, and he dipped his beak swiftly, furtively almost, to drink. Susan allowed herself to relax and absorb the blessing of this place that she loved. She rested her head back against the wicker chair and closed her eyes. The demon hovered. Why am I feeling so wilted? she wondered. Those years when I was working part-time and had the family to look after, I didn't feel tired like this. I'm so glad I decided to stop working when Richard did. I don't think I could cope now. She took a deep breath and blew out gently through her lips, coaxing the demon to retreat. Is it that I'm just getting older?

'Hello, only me,' a voice called from the back door. Joy.

'In the conservatory,' Susan called back.

Joy hugged her mother and kissed her on the cheek, like she always did. Susan felt the tickle of Joy's long hair and caught a whiff of Imperial Leather soap. Joy shrugged off her fleece and threw it down on a chair. Susan saw that she saw that she was wearing a long-sleeved tee shirt, body warmer and her trusty old denim jeans. But then, what did she expect?

'Coffee?' Susan offered.

Joy shook her head. 'No thanks, had one just before I came out. Then I walked here, over the footpaths. A bit muddy, but OK.' Joy looked at her mother. 'How are you?' She was one of those people who asked the question and then listened to the answer.

'Fine, thanks. Looking forward to us all being together.' It was clear that Richard had said nothing to Joy about her feeling tired, because if he had, Joy would have been round to their house like a shot, demanding a list of her symptoms, and why hadn't she been to the doctor's. 'Ed's in the study with your Dad. They're deeply involved in their research, so you won't get much out of them. Oh, did I tell you that Nicky's bringing Amita with him?'

Joy lifted her eyebrows. 'Nicky, bringing a girl home? Does this mean it's serious?'

Susan laughed. 'That's exactly what Ed said. Who knows? It's about time one of you settled down, anyway.' Susan regretted the words as soon as she had said them. She didn't want to be on Joy's case.

'Well, don't look at me. Does Dad like her?'

'Yes he does, but you know your Dad. He accepts and likes everyone.' Susan paused. 'Did I tell you that Amita's from India? Her parents moved here when she was small.'

Joy's eyes widened. 'Ooh, trust Nicky to choose someone exotic. Anyway, I'm going to wish Ed happy birthday.' She got up, slinging her fleece over her shoulder.

Susan went upstairs to change into the dress that she had laid out on the bed, thinking of Joy's words. The ease with which the younger generation accepted people from different backgrounds always surprised her and made her feel slightly ashamed. She sat down at her dressing table and picked up her comb, looking critically in the mirror for grey hairs. There were a few, but not too bad she supposed, for a woman in her fifties. I need a trim, she thought as she tidied her hair; it was nearly down to her collar. It was only a year since she had decided, for the first time in her life, to have her hair cut short, as befitted a middle-aged woman. Sometimes it was still a surprise to see this woman with short, greying hair looking back out of the mirror at her.

Richard came into the bedroom and leaned over her shoulder, looking into the mirror too. They smiled at each other's reflections.

He took the comb from her hand and began to comb her hair. Susan closed her eyes and yielded to the gentle movements. 'Still feeling a bit peaky?' he said.

Susan opened her eyes again. 'Oh, no, no... I'm fine. Don't worry about me.' She reached over to her jewellery box and picked out a string of fine grey pearls. 'I'm going to wear these. Can you fasten them for me?'

'Ah, the pearls I gave you for our silver wedding. Oh dear, I might have to get my glasses. The clasp is very small.'

Just then they heard the crunch of a car pulling up on the gravel outside. 'They're here already,' Susan gasped, jumping up from the dressing table, pearls forgotten, and looked out of the window at a sleek green BMW convertible in the drive. 'Quick, change your shirt!'

'Now, don't panic. Look, Joy and Ed have gone out to meet them. It might be rather nice for the young people to be together for a few minutes without us.' With irritating slowness he began to unbutton his cardigan as he looked out of the window. 'And it looks like young Nicky has bought himself a new car. That job of his in public relations must be paying him handsomely. Not that I've ever understood exactly what it is that he does.'

As Susan finished tidying her hair she looked out of the window and saw that Nicky and Amita had got out of the car. Nicky was carrying what was presumably a gift for Ed and Amita was carrying a bunch of flowers which Susan guessed were for her. A nice touch. There were a lot of introductions, hand-shakings and hugs going on between the four of them, and the sound of their chatter and laughter came faintly through the double glazing. Almost guiltily, Susan stopped dressing for a minute to observe the tableau from her unseen vantage point. Nicky and Amita made a handsome couple, both tall, slim and dark. In fact Susan often thought her elder son looked almost Mediterranean. Although Susan knew relatively little about clothes, she could tell that what Nicky and Amita were both wearing was expensive. In particular her eye was drawn to Amita, to her silk shirt in a subtle green hue, a single strand long gold necklace and well-cut trousers finished off with polished boots. Her long glossy hair was tied back in a bow. Seemingly at ease, she was chatting to Joy, who was smoothing her hair behind her ears. Then Amita said something and both women laughed. The men were standing with arms folded, looking at the car,

198

reverential awe on their faces. Then Nicky started gesticulating as if he was explaining something technical to Ed. Ed was nodding his understanding. Suddenly, this moment in time seemed infinitely precious. Susan had an urge to get her camera and capture it.

***

Lunch was a lively occasion. Everyone expressed their admiration of Susan's perfectly cooked spring lamb with all the trimmings and the conversation was animated, like it always was when the three children got together. Although, that happened less and less often nowadays. Usually there would be an edge to their banter; typically Nicky teased Ed, who rarely took the bait, but then Joy would leap to Ed's defence. Today though, there was a different dynamic because Amita's presence had disrupted the familiar pattern. Susan sat back, lightheaded, and watched with strange detachment while Amita asked Ed about his Physics degree course and Joy about her teaching career. Amita's skill had to be admired; she showed interest in others, and drew them out with questions, but stopped short of prying. A skill? Yes, it seemed so more than a genuine curiosity. Nicky dropped in the odd comment, and Susan's maternal antennae picked up how he and Amita sparked off each other. They're good together, Susan realised. And she's not afraid to stand her ground.

Unusually, today Ed was the one who was talkative and Joy was more reticent. Ed said to Amita that he had heard from Nicky that she was a lawyer. What was her specialism, he wanted to know. Although Amita spoke lightly, deprecatingly almost, about her career, it was clear that she was an achiever. Glass ceiling, what glass ceiling? laughed Nicky. Susan saw the look he gave her. He's proud of her, she thought.

On the other hand, when Amita said – not really patronisingly - how much she admired Joy for teaching special needs children, and asked what had influenced her to train for such a job, Joy stiffened into defensiveness. Don't, Susan said silently to her daughter. You are as good as any other woman, you are as good as this exotic, high flying woman. Just because you chose to come back to live and work in the village where you were brought up, it doesn't devalue you. You are

199

never less than amazing in my eyes, my darling girl. Susan drew in a breath, caught unawares by the sudden uprush of emotion. They were all laughing now at something Nicky had said. Susan looked to the other end of the table at Richard who, like her, was mostly an interested observer of the subtleties of the interplay. They caught each other's eye. He lifted his eyebrows slightly in a question and she nodded.

Richard got to his feet. 'It must be about time we opened this champagne,' he said.

The cork popped, and everyone had their glass filled, except for Nicky who accepted only half a glass because he was driving back to London later. Susan had suggested that they stay over, but he had said they preferred to go back. They were staying at Amita's flat in town that night, because the next day they were out for an early Sunday lunch with friends at a restaurant nearby. Susan didn't see why that meant they couldn't stay the night and make an early start the next morning, but she said nothing. Perhaps she was secretly rather relieved. Richard might not have been keen on Amita sleeping in Nicky's old room with him.

Richard raised his glass and proposed the toast. 'To Edward, on his twenty-first birthday. Our youngest son, now fully fledged into manhood. I can relax at last.' They all laughed dutifully.

'It's funny how the anachronism of the twenty-first birthday still persists,' said Nicky after they had drunk Ed's health. 'After all, it doesn't have any meaning now. Eighteen is the age of majority.'

'That's true, but it does seem to have more gravitas than eighteenth birthday celebrations,' said Richard. 'I remember on your eighteenth birthday, Nicky, you and your friends got rolling drunk and half of them were underage.'

'And anyway, this is a lovely reason for a family get-together,' said Joy, giving Nicky a pointed look. 'Happy birthday to you, Ed, and thank you for a lovely lunch Mum.' She drank again and then put her glass down firmly.

Nicky opened his mouth to reply but Ed interrupted him. 'Thank you everyone. I've actually got an announcement. I had the letter on Friday but I thought I'd wait until we were all together to tell you.' He cleared his throat and paused, a smile twitching his lips. Everyone clamoured for him to get on with it.

'Well, I applied to Cambridge to do a research project that they were advertising.' His voice was as quiet and diffident as usual. 'I didn't think I stood much chance, because they usually recruit in-house, but I had a go anyway, just for the experience.' Then a big smile captured his face. 'And I've got it! They didn't even interview me!' His cheeks flushed. 'It's all provided I get a First Class degree in the summer, of course,' he added.

Pandemonium broke out as they all congratulated him. 'I'm so proud of you,' Susan whispered as she had her turn to hug him. She couldn't say more because of the lump in her throat.

'So, tell us exactly what it entails,' said Joy, when they had all settled down again. 'It's all a different world to me.'

'It means I will be a research student, and work for three years on the project, then write my thesis and hopefully – if they approve it – get awarded a Doctorate.'

'A Doctorate from Cambridge, no less,' said Richard, the pride in his voice unmistakeable.

'So three or four more years before you get a real job then,' said Nicky.

Ed turned to him. 'I will get a substantial grant.'

'And with a Doctorate from Cambridge he'll be sought after,' added Amita.

Nicky held up his hands. 'Only joking, only joking! It's great for you, mate.' He clapped his brother on the back.

Susan stood up and started to collect the empty dishes together. 'After all that excitement, I'm going to put the kettle on. Who wants coffee?'

She carried the tottering pile of dishes out to the kitchen while the others started to get up from the table. Richard followed her out carrying the empty champagne glasses. Then suddenly, and she didn't know quite how it happened, the dishes had slipped from her grasp and crashed to the kitchen floor, splintering spectacularly and littering the floor with shards. There was a couple of second's silence before Susan burst into tears.

***

'Here, I've brought you some tea, like you wanted,' said Joy. She put the mug down on the low table in the conservatory, quietly, as though someone was sleeping. 'How are you feeling now?'

'Better,' said Susan. She felt the kind intensity of Joy's scrutiny and forced a laugh. 'I feel really silly now.'

'No real harm done, just a few broken dishes. We've cleaned it up. Shall I sit with you, or do you want a bit of quiet time?'

'Quiet time would be nice.' Susan picked up her cup. There was movement outside which caught her eye. Richard was showing Amita the garden – a tactful ploy of his to get her out of the kitchen when everyone had been exclaiming and fussing. She could see him pointing out various bushes, and Amita was nodding. Then they both smiled at something Richard had said.

'OK. In that case I'll go and get the others to help me clear up from lunch. No…' Joy added, putting her hand on her mother's shoulder as she began to protest. 'We'll do it all – you just rest. You can serve the birthday cake later.'

So Susan sat alone and listened to the sound of the dining table being cleared and the tap running in the kitchen. Voices floated in to her, carrying fragments of the conversation. Haven't you two ever heard of the menopause? she heard Joy say. Their reply was muttered. Then she caught Joy saying something about mood swings.

The menopause. Is that what this is? Thought Susan. I'm fifty-two, so I'm plenty old enough. And my periods have been erratic for the past couple of years. In fact, when was the last one? five or six months ago, surely. But there were no hot flushes, which is what she'd heard friends complain about. Only this crushing listlessness. That, and now these strange lumps. She gently touched the sides of her neck.

***

It was later on, after the birthday cake had been eaten, after Nicky and Amita had roared off back to London, after Joy had put her wellingtons on and set off over the fields for home, that Richard found

202

her. She was sitting on the floor of their en-suite bathroom, her arms around her knees. With a cry Richard dropped down beside her.

'Oh Richard,' she whispered. 'I just feel so ill.'

Chapter 18

It's no good, I can't do it. It was one thing writing about the Susan from decades ago, that excruciatingly shy girl who does indeed seem like another person and not me. But that doesn't work for these recent years. Not since it happened and my world disintegrated.

The words that I have just written are blinking at me from the computer screen. I remember that moment on Ed's twenty-first birthday so clearly. I don't want to, but I do. I remember how Richard tenderly gathered me in his arms, right there on the bathroom floor where I was sitting, and I told him about the lumps in my neck. He felt them and said nothing. I wanted him to say it's OK, I'm sure it's nothing, but he didn't. He said that we'd go to see the doctor on Monday, and so we did.

Of course the doctor, who we've known for years and who had seen the children through all the various ailments, was non-committal and said he wanted me to have tests. Soon. Eventually we ended up seeing Mr Evans, the specialist, and he confirmed what by this time I already knew. Well, sort of knew. You still hope that all you have read up about on the internet won't, can't possibly, apply to you. Cancer happens to other people, but not to me. I was fit and healthy and I looked after myself, so how could it be me? I only half listened while Mr Evans outlined the strategies of treatment – chemotherapy, radiotherapy, the support that I would get. This was a cancer of the blood, and quite a rare type, so there was no option for an operation. This cancer couldn't just be cut out. It was inside every part of me.

We drove back in silence and got home early in the afternoon. Joy was teaching at school, Nicky was working in London and Ed was now at his research post in Cambridge. We had said we would let them know straightaway, but I needed to summon my strength first. Richard put his arms around me and I blurted it out.

'Richard, I'm so scared. I don't want to die.' I could hardly breathe.

He tightened his arms. 'You're not going to die. You heard what Mr Evans said: there is a very realistic chance of recovery.' He took my face in his hands and looked into my eyes. I saw his pain as well as my own in the reflection.

'Because, don't you see, it would be so ironic,' I gabbled. 'You're sixteen years older than me. It always seemed a foregone conclusion that you would die first, but now it could be me. It could be me!' A strange sound ripped out of me, halfway between a laugh and a sob. And then I couldn't stop. The hysteria spewed from me, and Richard just held onto me until I was empty.

Oh, I don't want to think about that dreadful time any more, let alone write about it. I snap shut the computer screen and get up to look out of the window. By now I know every inch of that corner of the car park. Today the rubbish bin is full, and a polystyrene coffee cup is poking out of the top like protruding teeth from a mouth. Neither do I want to dwell on all the treatments that they gave me, those awful months, years in fact, of the gruelling cycles, the hair loss, the indescribable sickness and debility. I close my eyes and breathe deeply like I have learned to do. Let it go, Susan. It's past now.

It's past because the day came when we went to see Mr Evans and he gave us the news that we thought we might never hear. I was clear. There were no more traces of the cancer left in my body. Richard gripped my hand.

It's funny, the feeling when you get good news like that, what you've been hoping for, praying for. When it actually happens it feels like an anti-climax. You've kept your hopes firmly locked away, and so your mind won't allow the good news to penetrate. Mr Evans was talking quietly, sitting back in his chair, legs crossed and one ankle bobbing up and down. I nodded like I was taking his words in, and I said thank you when he passed me some leaflets.

It was only when we got outside and stood in the warmth of the sunshine that the truth started to tingle within me.

'Look,' I said to Richard. 'Look.'

'What?' he said.

I bent down and picked a wild flower that was pushing its way up through a crack in the pavement. Its petals were like butterfly wings. 'Isn't this the most beautiful thing you've ever seen?'

***

205

We stopped off at a Harvester restaurant to get lunch on the way home. Before we ordered our meal I texted to the family and close friends, to all those we knew who were waiting to hear the news: *'Cancer completely gone, I'm all clear! Can hardly believe it!! Thank you for all your love and support. Speak soon, S xx.'*

The restaurant shimmered and hummed around me with activity and life. Life. There were grandparents giving their pre-school grandchildren a treat, bunches of lunching women with heads bent close together to savour the latest gossip, and retired couples like us who had the luxury of choosing not to cook.

'We can book that holiday now,' I said, taking a sip from the celebratory bottle of bubbly that Richard had ordered.

'We certainly can. Let's do it soon – perhaps a last minute deal? We were going to have a holiday anyway, but now we can book it in a different frame of mind.'

A different frame of mind. It still wasn't real.

'Mmm.' Richard consulted the menu. 'I think I'm going to have a steak. With a jacket potato, though, not chips.' He looked up at me over the top of his reading glasses for approval. 'Of course,' he went on, putting the menu down, 'Before we settle on any dates for a holiday, you should think about what Mr Evans said about harvesting your stem cells.'

'It was hard to focus on what else he said after he told me I was all clear. I didn't take in all the details.' I tried to concentrate on the menu. Not that it mattered what I ate; it was all wonderful. 'I'm think I'm going to have the fish and chips. No, the chicken breast with barbeque sauce.'

Richard reached across the table for my hand. 'I can understand you not wanting to think about anything else now after what you've been through, but it does make sense, darling, for them to collect your own white blood cells now that you are totally free from cancer.' He hesitated. 'The cancer probably won't come back, but just in case... well, you heard what Mr Evans said. If it does, then have your own healthy cells ready to transplant back into you. Simply an insurance policy, he said. It does make sense.'

A young waitress came to our table. According to her name badge, she was called Stacey. 'Are you ready to order, or do you need a few more minutes?' She had a perky smile only slightly marred, in my opinion, by a piercing through her lower lip. We ordered our steak and chicken, and declined her suggestion of garlic bread or any other accompaniments.

I picked my glass up, then put it down again without drinking. 'I do see all that. But Mr Evans said I would have to have another big dose of chemo before the procedure and I don't think I can face that again. Then didn't he say that after they harvest the cells I'd have to be in isolation in a clean environment for a while, while my immunity builds up again? Solitary confinement, by any other name. I don't fancy that.'

After a moment Richard nodded. 'As you wish. Let's just make today a celebration, shall we? Now, shall we start on the salad bar?'

We came back from the salad bar with our little dishes loaded to the brim with cherry tomatoes, coleslaw and other crispy goodies.

We ate in silence for a while. 'I'll read the leaflet and then I'll think about it,' I said, a piece of cucumber speared on my fork. 'After we've had a holiday.'

***

'All packed up and ready, are we?' said Matthew. 'The great day has finally arrived!'

'Do you mean the great day when I can go home or the great day when you take off that surgical mask and I see what you look like?' Matthew and I were well onto teasing terms by this time.

The crinkles that appeared around his eyes above the mask told me that he was smiling. 'Ah, you can't wait to be dazzled by my good looks, can you?'

'You could give me a quick peek now. After all, I'm going home in an hour or two when my husband comes.'

He shook his head. 'At all times while in the isolation room, nursing staff shall wear the appropriate protective clothing,' he intoned. 'You'll just have to contain your excitement until I walk you down the corridor. And seriously, you know you're still very vulnerable to infection, don't you?' He tapped the information leaflet that he'd left on the table for me. 'It's all in here.'

I nodded. 'And talking of seriously, I do want to thank you for all you've done for me, especially in those early days.'

'All in a day's work, my dear. Anyway, you've been no trouble. I wish all my patients were like you. Oh, and when the book comes out, could I get a mention? You know, in the acknowledgements?' He clasped his hands together on his chest like a heroine in an old romantic film.

'I keep telling you, it's not anything that's going to get published. It's just the story of a girl's life. Part of it, anyway.'

He persisted. 'Do you at least know how it's going to end? It will be a happy ending, won't it? I can't bear an unhappy ending. I couldn't stop crying after I finished *Gone with the Wind*.'

'I don't yet know how it ends. But I agree, a happy ending is what we all like best.'

'Oh yes.' He sighed theatrically. 'Well, I'll come and get you when your husband arrives. And Susan...' he paused at the door, his gloved hand on the handle. Quick as a flash he whipped his mask off to one side and grinned at me. He looked just as I had imagined: smooth cheeked, boyish good looks, white teeth. Then with a wink he hooked his mask around his ear again and he was gone.

I looked around the room and checked under the bed, backs of drawers, to make sure I'd got everything. Then I put my laptop on the table, turned it on and waited while the words filled the screen. My words. I scrolled down and down; I couldn't believe how much I had written, how it had all simply deluged out of me. I hadn't re-read any of it, but sometime, in the quietness of home, I would sit down and ponder on it. I would make friends with young Susan and bridge the gap between that awkward, naïve girl and the woman I am today. That, after all, was the whole point.

But for now, I was searching through the text to find where I had written about that particular morning in May, when there was warm spring sunshine and it felt to me like the world was uncurling. The time when young Susan walked along the cliffs to the secret beach and saw a man swimming in the sea. If I closed my eyes I could see the scene now. I found the passage that I wanted, and highlighted that and several subsequent pages. Then I hit 'delete.' '*Are you sure?*' said the message on the screen. I hit the 'yes' button. I was sure.

Chapter 19

A few days after coming home I was still noticeably weak and had to guard against infection, but I knew that was normal and I chose not to fight it. I had become accustomed to choosing my attitude, rather than letting events toss me and control me. We were eating our normal breakfast which, apart from on a Sunday when we treated ourselves to bacon and egg, consisted of fruit and wholemeal toast with cups of fragrant coffee. We would sit together at the kitchen table, with Radio 2 emanating cheerfully in the background. This and other familiar routines settled themselves around me like a comforting blanket. The little things of life; so infinitely precious, so often taken for granted. After we had eaten, Richard would usually unfurl his newspaper to read with his second cup of coffee, and I would open my laptop to read my emails, or to check the weather or to browse the internet. A gentle morning routine.

'Aha,' I said. 'I've got an email from Nicky. He's asking how I am, he says he and Amita are both well, work busy for them both and – hey, get this – he asks would I like him to pop down and visit!'

Richard ruffled his newspaper and raised his eyebrows. 'About time.'

'Oh, you know what long hours he works and it's a long journey. He texts and emails to keep in touch. Well, sometimes anyway.' It wasn't something I wanted to argue about.

Richard folded up his paper and grunted. 'I've realised that today's the last day for me to reply to that email about my university reunion, because it's only two weeks away now. I should reply, even though I'm not going to go. I'll do it now.' He didn't move from the table. Richard and electronic communication were not the best of friends.

I looked at him, assessing if it was worth one last try to get him to change his mind and go to this reunion. The last university reunion of his class had been twenty years ago and, as I pointed out to him, it was no good waiting for the next one in another twenty years because most of them would be dead. The invitation had arrived a couple of months ago, and he had said that he wanted to see how I was after my cell harvest before he committed himself to going. Always so caring, this dear man. A little over protective, maybe, because I knew I would be fine on my own. Then we discovered that the reunion was going to be on a weekend when Joy was going to be away at a hen party in Marbella with all her work friends (would it ever be Joy who was the bride, I wondered). So the reunion was definitely out of the question, Richard had said - and anyway, why would I want to see a bunch of old men with whom I no longer have anything in common, some even more doddery than me, no doubt. I couldn't quite work out if he really wasn't very keen on going and I was a convenient excuse, or he was genuinely concerned about leaving me without backup.

Then the light bulb went on in my head. 'I've had an idea,' I said. I nodded at the computer screen. 'This email from Nicky. He says he wants to come and visit. So how about if I suggest that he comes the weekend after next, and then you can go to the reunion!'

Richard turned his loose change over in his pocket – something he did when he was thinking. 'I suppose that could work,' he said, cautiously.

I got straight up from the table to get my phone, before he changed his mind. 'It's Saturday, he should be home.'

And so it was all arranged. Nicky seemed almost eager to come, which pleased me, yet I was just a tad mystified. I dismissed the latter as Mum paranoia. Amita probably wouldn't be coming, he said.

Richard went to his study to send the email to confirm that he would be attending the reunion, and to book his accommodation. I sat back and looked out of the window at the sky, which was something I did more often nowadays, just for the simple pleasure that it gave me. I watched the clouds drifting in the wind. Clouds. Were there clouds in my own sky? Because life was so precious to me nowadays, I could usually rationalise all the standard worries and 'what ifs'. But there was one thing that sat in the corner of my mind and nagged at me.

I turned to my computer again and clicked on my story. I opened a chapter and scrolled down to where it said 'Dear Susan'. My eyes flicked over the words until I came to 'Love, April'. I sat back and stared out at the clouds again.

What had happened to the original April letters?

***

'Surely we're not going to have the roof down,' I said as I sank into the passenger seat of Nicky's convertible BMW. 'It's late October!'

'You've got a thick coat on, and it will be much warmer than you think,' said Nicky. When he turned the ignition and pushed a button the hood of the car peeled discreetly away, letting in the expanse of sky above us. 'Where to, my lady?'

I liked this playful, boyish Nicky. He had arrived in time to see Richard for half an hour before he left to drive to the main reunion event, which was to be in the evening. Then Nicky and I set off for lunch. Amita, apparently, had gone to visit her parents.

'I've booked a table at the Orange Tree, if that's OK,' I said. I had thought about Nicky's sophisticated London tastes nowadays, and decided that it would be nice to go a bit upmarket. And anyway, this was a special occasion, a visit from my son, so I fancied the treat of lunch in a fairly posh restaurant. Why not?

We picked up a bit of speed though the lanes and I felt the luxurious warmth pervading me from the heated seat, contrasting with the cool breeze that lapped my face and ruffled my hair. I looked up at the branches of trees gliding overhead and the overarching sky and I laughed with delight.

'This is just amazing! How can I have lived to the age of fifty-four and never been in an open-topped sports car? I thought it would be cold but it's not, it's just... free! Oh, I could get used to this!'

The magical, carefree mood continued. We arrived at the restaurant where a suitably obsequious waiter took our coats and showed us to our table. The linen was so white you almost needed sunglasses. With a flourish he placed napkins on our laps and left us to the menus. The food, when it came, was excellent. Old fashioned dishes with a modern twist. And I confess that I indulged in the best part of a bottle of wine, because of course Nicky could only allow himself two small glasses. He talked a lot, and I sat back, rather enthralled. In fact I learned more about his job in those three hours than at any time previously. By the time we had eaten an excellent homemade trifle (I couldn't manage all of mine) we had got onto old times and holidays from his childhood. I knew that he was making an effort for me. I sat back, replete and slightly tipsy, and abandoned myself to the sheer pleasure of this moment, without thought for the future or the past.

Then we drove to the beach and strolled for a while on the sand. It was just right. Enough to aid our digestion and get some fresh air after the big lunch, but not enough to tire me too much. Afterwards at home we lolled in armchairs and the conversation slowed as I got sleepy. So Nicky went to his old room to look through some of his books – and to take them back to London, I couldn't help hoping – while I put my feet up on the sofa. After about half an hour he came back and slumped silently in the armchair, his face turned away. Here we go, I thought. I was used to how quickly his moods could change, but it did seem a shame after the lovely shared time that we'd had.

'I've been thinking,' I said, ignoring his change of mood, 'I can't remember a time in the whole of your adult life when we've had quality time together like this, just you and me. I'll treasure this day. Thank you for making it happen.'

At first I thought he wasn't going to answer. Then he said, 'I know I haven't been in touch much, Mum,' he said. 'While you've had... *the thing.*' He concentrated on picking at a thread on the cuff of his shirt.

'Cancer,' I said gently.

He shot me a glance and looked away again. 'I just... I just couldn't handle it when you were so ill.'

'I'm not ill now,' I said, feeling my way. 'The cancer's gone. I'm just a bit weak after the cell harvest and the chemo I had to have beforehand. I'm getting stronger all the time.'

He sat forward on the edge of his chair, clasping his hands together between his knees. 'But if the cancer's gone, then why did you have to have your cells harvested? Surely that means they think it's going to come back?'

I shook my head. 'No it doesn't. It's simply a precaution. It means that, if the same cancer *should* come back some time in the future, they can transplant my own white cells back into me as a way of treating it.

213

For many people, it doesn't ever come back. So, my chances of staying healthy are excellent.'

He got up abruptly and walked to the window, thrusting his hands in his pocket. Then he turned around and sat down by me on the sofa. 'So it might come back then,' he said. He took hold of my hands and looked at me directly. I saw the fear. 'I don't think I could bear to lose you.'

I admit I was taken aback. All the time during my illness when he had seemed so distant, this was why. I wanted to put my arms round him, like I used to when he was a little boy. I wanted to soothe him and tell him everything would be alright, that I wouldn't let anything hurt him. Instead I said, 'Look Nicky, life is uncertain. I can't guarantee, absolutely guarantee, that I'll still be alive in ten years' time. But then neither can anyone else. All this has made me realise not only how uncertain life is, but also how precious and wonderful it is. Every day is a gift. You realise that it's only really *now* that's important. Not the past, not the future. The past you should make peace with, acknowledge your mistakes, forgive, and move on. The future you should allow to unfold.'

I was breathless after that speech, and rather surprised at myself. But I think I got through to him. He lifted his eyebrows. 'What mistakes can you possibly have to acknowledge? You've always been such a perfect wife and mother.'

'Not quite, but thank you. I've made mistakes. Perhaps everyone does,' I said, half to myself.

'If you say so.' He let go of my hands and his gaze roved over me. 'I must say you look better than I thought you might. Your hair's grown back great. I hated seeing you a couple of years ago when your hair fell out. That's why I didn't come again.' He looked away. 'I should have done.'

Then I reached out and hugged him, and he hugged me back. We both needed it. 'It's OK,' I said. I wondered whether to tell the truth or leave him with his illusion. But then it occurred to me that he might see me in the night, so I added 'Actually, it's a wig. My hair fell out again with the chemo I had to have before the cell harvest. But it will grow back, like it did before.'

His eyes widened but he just nodded. I sat back. Now would be a good time to change the subject and broach what had been tickling at the corner of my mind ever since we had got home.

'Nicky, do you think you could do me a favour? There's some stuff of mine in the loft, things from before you were born, which I've been thinking about lately. It's nothing important, just some jottings that I did. I used to do a bit of writing then, and when I was in school.' I looked down at my hands. 'I don't want to trouble your Dad about clambering up into the loft. I'd have to go up there myself to locate the exact box, and that would worry him, me going up and down the ladder, and then I wouldn't be able to carry the box back down again.'

It had been some years since I'd been in the loft. When we got up there I was quite shocked by how much junk had accumulated. Close to the hatch entrance, where we climbed in, were our two big suitcases for holidays, and the Christmas decorations. Next there were various boxes from recent (and not so recent) household purchases – the microwave, the new TV, etc., – kept in case the items needed to be returned. There was an old vacuum cleaner; why on earth were we keeping that? It hadn't worked for years.

Towards the back the boxes were stacked in a more orderly fashion. These were the ones that had come from the cottage. I pointed to them. 'It'll be back there.' We crawled towards them.

'It's like Aladdin's cave in here,' said Nicky.

Most of the boxes were Richard's; books and more books, and one containing trophies, a cricket bat and a tennis racquet. I found a box of mine. Was this what I was looking for? No, it contained my school books. A big bag was in our way. I gasped when I opened it up and found my wedding dress. 'Oh, look!' I said. 'It was my mother's. It still looks in good condition. Maybe it could be passed down another generation.' I stroked the shiny fabric.

He grunted. 'It's awfully hot up here.'

I covered the dress over again. It wasn't the right time for nostalgia; I had other things on my mind. 'I think that's it,' I said, pointing to a box containing notebooks, letters and some photographs. On top I recognised one of Mum and Dad from when they were courting. He dragged the box out nearer the light. I pulled a letter out at random and saw my name in spidery writing on the envelope. My heart lurched. Yes, this was it. The April letters.

***

We washed the dust of the loft off our hands then I made ham and salad sandwiches and opened a bottle of wine. We sat in the living room and picnicked. The thought of the box which Nicky had just carried down from the loft, and that was sat waiting for me in my bedroom, puckered the edges of my mind. I pushed it away.

I wasn't very hungry; I put my sandwich down on the coffee table and instead had a hefty swig of my wine and took some deep breaths. Nicky was sitting cross-legged on the floor, wine glass in one hand and texting rapidly with the other in the way that young people do, that half impressed and half irritated me. He had changed into an old T-shirt and jeans, and looked younger than his thirty years.

The wine seeped along my veins. 'Do you know what would be nice?' I said.

'What?' he didn't take his eyes off his phone.

'A log fire. The first one of the autumn. It would be lovely and cosy for the evening.'

That got his attention. What is it about men and fires? 'It's not really that cold, but yeah, I could light a fire.'

He brought the wood in, and I suggested some coal too. He got the fire going while I closed the curtains and turned on the lamps. Soon it was crackling away and we both sat and basked in its glow.

'How's Amita?' I said, following my train of thought that it was probably to her that he'd been texting. 'Didn't you say she's gone to visit her family?'

'She's fine.' He picked up the tongs and opened the front of the stove to add a few more coals.

It dawned on me that he hadn't said much about her all day. 'Where did you say her parents live?'

'Kent.' He closed the door of the stove and continued to watch the flames.

'Ah. I've never been to Kent.' A pause. 'You could have brought her with you, this weekend. I do like her, you know.'

'Do you?' His look was enigmatic. Then, 'Actually, we'd both like to visit the weekend after next. When Dad's here. If that's OK.'

'Oh... well, of course that would be fine. You're always welcome, you know that.' I tried to keep the surprise out of my voice. Two visits in a month was unprecedented. 'But... perhaps you'd like to leave it a couple more weeks, you know, space it out between now and Christmas?'

He picked up the wrought iron poker and twisted it in his hands, as if examining the workmanship.

'Nicky?'

'I'm not supposed to tell you...'

'What? Tell me what?' I automatically panicked. 'There's nothing wrong is there?'

'Oh no.' He put the poker down and sprang up to sit by me. 'It's just..., well, Amita and I wanted to both come and tell you and Dad together.'

'You're not getting engaged, are you?' I gasped.

He shook his head. 'No. Better than that. Mum, Ami's pregnant!' It was like the sun had come out on his face. 'We said we'd wait until she's three months before we told anyone. That'll be next week. But it's been on my mind all day and I've hardly been able to keep it in. I thought you might guess that I was... well, different.' He was almost bouncing up and down.

All I could do was stare at him. And I thought it had been our day, his and mine, that that was why he had come. How foolish of me. 'This is so unexpected,' I managed. 'I don't know what to say.'

'You could try congratulations.' He looked so boyish, so eager.

'Of course. Of course, congratulations.' I tried to sort out the questions that were crowding my mind. 'So, when will you be getting married?'

'We're not getting married. Maybe later, but we haven't really thought about that.'

I absorbed that. 'U-huh. So will you both be living in your flat or Amita's, or buying somewhere new?'

He shook his head. 'Neither. We're going to stay just as we are. Ami's flat is central and convenient for her office, but it would mean

217

nearly a two hour commute each day for me to get to work, rather than the twenty minutes I have now, on a good day.'

He went on to explain that they would spend all weekend together, just like now, and he would see the baby then. And Ami's flat had three bedrooms, so there was plenty of room for the nanny.

'The *nanny*?' I wasn't quick enough to control my expression. My grandchild was going to have a nanny.

'Mum I thought you'd be pleased.' The eager look was gone. 'This is your first grandchild. I know you wanted grandchildren.'

Yes, I wanted to say, but not like this. There was supposed to be an engagement, a big white wedding with a cake and bridesmaids, a nice house, and then, a year or so later...

I dropped my eyes and stared at the fire. 'It's just such a surprise. I... I can't get my head around it all.' I searched for the right thing to say. 'I can't see how it's going to work, this living separately. Amita will need your support every day, not just at weekends, believe me. And, well, it just doesn't seem right. Fatherhood's not a part-time occupation, Nicky.'

Nicky poured us both another glass of wine and folded his arms. 'We've thought it all through, Mum. We're not stupid. And things are different now.'

Things are different now. Every parent hears that at some time, and every parent wants to say *yes, but not necessarily better.* I searched for a way to bridge the gap that had opened between us. 'Do Amita's parents know?' I said. 'Is that why she went to see them?'

'It isn't exactly why she went. We planned to go next weekend, together, and tell them. But her Mum guessed – Ami just texted me and told me. I think Ami knew that would happen, but it's cool.'

'And are they pleased?'

He shrugged. 'They're very traditional, but they don't try to impose their views on Ami.'

In my imagination I saw a woman in a sari, a tall, dignified woman with a handsome husband, and I felt a surge of empathy with this unknown person. Was she thinking too, that the baby would be half Indian, half white? Ironically, Nicky's ambiguous reply had given me some comfort and perspective. I took a sip of my wine. 'Look, you know I love you very much and I will support you in whatever you do. I admit I'm shocked about how you and Amita are going about this, but it's your choice. And yes, our first grandchild.'

We hugged, and firmed up the slightly prickly truce.

'What do you think Dad will say?'

I reflected. 'He's bound to be disappointed that you're not going to get married.'

'Don't tell him yet, Mum,' he pleaded. 'Wait until Ami and I come to tell you both together. Dad and Ami get on well together, and she'll know exactly how to handle him.'

I was doubtful. I would have to pretend my surprise when they came to announce the news. And the truth was I badly wanted to discuss this with Richard.

'Please, Mum. Telling both of you together is what we originally intended to do, anyway.'

So I ended up agreeing. We talked for a few minutes more, then I excused myself, pleading tiredness from the exciting day, and went to bed.

Light brown, I thought. The child will probably be light brown.

***

I slumped on the chair in my bedroom and covered my face with my hands. I peered through my fingers at the box lying on my bed. The last thing I wanted to do after the emotion of the last half an hour was to unpack those letters, to unfold the old pages and see in black and white the words, the actual words, for which I had had to rely on memory – and imagination – to write about. But it had to be tonight, before Richard came back. I knew that.

Only three of the letters were in envelopes. I pulled one out and read it, and there it all was; the flamboyant phrases, the breathless descriptions of parties and boyfriends. April's inimitable style. I found that my hands were trembling.

Then I emptied out the rest of the letters. Straightaway I recognised the battered notebook that I used to write in. Of course, I had the choice not to sit there and re-read the letters, but inevitably I turned to each one and at least glanced through it. Oh yes, I'd been accurate when I wrote my memoir. It was all there – the complaining, the shyness, the discontent, and then, the blow-by-blow account of the shabby affair with Phil. I had had a crazy, foolish notion that, given how I had liked to make up stories back then, I had actually just conjured up the whole thing in my imagination. But I knew that was ridiculous. And reading my actual words, in my own handwriting, crashed open the portal to the past; I could smell the fetid caravan, I could feel the enslaving, compulsive lust.

With a whimper I dropped the letter. I curled up on the bed and screwed my eyes shut, but I couldn't block it out. I wasn't me anymore, a woman in her fifties, I was that young woman, that pathetic girl who was too scared, too insecure, to just realise how blessed she was. I could sense her with me in the room, I could see her. God, I *was* her. I *am* her. I didn't know which was the worst – the fact that I could have had a tawdry affair or that I could have contrived an imaginary friend to pour out my troubles to.

I heard Nicky's footsteps on the stairs, and I froze. He mustn't see me distraught like this. I fumbled with the light switch, turned off the light and lay in the dark, breathing as heavily as if I'd been running. It worked; he didn't knock my door to say goodnight but went straight to his own room. Gradually my breathing slowed and I dared to examine my wretchedness. April, my alter ego. Daring, outgoing, friendly, carefree. The girl I thought I wanted to be, but was too afraid. Thank God that Joy came along and set me on the right path. That, and that Richard loved me steadfastly and believed in me. I came so close to losing all that.

It had been more than half an hour now since I'd heard Nicky's door close. I dragged myself off the bed and collected together every one of the April letters from my notebook. Leaving my shoes off, I gently opened the door and listened on the landing: nothing. I clutched the letters to my chest and crept downstairs, conscious of every tiny creak. In the living room I carefully closed the door and saw that the fire was still glowing, thanks to the coal that I'd asked Nicky to put on. I sat down in front of it and fed the letters into the red mouth of the fire. I watched the flames carry them into oblivion. Even then, I used the poker to disperse their ash to convince myself that they were gone. *The past you should make peace with, acknowledge your mistakes, forgive, and move on.*

Chapter 20

The church clock chiming two o'clock sounded faintly in the quiet of the night. It wasn't loud enough to wake you; you'd only hear it if you happened to be lying in bed awake. I sighed and turned over.

'Still awake, darling?' Richard's voice came out of the dark.

'Afraid so. I did go off for an hour or so, but I was awake again to hear the church clock strike one.' I turned over again onto my back and wriggled my legs, trying to get comfortable. 'Sorry if I disturbed you.'

'No matter.' He reached from his side of our large bed and laid his hand on my arm. 'This is the third night you've been restless.'

So he had noticed. 'Mmm. It's just one of those things. I was hoping that by tonight I would be so exhausted I'd stay asleep, but it seems not. It probably has to run its course.'

'You poor old thing. Come and have a cuddle.' He drew me under his arm and I nestled against him. After all these years we could instinctively find the position where our bodies fitted like jigsaw pieces.

'Is there anything on your mind?' he said after a moment.

I tried not to tense up. 'No… not really.'

'Only, this has been happening since the night I went away to the reunion. The night when Nicky stayed.' My eyes flitted backwards and forwards in the dark. 'You did seem a bit reluctant to talk about his visit. Was everything alright?'

Richard was always so perceptive. 'Yes, Nicky's fine. Honestly.' I was aware that, lying together as we were, he would be able to feel the increase in my heartbeat. I felt myself starting to sweat.

'I still feel there's something troubling you.'

I moved back to my own side of my bed and pushed the duvet down off my shoulders to cool down. 'I have secrets,' I murmured, half to myself.

'Ah. Secrets. Never good for peace of mind. Are you allowed to tell me?'

The dim outlines of the bedroom furniture were humped and

menacing in the gloom, like large crouching animals. 'I said I wouldn't...' I hesitated, but I was too near the brink to pull myself back. 'Oh, but you're going to find out soon anyway, and you know there's something wrong.'

So I told him. I told him about the baby, and that Nicky and Amita weren't even going to live together, let alone marry. I told him that they planned to visit and tell us in a couple of weeks' time, and that we would have to act surprised. And pleased.

'I don't think I handled it very well,' I finished. 'I hope I haven't alienated him.'

I must say Richard took it calmly. Perhaps he might have been imagining something worse. 'Their plan to live separately may well change as time goes by,' he said. 'And plenty of children get looked after by a nanny.'

'But not our grandchild.'

'Darling, we can't live their lives for them.'

I lay silently. His reasonableness was not making me feel any better. 'How do you feel about the baby being, well, you know...'

'What?'

He was going to make me say it. 'Half Indian.'

'It hadn't occurred to me. But now you come to mention it... yes, the child will probably be a lovely golden colour.'

I turned on my side towards him so that I could just see his profile in the dark. He turned his head towards me and I caught the glint from his eyes.

'You put me to shame,' I said.

'Well, it was all a bit of a shock to you,' he said generously. 'And because it's upsetting you, I think you did the right thing telling me.'

We kissed and I turned over to settle down. A golden baby... I was just starting to relax when Richard said, 'Secrets.'

'What?'

'You said 'secrets'. Plural.'

I heard a car in the distance. You had to wonder who was out and about in the middle of the night. Had I really said 'secrets', not 'secret'? The bedside clock ticked away the slow seconds. Suddenly my mouth was very dry. 'I need to get a drink of water,' I said, fumbling for my bedside bottle. I lay back down, the water cold in my stomach.

It's easier to talk when you are in the dark, when both you and your listener are disembodied. 'It was all a very long time ago, and it's not really important. I've never told anyone…'

'Take your time,' Richard said.

The darkness enveloped and emboldened me. 'You probably don't recall this, but back when we were first married, I used to have letters from a friend, a friend called April.'

'Yes, I do remember. She was a friend from University. A very outgoing girl, you used to say. You used to exchange letters quite often.'

My eyes opened wide in the blackness. 'Goodness, I'm surprised that you should remember.' I paused, unsure if this made it better or worse. I took a breath. I had to go through with it now. 'I don't know quite how to say this, but, you see, I sort of made her up. She wasn't a real friend.' There, I'd said it now. The rest would be easier. 'Oh, Richard, it sounds ridiculous now, but you know how shy I was. I didn't have any friends, I liked writing and making up stories and well… it was just something that I did.' The words were coming out in a rush. 'I feel so embarrassed now.' I turned over towards him. 'Do you want to know just how pathetic I was? Sometimes, three times in fact, I'd actually put the letter that I'd written, pretending to be from April, in an envelope and posted it to myself.' I gave a dry laugh. 'I even used my left hand to write the envelope, to make my writing look different. I'm not sure now if that was to stop you finding out or to take the game to a higher level for me.' I groaned. 'How sad can you get?'

'I knew.'

At first I thought I'd misunderstood. 'What do you mean, you knew?'

'I mean, I knew April wasn't real.'

I sat bolt upright in bed. 'You *knew*?'

'Well, I guessed. But darling, it doesn't matter.'

I threw back the duvet and jumped out of bed. I was trembling. 'You *knew*? All this time you knew and you said *nothing*?'

He sat up in bed. 'I didn't think it was of any importance. Susan, there's no need to be so upset.'

I clawed at my dressing gown and bundled it round me. Strange noises were bursting out of my throat. In the dark I couldn't find my slippers so I stomped downstairs in bare feet.

The fluorescent light in the kitchen was harsh. A tornado of anger was sweeping through me. How *dare* he? How dare he make a fool of me like that? I knew really that my response wasn't entirely rational, but it was consuming me like fire and I was out of control. I prowled up and down the kitchen, waiting to hear the creak overhead indicating that Richard was getting out of bed to follow me. I waited, glaring at the ceiling. *Damn him!* Why wasn't he coming after me? I clenched my fists and looked wildly round the kitchen. There was a large bowl on the counter and I grabbed it, lifted it up, up right above my head, and smashed it on the floor with a cry like a wild thing.

That did it. I heard the tell-tale footsteps overhead and Richard appeared in the doorway. We both stared at the broken crockery on the floor.

'Susan, stop it,' he said. He didn't shout, but his voice was firm.

I crumpled. My outburst had frightened me and I began to sob. He was beside me in an instant. 'Don't move,' he said. 'You'll cut your feet to ribbons.' He, of course, had put his slippers on.

He insisted on cleaning up the mess with a dustpan and brush while I sat on a kitchen chair and sniffled. I felt curiously remote, the lightning strike of anger now conducted to earth.

A few minutes later, when we were sitting with our hands around mugs of cocoa, I asked him how he had known.

'First of all I only wondered, knowing how you used to like to write and use your imagination. But then one day a letter arrived for you and I picked it up off the mat. You opened it and said it was from April. But I had looked at the postmark and had seen that it was local. So I put two and two together.'

'The postmark. Of course! It never occurred to me.' I struck the palm of my hand to my forehead. 'Oh, how stupid can you be.'

'The letters didn't do any harm, you know,' he said. 'I didn't tell you that I knew about them simply because you seemed to want to keep it private, like a diary.'

I nodded. 'Yes, I suppose that was it. I used my letters to her like a diary, to pour out my feelings. And April's letters to me... well, I guess she represented the person I thought I wanted to be but didn't have the nerve. I'd seen girls like her in school – outgoing, confident, pretty, lots of friends. Now I feel so ashamed, an adult having an imaginary friend.'

'You know, it was probably therapeutic for you, having a sort of ready-made agony aunt to hand.'

I smiled at that. 'Maybe. But the thing was she always said what I wanted her to say.' I stopped abruptly. I didn't want to go down that road. 'Actually, she was a real person. From university.'

'Oh? You knew her?'

'Well, sort of. On the day when I went to enrol, I was having a real confidence crisis because I couldn't find where to go. I was in the ladies' room and she was there. She was a third year student, and she asked if she could borrow my comb. She had the most beautiful wavy blonde hair. She said she knew how difficult the first day was.'

I stared across the kitchen, seeing again, like a bright butterfly, the girl with cornfield hair and red lips. 'Without that conversation, I truly think I would have turned around and gone home. Afterwards I used to see her now and again in the refectory, always with a crowd of others. They would be laughing and joking, and she would be right in the centre of things. I tried to catch her eye once, but it was obvious she didn't remember me.'

The fridge gurgled. It's funny, you never notice it in the daytime. 'I never knew her name. Do you know why I named her April? Well, the first time I came to visit you in the cottage, at Easter, you were pressing me about if I had any friends at university. So, to divert you, I mentioned this blonde girl – although I could hardly call her a friend; I'd only had one short conversation with her. I had to give her a name, and there was a calendar on the wall opposite me, so on the spur of the moment I called her April. April from the month that the calendar was turned to.' I spread my hands. 'And there we have it.'

We sat quietly. My cocoa had gone cold. Then Richard said, 'Why all this now, after all these years?'

'Because while I was in hospital I spent a lot of time writing my life story – at least, the early years, mostly up until Joy was born. First of all it was a way to pass the time, but then – or perhaps afterwards – I realised I wanted to make peace with that Susan from back then.'

226

'Can I read it? It would be quite like the old days when you were at school. I used to delight in reading your work back then.'

I hesitated. 'Let me edit it first. It's still full of errors.'

We climbed the stairs back to bed, to make the most of what was left of the night. As we settled ourselves under the duvet Richard said 'We could call this 'the Night of the Secrets'. I hope there's nothing else that you need to tell me?'

'No,' I said. 'There's nothing else that I need to tell you.'

***

I woke up the next morning to find that Richard was already up. He must have crept out of bed, because I hadn't heard him. I looked at the clock and saw that it was ten-thirty. Ten thirty! I never sleep that late. But then I'd had a few broken nights so I had needed the sleep.

I turned over and stretched luxuriously, and gradually the bizarre scenes of the night unrolled back into my consciousness. Did I dream it? I unpackaged it all and laid it out for inspection – the golden baby, the big confession, the bombshell from Richard, my misdirected anger, the final dissection of the April letters. It was all finished now and I could let it go. I lay and basked, letting myself feel the clouds dispersing.

But wait. Suddenly my body tensed. No, that couldn't possibly be right... I must speak to Richard. I got up and dressed quickly, splashed some water on my face and hurried downstairs. He wasn't anywhere in the house. I looked outside and saw that he was in the garden, sweeping up autumn leaves dropped from the horse-chestnut tree that nodded over the fence from the copse behind our garden. I put on my fleece and boots and went to join him.

He greeted me with a smile, his shabby old gardening jacket hanging loosely about him. 'Good morning, my love. I'm glad to see that you had a nice lie-in.'

'I need to talk to you,' I said, without preamble. 'It can't be true, what you said last night.'

'What can't be true?'

There was a tightness in my chest. 'About you knowing that April

227

was make-believe. It can't be true.'

He propped the broom up against the horse-chestnut tree and led me to the garden bench that was next to it. We sat down together. 'Now tell me what you mean,' he said.

The words came out in a rush. 'Do you remember that first summer after we were married when I… when I was depressed and I went away for a few days? Well, it was you who suggested that I went to stay with April. *You* suggested it, not me. I distinctly remember. So you can't have known.'

He took off his gardening gloves and laid them on the bench. The arthritis that was starting to claim his hands made them look gnarled. 'Yes, you're quite right. I suggested it.'

'Then… how could…'

He interrupted me. 'You see, you were acting so strangely, and I could tell you weren't happy. I could feel you slipping away, and I thought a change, any change, some time away from me, might help you to see your best way forward. You didn't want to go back to your family home. So, on the spur of the moment I suggested that you went to stay with April.'

'You mean…. even though you knew she was fictitious, you still suggested it?'

'I told you, it was on the spur of the moment.' He turned his face away from me and stared towards the house. 'I was desperate, Susan, so I took a gamble that a short separation would be better than continuing the downward spiral that you were in. I prayed that it wouldn't be a permanent rift.'

I looked at his profile, and at the lines on his face. His thinning hair was sticking up where he had dragged a hand across it. I put my hand to his cheek. 'And when I agreed to go off and stay with this non-existent person, where did you think I was going to go?'

'I had no idea. My guess was that you were going off somewhere on your own.'

'And you were right, of course. I went to Tenway. It was awful.'

He turned to me and smiled. 'It didn't matter where you went, it only mattered that you came back.'

A leaf, russet and crispy, fluttered down from the horse chestnut tree. I caught it and held it gently between my fingers. I returned his smile. 'You are an extraordinary person. I don't quite know how I've come to deserve you, but please know how grateful I am to you and that I love you very much. I always have. It just took me a while at first to realise it.'

***

It wasn't as convenient to walk to the beach from this house as it had been from the cottage, where it was only half a mile down the lane. Nevertheless, it was only a couple of miles and I could do it easily in forty minutes. The day was fat with late spring sunshine, the warmest day of the year so far, and I stood on the cliffs breathing in the exciting promise of the summer to come. The tide was in and the waves caressed the beach with a sigh. A few people were strolling on the shore, exercising their dogs or simply exercising themselves, and a few mums sat watching their pre-school children playing in the sand. It might be the computer age, but kids still love to play on the beach.

I gloried. I gloried in the fine weather, the vista of sea and sky, and in my own vigour. Vigour. I could never have imagined using that word in connection with myself last year, but now I felt truly well and I could feel the upsurge of vitality in my body. I drew the sea air deep into my lungs. So, what to do now? Would I flop on the beach with my picnic or would I walk for a while along the cliff? Even though the notebook in my backpack was calling to me, I thought I would walk on. I turned right and took the footpath as far as the Big House. I hadn't been this way for a while, because last year I hadn't the strength to walk this far. The gate from the footpath into the grounds of the house had long since been padlocked and was overgrown with greenery. The Big House itself had been sold several years ago and was now a nursing home. Through the trees I could just see a corner of it.

On an impulse I decided to leave the main path and drop down to the beach and scramble over the stones to the tiny secret beach. When was the last time I was here? I couldn't recall. Possibly I'd never been back. I picked my way over the rocks, but as soon as I was down on the shore it was obvious that there was no longer any beach. The crescent of enticing sand that had been there thirty-five years ago was now buried beneath layers of stones, and the sea now beat in over harsh rocks. Surveying it now, it was hard to imagine how it had been all those years ago. Everything changes. I said my goodbyes and left.

I walked back to the main beach and arranged myself on the sand, at the far end of the bay where it was quietest. It was good to be alone sometimes, allowing my thoughts and imaginings to come out to play. Richard rarely came to the beach; he said he preferred his sandwiches without sand, thank you. Today I had left him happily working in his study on his project. I lifted my face to the blessing of the sun and allowed my thoughts to wash to and fro like the waves. Then I took out my notebook. It was battered and dog-eared and had a big number three on the front. Hard to believe that I had filled two and a half notebooks since last autumn with my scribbling, notes and outlines, not to mention the pieces that had found their way onto my wordprocessor and had actually emerged as finished compositions of one sort or another – poems, short stories, essays. As yet, nothing longer.

I flicked the notebook open and got out my pen. Above me seagulls were wheeling and screeching their chainsaw cries. I stared at the vacant page, and wondered if I dared. The idea had been swirling around inside me these last three months or more. Would it do more harm than good? I didn't know. I picked up my pen and started to write.

8 May 2008

Dear April

Well, well, after all this time. Who would have thought that I would be writing to you again, thirty-five years on.

I paused and looked at the words I had written, and there I was, back in time watching over the shoulder of young Susan as she sat writing at the kitchen table, hair falling down in waterfalls around her face and the clock ticking out the minutes of her life. Or was it she who was looking over my shoulder now, as I sat on a beach in the drift of a sweet sunny afternoon? Perhaps it was both, the words on the page reaching back and uniting us, completing the circle. I picked up my pen

230

again.

My years have been mainly good ones. Richard and I share a deep and abiding love, we have three grown up children who are well and happy and following their chosen life paths, and we have our first baby grandson who is the colour of caramel and just as sweet. I have also had cancer. Yet I don't consider that as a bad thing now that it is gone. I have lived through it and it has altered my perspective on life forever. Nowadays I wear life loosely. It was a wake-up call not to waste any precious time, and it has made me consider exactly what it is that I want to do: write.

And now I think I know what I want to write about. You! The fabric of your life, the unfolding, the dreams, the people, the adventures, both planned and – the best ones – unexpected. I'm going to write a story based on your life. And the best thing of all is that it will be mine. I will create it, I will shape it. But I suspect it will take charge and shape itself. Yes, I know it is fantasy. Stories are not real, and yet they touch us profoundly and make us believe in them.

What has happened in your story, I wonder? Relationships that turned you inside out, journeys into strange places, life lived in the fast lane? What fun it will be finding out. And there will be a happy ending. Everyone loves a happy ending.

And, April, one more thing. You were my friend when I thought I didn't have any. Thank you.

With love,

Susan xx

Also by Valerie Norris published by Cambria Publishing.

In the Long Run
ISBN 978-1-9996129-6-2